THE KILLER WITHOUT A FACE

HELEN STARBUCK

The Killer Without a Face
Published by Routt Street Press
Arvada, CO

Publisher's Cataloging-in-Publication
(Provided by Cassidy Cataloguing Services, Inc.).

Names: Starbuck, Helen, author. Title: The killer without a face / Helen Starbuck. Description: Arvada, CO : Routt Street Press LLC, [2024] Identifiers: ISBN: 978-0-9992461-8-4 Subjects: LCSH: Witnesses--Fiction. | Colorado--Fiction. | Escape (Psychology)--Fiction. | Secrecy-- Fiction. | Suspense fiction. | Romance fiction. | LCGFT: Thrillers (Fiction) | Romance fiction. | Detective and mystery fiction. | BISAC: FICTION / Romance / Suspense.
Classification: LCC: PS3619.T3727 K55 2024 | DDC: 813/.6--dc23

Cover and Interior Design by Victoria Wolf, wolfdesignandmarketing.com. Copyright owned by author.

For information, email info@routtstreetpress.com.

Routt Street Press
Arvada. CO
info@routtstreetpress.com

*This book is dedicated to Friscus, a very good boy
who, like Elmer, was a comfort and very loved.*

"We all make choices, but in the end, our choices make us."

—Ken Levine

ALSO BY HELEN STARBUCK

THE ANNIE COLLINS MYSTERY SERIES
The Mad Hatter's Son
No Pity in Death
The Burden of Hate
A Cold Case of Conscience

STANDALONE ROMANTIC SUSPENSE
Legacy of Secrets

THE DENVER MAJOR CRIMES SERIES
Finding Alex
The Woman He Used to Know

PROLOGUE

THE SOUND OF HIS VOICE raised the hair on the back of her neck. He made small talk as he drove, and the more he talked, the more insistently a warning alarm deep inside her sounded. It was nothing he said, really, and she couldn't figure out why she was having a hard time breathing or why her heart had begun to race.

She turned toward him as he pulled up to the junction that would take them to the interstate. He looked to the left for oncoming traffic, and the alarm went ballistic. *Get out,* she thought frantically, *get out now!* She quietly unlatched her seat belt, gripped the backpack that sat on her lap, and, as he pressed the accelerator to merge onto the highway, grabbed the door handle, jerked it open, and bailed out of the SUV.

He lunged for her but missed. In his attempt to grab her, he jerked the steering wheel and lost control of the car as it slid on the icy pavement. He overcorrected, which sent the car into a 360-degree spin across the highway and off the opposite edge. She landed hard on her left shoulder and hip and rolled several feet before coming to a halt. Despite the searing pain in her shoulder, she staggered up, pulled her backpack onto her other shoulder,

and took off running into the snow-shrouded trees without a
backward glance.

CHAPTER ONE

THAT STUPID FUCKER TULIO. *Listening to the voice on the other end of the burner phone, he squeezed his free hand into a fist and bounced it against his thigh, keeping time with the headache that pulsed in his head. Tulio had been released from the county jail after serving six months on an assault charge and had gotten high as a kite. He was stopped for speeding and tried to pull a gun on two cops. For Christ's sake, what the fuck had he thought he was going to do? Shoot two police officers? And then what? Benny Tulio liked to brag. He had a record an arm long, so he would want a deal, and that would require naming names.*

He should have taken care of Benny a long time ago. This wasn't his first screwup that had landed him in trouble with the law. Well, it was a done deal, and now the cleanup had to begin. Benny was just one of many things that he needed to take care of. He would, but the next couple of problems, he'd take care of himself.

"Major fuckup on Tulio's part. See to it before he decides to talk to anyone." The man disconnected. On his way across the street toward his car, he removed the SIM card, dropped the phone in a garbage can, and ground the SIM card under his heel.

Lieutenant Kaye Jagerski's phone vibrated in her pocket. She sighed. It was late. She'd actually thought she'd be able to eat and maybe get some sleep, but apparently not. Head of Vice meant long hours and disrupted plans. She reached for her phone as she walked to her car in the precinct parking lot, the cold wind of an October evening in Denver playing with her dark, curly bob. She was a woman who might, at first glance, make you think she was harmless, but she had served her time on the streets and in Vice and had made a name for herself for all the connections she could tap. At last, she'd been rewarded with her boss's job when he retired. Kaye wasn't sure it was a reward. A promotion yes; a reward not so much.

Raising her phone to her ear, she got in her car and answered. "Jagerski." Kaye listened intently, a frown on her face. "What the hell happened? Where were the guards?" She listened for a few seconds longer. "I'll be there shortly. Separate the guards who were involved, if you haven't already, and put them in different interview rooms. I want to talk to them. Keep the inmates involved isolated. I'll want to talk to them too."

Benny Tulio had been arrested earlier in the day during a traffic stop. It had ended in a charge of carrying a concealed, unregistered weapon and possession of a shitload of meth and fentanyl. He'd been booked and sent to the Denver Detention Center, where he'd been found in the men's showers with a bar of soap shoved down his throat. No one saw anything or heard anything, if the guards and the inmates were to be believed. The guards had been standing outside the shower area while Benny and four other men showered.

Everything had sounded normal, both guards claimed—no noise or indication of trouble—until Tulio didn't exit the showers with the others. In the chaos that ensued, the remaining inmates claimed to know nothing. With a smirk, one inmate had actually suggested that Tulio had committed suicide. The inmates were involved, little question about that, but the guards had to be complicit, Kaye thought. The task ahead would be proving it.

There were no injuries to the inmates or the guards, but the marks on Benny indicated he'd been restrained while the bar of soap had been shoved down his throat. Figuring out who was to blame would have to rely on forensics, assuming there was anything that was usable. It was doubtful; Tulio had been left under a running showerhead. None of the inmates involved were talking, other than to claim innocence, without their court-appointed lawyers present.

Inmates got injured occasionally at the DDC or died from other causes as they waited to be sentenced and transferred to the Department of Corrections jail. There'd been an inmate who died as a result of a confrontation years ago. He'd been put in a headlock, sat on, and tasered. Kaye couldn't remember what had caused that confrontation. Despite the coroner's ruling of homicide, prosecutors hadn't filed charges. But intentionally killing an inmate at the DDC had never happened.

After the interviews, she sent the guards home on suspension pending an investigation, and the inmates involved were isolated until their bond hearings. The incident report would be included for the judge to rule on whether any of them got bail. It had been a long shot whether they would have been offered bail, but this incident had ended that possibility. Kaye planned to press the inmates, and after a conversation with the DA's office, perhaps offer a deal that would encourage one of them to give up the guilty parties.

Locking the barn door after the horse has escaped, Kaye thought on her way home from the DDC. The guards had been involved, had to have known what was going on, and stood outside the shower area, pretending not to hear or see anything. Kaye didn't see how it could have happened otherwise.

She'd have to do a deep dive on the guards to see how they'd been compromised and vulnerable to someone on the outside needing a favor done or whether they had a side hustle to pad their wallets. She'd get warrants to have their bank accounts searched for any unusual spending or the appearance of unexplained money in their accounts and get their phone logs to review all calls.

Any of the inmates showering with him could have held a long-standing grudge, seen him as a rival, or been asked to take care of Benny in return for favors of some kind. The end result was, somebody hadn't wanted Benny Tulio to talk to anyone. Now he couldn't.

She wasn't even sure he'd had anything to talk about. He wasn't a major player in the local drug business, just a low-level repeat screw-up, but she'd hoped to interview him and see what he could tell them. He'd been too high when arrested to bother trying to interview him, so he'd been charged and sent to the DDC.

The stash of drugs found in his car, though, represented a lot of money. Someone might not be all that forgiving when an employee fucked up and lost that much product. Benny was in serious trouble legally, and he might have volunteered to rat out the higher-ups in exchange for a lighter sentence, or, depending on who he ratted out, no sentence at all.

She sighed as she let herself into her small bungalow, locked the door, reset the alarm, and made her way to the bedroom. She thought about a shower, but with the shower death fresh in her mind, she decided to pass until morning.

CHAPTER TWO

LYING IN BED WITH HER eyes closed and savoring the fact that she didn't have to work, Danielle Calderwood began to think about what she had to do today. Her nine-to-five job as an accountant in a busy firm often meant staying late to get work done. That left her with little time to catch up on other tasks. Saturdays were always busy. Her eyes flew open, and she sat up abruptly, startled by the insistent pounding on her apartment's door.

A loud voice announced, "Police! Open up."

She got up and hurried to the door. Peering through the peep hole she found herself staring directly at the chest of a Denver police officer. A badge on his chest said Kurtz, his name presumably.

Christ, what now? Dani thought. She hesitated for a moment trying to decide whether she should open the door or pretend that she wasn't home but the pounding began again.

"Okay, okay! I'm opening the door." She opened the door as far as the security chain would allow. A tall, heavyset police officer with a deep scowl on his face stared at her. Another officer stood to his side, hands hooked into his duty belt.

"How did you get into the building? You didn't buzz me."

His face was cold and he didn't answer. Dani sighed. They'd probably buzzed the manager and he'd let them in.

"Can I help you?" she asked, pushing her long blonde wavy hair away from her face.

"Hannah Calderwood?" he barked.

"N-no. I'm her sister."

He held a piece of paper up and looked between it and her face. "Can I see some ID?"

"What's this all about, officer?"

"ID, please."

"Okay, hang on a minute." Dani retrieved her purse from the coffee table and fished out her driver's license. She passed it to the cop and watched as he looked at her license and looked at what she assumed was a photo. He looked puzzled, and she took pity on him. "Hannah is my twin sister. Is she who you're looking for?"

"Yes, ma'am. Can we come in and talk to her?"

"She's not here." She saw the look of suspicion on his face, and she saw her neighbor across the hall emerging from the stairwell and heading to his door. "Look, come in and tell me what you're here for. I'd just as soon my neighbors not get an earful." She started to close the door and the officer blocked it with his hand. "I have to take the chain off," she said, raising her eyebrows at him. He removed his hand and she finished closing the door and sliding the security chain off.

They entered the small one-bedroom apartment and glanced around. "Where is your sister?"

"I have no idea. She doesn't live here, and I haven't talked to her recently."

"She listed this address as the place she lives."

Dani made a sweeping gesture with her hand at the small, tidy apartment. "Take a look around, officer. She doesn't and never has lived here. What's going on?"

"She's missed her last two appointments with her parole officer, which violates her conditions of parole. It's been revoked. We're here to take her to jail."

"As I said, she doesn't live here. Feel free to look around if you think I'm lying about it."

Dani watched as the other cop entered her bedroom, opened the closet and bent to look under the bed. He went into the bathroom, and she heard him slide the shower curtain open. He returned and shrugged at Kurtz.

"I'm sorry I can't help, but I haven't seen her in more than a week."

Kurtz handed her his card. "And you have no idea where she might be?"

"No, I don't. I'm sorry."

"If you hear from her, please let me know. Or, if she'll cooperate, bring her into the precinct. The address is on my card."

Dani nodded as she took the card, closing and locking the door after them. She'd lied. She knew where her sister was and should have told the officers, should have allowed her to suffer the consequences of her poor decisions. Dani leaned against the apartment door with her eyes closed as a familiar wave of depression washed over her. Hannah had listed Dani's address as her own. No big surprise. As usual, Hannah hadn't asked, hadn't even mentioned it, leaving Dani to deal with the blowback.

She changed into clothes a bit more suitable for going to visit a parole officer than an oversized T-shirt and pajama bottoms. Brushing her hair in front of the bathroom mirror, she stopped and looked at herself—*really* looked, instead of a quick glance, which was her usual habit. A worried frown drew her brows together, and her mouth had taken a more decided downturn in the last year.

Twenty-nine just a month ago, but she looked far more worn than she thought someone her age should.

The last year had been hard as Hannah had spiraled more and more out of control. Arrested six months ago for selling drugs, she'd reached a plea deal that resulted in a minimal jail sentence, but she had to complete a year's probation. If she failed to comply, she was looking at two years in jail. Hannah had sworn she'd do anything to avoid going back to jail, and Dani had thought perhaps the threat of a two-year sentence had finally made her decide to turn her life around.

With the visit from the police, it was clear Hannah had no intention of changing. Using Dani's address had once again pulled Dani into her messy life. Hannah had always used Dani as a last resort lifesaver—the person she could grab onto when everything went to shit and everyone else had abandoned her. Hannah was the millstone around Dani's neck. She should walk away and refuse to rescue Hannah. But she had never figured out how to do that.

Being Hannah's twin had meant people assumed she was just like Hannah—up for anything, happy to take drugs or get drunk with abandon. Men who knew both of them assumed she was an easy lay as well, and she'd spent far too much time correcting their mistakes. Women judged her with that yardstick if they knew anything about her sister, so Dani had built a high wall around that part of her life. Unless a person had known her growing up, most people would have been surprised to find out she had a sister.

There was no way to shield the men she had dated from her sister, however. Hannah would show up unexpectedly, drunk, high, or belligerent, which was as hard to explain as a call from her sister, who was in jail or the ER, asking Dani to help. Dani hadn't had a serious relationship in four years since the last guy had walked out the door after a couple of months.

Standing in the doorway of her apartment, he'd said, "I've had my fill of your sister and the chaos you get into with her. We've never had a chance to have a relationship because our time together is constantly derailed by your sister. I barely count, and I don't like that. I'm done with this."

Dani gathered her purse and coat, the millstone firmly back in place. Getting into her car, she knew, as sure as she knew anything, that this would be as pointless as every other time she'd bailed Hannah out or tried to get her to stop fucking her own life up or, at the very least, to stop fucking Dani's life up. She'd never been successful at either effort and admitted to herself that, although she should have, she'd never stopped trying.

"Hannah's just being Hannah—that's not going to change. *You're* the one who has to change, *you're* the one who has to walk away, now, forever, unless you want to continue to throw your life away."

Her best friend, Elaine, had been saying that since at least high school. She'd been supportive, and Dani had agreed with her and then ignored her for just as long. The eldest by five minutes, Dani had always felt responsible for her twin, for which her mother was partly to blame.

Mary Calderwood had been unprepared for marriage, but she'd been a dutiful, if not enthusiastic, wife, and pregnancy had ensued. After the birth of the twins, Mary lost interest in being a dutiful wife and refused to have sex with her husband to ensure no further children would be created. Dani's parents slept in separate bedrooms, and once, after a nightmare, when she went to her mother's room, she found the door was locked.

Mary had also not been prepared for children, certainly not twins, but she made a feeble effort to care for them. Hannah had been a small, sickly infant, and Mary had basked in the sympathy from friends and family for her martyred lot in life. She favored Hannah to the exclusion of Dani; she received far more attention for her sick child than she did for her healthy one.

It didn't take long for Mary to lose interest in the twins altogether. People got tired of hearing her tales of woe and began visiting or including her less and less. Without the attention as a reason for her attempts at mothering, she'd handed over the responsibility for the twins to neighborhood babysitters. When money was tight, she let the twins fend for themselves as best they could. Sporadically as a young child, then permanently as they grew older, Dani had stepped in to care for herself and Hannah, and those responsibilities had worsened as she and her twin grew up.

Mary's neglect had begun as confusion and inadequacy, morphed into detachment, and turned into absence after her husband had finally disappeared. Her response to his abandonment was to lapse into a haze of drinking.

As she left her apartment, Dani's last conversation with Elaine played in her mind. "I can't … I don't want to keep talking about this," Elaine had said a year ago, the last time they'd talked. "I'm enabling you just like you're enabling Hannah. I can't stand by and watch you throw your life away thinking you're going to have any effect on Hannah's life. Dani, please, get some help, some counseling, a support group for families of addicts, something."

But she hadn't. Now all she had left was her twin sister, the sister she wished, in the most angry, desperate part of her heart, didn't exist. The sister who would never go away and would never change. The shame that she simultaneously wanted her sister dead and couldn't seem to walk away from her weighed on her.

Dani huffed out a breath in defeat and drove toward the run-down house Hannah shared with her drug-dealing boyfriend, Billy Alphonse. Another Saturday gone to hell.

CHAPTER THREE

IT WAS A DEPRESSING PART OF DENVER, a street filled with derelict houses covered in graffiti. The houses that were occupied had been neglected for such a long time, they appeared as if they had given up. What paint existed was peeling, and yards were nothing but hard-packed dirt and weeds. The occasional old, poorly maintained car sat in the street in front of a few houses. While the house was in no better condition, Billy Alphonse's luxury car sat in pride of place, where he could easily see it, on the front patch of dirt that had once been the lawn of the ramshackle house he and Hannah lived in. Dani crammed her small purse under her car's front seat out of sight and got out.

"What're you doin' here?" Alphonse asked, as he held the door to the house open.

"I want to see my sister," Dani said, giving him a cold, belligerent look.

"Yeah? Maybe she don't wanna see you." His cigarette-tainted breath and body odor hung in a cloud around him, making Dani grimace.

He was borderline good looking, in a dangerous sort of way. Tat sleeves covered both arms and were currently on display because of the unfortunately named wifebeater T-shirt he wore. At five foot eight, Alphonse wasn't a tall man. To make up for not having an impressive figure, he resorted to being mean, pushy, and demanding. He'd never liked Dani because she had never allowed him to bully her and she'd scornfully rebuffed his pathetic attempts at seduction. Dani had dealt with a lot of disagreeable people and situations thanks to Hannah; Billy Alphonse was just one more.

"Then she can tell me that herself," Dani said, pushing past him. The house smelled of old food, unwashed bodies, and the remains of cigarettes. Several plates and take out containers that were overflowing with cigarette butts and ashes covered most of the flat surfaces in the living room. Drug paraphernalia sat on the coffee table, and empty beer and liquor bottles were seemingly everywhere. Hannah had never been big on housekeeping, and Alphonse thought it was beneath him. Dani glanced around and finally saw her sister in the kitchen.

Hannah looked up from the small kitchen table, where she sat eating a fast-food burger. Technically they were identical, and there was still a resemblance, but drugs and Hannah's lifestyle hadn't been kind to her. There were dark circles under her eyes. She was thin, her blonde hair was limp, dull, and greasy, and there were scabs on her arms where she had picked at her skin.

Gone was the wicked sense of humor, the shining wavy blonde hair, and the dancing sea-green eyes that Dani remembered from before Hannah had fallen in with the wrong crowd in high school. It had been a steady downward path since then, like slowly and inexorably committing suicide. It was such a waste, and Dani hated Billy Alphonse for his part in it.

"What're you doing here?"

"I'm here to see you." Dani eased into the chair opposite her sister and set her phone on the table.

"What about?"

"The police showed up at my place this morning. You were supposed to report to your parole officer and haven't shown up for the last two appointments. They thought you were living with me. Why'd you give my address to your parole officer?"

"I had to. I can't very well give them Billy's address. You didn't tell them where I was, did you?"

"I told them I hadn't seen you and that you didn't live with me. Hannah, this is the last straw. I can't have cops showing up at my door looking for you."

"Yeah, yeah, I hear you."

Dani could hear the sarcasm in Hannah's voice. Both of them realized Dani's threat was a bluff, as it had always been. There was always a "last straw" followed by a "maybe if I help, she'll turn herself around this time."

"Let's go now and take care of this parole issue so they don't arrest you. Then I'll bring you back and leave you to your glamorous life here with Prince Charming."

"Fuck that, I'm not going anywhere. They don't know where I am, and as long as you don't rat me out, they won't figure it out. Go away Dani. I'm not going with you to the parole officer. I'm not going anywhere with you."

Dani watched her sister in despair. "God! Do you *want* to go back to jail? Why won't you help yourself?" she cried.

"You don't get it. You never have. I don't *want* to live like you do. Miss Accountant, working at a dead-end job, following the rules, never having any fun. Your life is so boring I don't know how you stand it. I *like* my life, I *like* Billy, and I'd *really* like it if you'd fuck off and leave me alone."

"Leave you alone? Gladly. Until I get a call from the hospital ER asking me to come get you, or you come by my apartment begging for money, or the police show up. What would you have me do then?"

"I want you to get a life for God's sake and stop hounding me."

"How am I supposed to get a life when you drag me into your disaster of a life every time I turn around?"

"You wouldn't know how to have a life if I was gone. You have no real friends, haven't had a lover in ages, no fun, no nothing. You're pathetic, you know that? You just …"

Hannah started to say more when she glanced behind Dani toward the living room, stood up from the table abruptly, and her eyes widened in alarm. Dani turned and caught a glimpse of someone passing by the front window. Hannah grabbed her arm, knocking Dani's phone off the table, where it landed out of sight underneath. She hustled Dani over to a door leading to the basement stairwell and opened the door.

"Stay here and *don't make any noise*," she hissed at Dani. "I'll come get you when he's gone. He can't know anybody besides Billy is here."

"Come down here with me and let Billy handle whatever is going down," Dani protested as her sister forced her down the stairs.

"*Shut up!* Sit here and shut the fuck up. I have a place to hide. I'll come get you when he's gone. *Listen to me for once!*" she said and hurriedly closed the door.

Dani quietly cracked the door hoping to better hear what was going on and to try to find out what had frightened her sister. Her phone lay out of reach under the kitchen table, and she couldn't call for help if things got out of hand, so she listened and prayed it was nothing serious. She heard the front door open and the sounds of an argument between Billy Alphonse and the person he'd allowed to enter. She could hear the men's voices, one angry, the other defensive.

"My guy warned you about this, Alphonse. He warned you not to piss me off."

"A man's gotta make a living, and this is my territory. Can't have my boys thinking I'm a pussy."

"Wrong choice, man."

"What're you going to do about it?"

"That's the question, isn't it?"

The pops that had suddenly erupted and the sound of something heavy hitting the floor had made Dani jump, and she slapped a hand over her mouth to keep from crying out. A few seconds later, she heard the sound of a door banging open and Hannah screaming, then running footsteps before she heard another popping noise closer to the kitchen. Shots? They sounded … muffled … Not what she'd imagined gunshots sounded like, but what else could they be? It was all Dani could do not to leave the safety of the basement stairs and go to Hannah, but she forced herself not to.

In the silence that followed, Dani heard someone come into the kitchen, walk past the stairwell door, and out the back door. A quick glimpse as he passed, a brief side view of his face and dark-brown hair, was all she saw. It was clear he didn't realize anyone else was in the house but equally clear that, if he found her where she hid, he'd kill her too. Her heart was racing so fast it was hard to draw a breath. She forced herself to slow her breathing down, knowing that if the killer heard her gasping for breath or crying, he'd find her.

Afraid he'd see the slightly open door, she closed it softly with a shaking hand and listened at the gap between the bottom of the door and the floor as he returned to the house with something that crackled and sounded like plastic. A few minutes later she heard him dragging something across the floor and out the back door. Something that made a sickening thump as it was dragged down the back steps.

She heard him return to the kitchen, opening and closing several cupboard doors until he found what he was looking for. During the course of the hour or more that elapsed, he made several trips to and from the kitchen, where it sounded like he was emptying and refilling a bucket. Dani waited for him to leave, trembling, trying not to cry or make any noise. What the hell was he doing? Would he ever leave? After what seemed like an eternity, he passed through the kitchen, out the back door, and didn't return.

She waited another half hour until she was fairly sure he wasn't coming back. Easing the door open and cautiously exiting the stairwell into the kitchen, which reeked of bleach, she walked into the living room. Alphonse's body was missing, and Hannah lay face-first in in a pool of blood from a shot to the back. *She saved my life by forcing me into the basement*, Dani thought, so shocked by what had happened that she couldn't cry.

The wall and the floor in the entryway had been had been wiped up, and like in the kitchen, there was a strong stench of cleaning product and bleach in the air. Dani crouched next to her sister and stroked the side of her face, trying to decide what to do. Should she call the police or just leave and hope they didn't discover she'd been there?

She couldn't ID the killer, and calling the cops would only involve her further in Hannah's chaos. She didn't want anyone knowing she was related to Hannah—hell, she didn't want anyone knowing she'd even been here—but it was only a matter of time until they knew who she was. Hannah had been arrested and fingerprinted; once they ID'd her, they'd see that Dani was her next of kin.

Dani flashed back to closing the basement door; her fingerprints would be on the handle and she couldn't remember what else she'd touched. She heard sirens in the distance and panicked. Time was running out for her to get away unnoticed. She didn't have time to wipe the door or the kitchen table down or try to figure out what else she might have touched. She couldn't stay, couldn't risk being there if the killer returned or the cops arrived.

She couldn't ID the killer, hadn't actually seen his entire face. All she could remember was that he was a white guy with brown hair. The glimpse of him had been so quick she couldn't remember if his hair was curly or straight, couldn't even guess at his height. She had to leave and hope no one, especially the killer, would know she'd been there. The sirens were getting closer so it was now or never, stay or run.

Her legs shook, and she had to grasp the arm of the couch next to where her sister lay to stand up. As she started to push up, she noticed a backpack sitting between the coffee table and the couch. In it, she found Hannah's wallet, two phones, a bundle of money rubber banded together, a gun, and a couple of ammunition clips. There could be a license of Hannah's or something else that would help the police connect Hannah to her, so she decided to take it with her. She'd sort through what to keep later. Dani glanced around and found a cell phone charger plugged into a socket in the living room. She pulled it from the socket, threw it in the backpack, retrieved her phone from under the kitchen table, and ran out the back door. The neighborhood seemed quiet, so she purposefully walked to her car, all the time crossing her fingers that no one had seen her.

Dani drove away, assuming police cars would arrive any second, but the sirens had faded. Maybe they'd been called to another emergency. After pulling into a convenience store parking lot several blocks away, she used one of the phones she'd found in the backpack to make a call to 911. She told the operator she'd heard shots, gave her the address, and hung up. Fearing the phone could be tracked, she checked to make sure the charger she'd taken would connect to the other phone. She got out, put the phone she'd used in front of her car's front wheel, and drove forward until she heard it crunch under her tire.

A mile or so away, she pulled over to the side of the street and rested her head on the steering wheel. Between sobs and the shakes that ran through her, she was panicked about what to do. Dear God, she was an accountant. She took comfort in the same, dependable monotony of the job. Now? She had no idea what to do other than avoid the police and hope it would prevent the killer from realizing she'd been at the house and that she was a witness. A witness he would think could identify him. She had to leave town, go somewhere and wait until the police found him.

In the midst of the panic, she realized that her darkest wish had come true, Hannah was gone, permanently gone.

CHAPTER FOUR

LOOKS LIKE WHOEVER THE SHOOTER was cleaned up after himself at least enough to make DNA retrieval difficult if not impossible. Used an oxygen-based bleach and regular bleach," Elly Mason, the crime scene tech said. The cops in Major Crimes were always relieved when they saw Mason at a crime scene. A petite black woman, she was meticulous, took her time, and refused to let anyone influence her processing of a crime scene, or hurry her along, or tell her what to collect. A scene processed by Elly Mason was evidence you could rely on.

"Cleaned up his shell casings too, unless he used a revolver. That says calm and organized to me. Maybe it was a professional hit," Detective Charlie Sanders said. Alphonse was well known to Vice.

"Where the hell have you been?" Sanders asked when his partner, Jack Michaels, stepped through the front door and slipped on booties over his shoes.

"I had a meeting with one of my confidential informants about some possible shipments coming in. I got your text and got here as quickly as I could. What's up?"

"Shooting was called in anonymously by a 'neighbor,' except, according to the uniforms canvassing the neighborhood, none of the neighbors who were home say it was them. Looks like there were two victims, but one's missing. It's Billy Alphonse's place, and he's nowhere to be found. Not sure yet who the dead woman is."

Elly used her chin to indicate an area on the old wood flooring that still looked damp and had probably been covered by a pool of blood in the entryway to the small house. "As I told Sanders, the shooter cleaned up after himself at least enough to make DNA retrieval unlikely. I'm gonna see if I can pry up a board or two—blood probably seeped into the joins in the wood. Blood gets into everything, but the cleaners the killer used can seep into cracks, too. I'll take samples to see what I can get, but don't get your hopes up. He was pretty careful."

"You're assuming it was a 'he,' Elly," Michaels said.

Elly rolled her eyes at him and waved a hand in front of his face. "It's my generic pronoun, Michaels. Don't get all worked up about it."

"So the question is, who's dead and who's the killer?" Michaels said, standing out of her way and that of the other techs gathering evidence. The EMTs had removed the woman's body after Michaels had taken a look. Now it was just a matter of getting her identified, notifying relatives, and waiting for the autopsy report. They had been unable to find a purse or any identifying information on her or in the house.

Michaels ran a hand over his forehead and back through his brown hair that was long enough to spill over his collar and let out a frustrated sigh. "Billy Alphonse killed one of his associates or they killed him, but with no body and the fucked-up DNA, no way to tell. My money's on Alphonse doing the killing. I think he's cleaning house. That guy Tulio got offed, then those dealers a couple days ago. Rumor has it that Tulio was working for Alphonse and the others had been double-dipping with Alphonse and his competition. Alphonse probably found out and took them out."

"Why the woman? Did you recognize her? You're more familiar with who Alphonse hangs with than I am. Is she a dealer?" Sanders asked.

They'd been informal partners for a year, but Vice cops often worked solo, so their partnership hadn't quite gelled yet, and Sanders was new, relatively speaking. He still looked like a patrol officer. He kept his hair short, was in good shape, and always wore a tie and a jacket—not someone who could pass undercover. He was good with tech stuff, so there had never been any suggestion that he work undercover. That took a special personality, and Sanders didn't have it. Michaels had it, but after he'd transferred from Sex Crimes to Vice he'd only been undercover for a couple of years. He still mostly worked alone, though, despite having a partner.

Michaels shrugged. "I don't recognize her. Collateral damage, I guess. A customer, a girlfriend, maybe a prostitute he was involved with. She looked like a meth head to me, so she could be all three. Once we know who she is, maybe that'll clear up some things." He and Sanders watched as the videographer finished up his work.

"Sanders! Michaels!" a voice from the kitchen called out. "Come here a sec."

Rick Kelly, one of the forensic techs, stood up as Sanders and Michaels entered the kitchen. His gloved hands were covered in fingerprint dust. "Whatcha got, Rick?" Michaels asked.

"This place is disgusting, and most of the fingerprints in here probably belong to the residents, not the perp. Look at this, though," he said, pointing to the basement door across from the kitchen cupboards. He walked over and swung open the old wooden door. It's interior handle was covered in the same black powder as pretty much everything in the kitchen.

The stairway light, a bare bulb that dangled from a socket and had a string pull chain to turn it on, dimly illuminated an old wooden staircase leading to what was little more than a walk-in-closet-sized dirt-floored basement that housed a water heater and a furnace. Rick pointed to the top two stairs. "Somebody was sitting there recently. The dust is disturbed and we got fingerprints off the interior door handle." He raised his eyebrows questioningly.

"So we have a potential witness," Michaels said. "Get those fingerprints into the lab right away so we can get an ID. You took photos of everything, right?"

"Of course. I'll send them to you when I get back to home base."

Sanders stared at the disturbed dust on the stair tread and shook his head. "Whoever was here is wearing a big target on their back and needs to be found."

Michaels frowned deeply and nodded. "That is one dead witness, if we don't find them first."

Dani's hands shook as she frantically threw clothes, along with other personal items from the bathroom, into a small suitcase and fought back images of what had happened at Alphonse's house. It was late October, cold but no snow yet. Although she had no real idea where she was going or how long she'd be gone, she grabbed her winter coat, a warm hat, and gloves and threw them into her car.

She was still debating what to do—call the cops and tell them she'd been there, do nothing and hope they didn't discover she had been there, or just flee and hope they couldn't find her. She'd already made the mistake of leaving the scene and making the anonymous 911 call. That didn't look good, nor did the fact that she'd lied to the officers looking for Hannah that morning. If they found her fingerprints, and they most likely would, they'd probably think she had killed Alphonse and her sister.

The news of the killings would be reported in the media, and it wouldn't be long before everyone, including the killer, would know there'd been a witness. And once the police knew who she was, her name would be out there as well. She'd be a sitting duck. The killer wouldn't know what she did or didn't know. She'd be a witness who needed to be silenced before she could ID him.

The only thing she could think to do was leave before the police put two and two together and found her. She called her boss at the accounting firm and told her she had to be off work for a week due to a personal emergency. Not really a lie, but it would keep her boss from wondering where she was come Monday and possibly contacting the police. After the call, she turned her personal phone off, tucked it into her bag, picked up her suitcase and Hannah's small backpack, and left.

Half an hour later, she entered a beauty supply store in a nearby strip mall. She purchased several boxes of hair color, a pair of scissors, a box of disposable gloves, and an aerosol bottle of spray-on color the employee recommended to cover regrowth and prolong the time between dye jobs. She stopped at several ATMs to withdraw as much money as she could from her checking account, then drove out of the city toward the mountains.

The news station on the radio had broadcast a report of the murder, not so much because drug-related murders were a top media concern but because the police were looking for an unidentified witness and wanted anyone with information about the murder to call an anonymous tip line. She had hoped for more time, but the search for her had already begun.

She stopped at a motel near Interstate 70 and Colfax in Golden, Colorado. Sitting in the parking lot several spaces away from the office, she shook out the contents of the backpack she'd taken from the house. There was a stack of bills rubber banded together that came to $500 dollars. There was a credit card in the name of Beth Caldwell and a driver's license in the same name bearing Hannah's photo, and the gun. What the hell had Hannah gotten into? What had she been doing for Alphonse? Dani shook her head. There was no way of knowing now.

The credit card and the license were a huge relief, though. Dani didn't know of any motels or hotels that didn't require a credit card to get a room. Dani just hoped the credit card wouldn't be declined or cause the clerk to call the cops. She had her own ID and credit card, but using either would need to be reserved for emergencies only.

After checking in, relieved the card had been accepted, she headed for the ground floor room. It was clean, which was about all you could say about it, but it was out of the public eye. Standing in front of the bathroom mirror, she gazed at herself. She'd always liked her hair, but it had to go. She frowned as she picked up the scissors and squeezed her eyes closed for a second, opened them, and began to cut off her hair.

When it was done, there were hanks of hair lying in the sink and on the vanity, and to her eye, she looked naked. Her hair was now chin length and a little uneven on the right side. She collected the hair, put it in the wastebasket, and began to unpack the hair dye. A medium brown had seemed like a good choice, not black and not a lighter color. After carefully reading through the directions, she pulled on a pair of gloves and began to apply the color.

Staring in the mirror when it was all done, she wasn't sure it was much of a disguise. The only advantage was, when they finally ID'd her, they'd be looking for a woman with long blonde hair, not chin-length brown hair. She pulled out the plastic waste bin liner with its contents, tied it closed, and put it near her suitcase. No point in leaving evidence behind. If she'd had time she'd have invested in colored contacts, but perhaps the hair would be enough of a disguise, she thought as she climbed into bed and pulled the covers up around her.

She stared into the darkness, listening to the traffic noise outside the ground floor room, and tried to erase the memory of her sister lying on the floor in a pool of blood. Her grief was accompanied by an uncomfortable, guilty relief that Hannah was gone.

She'd failed to keep Hannah safe. According to her mother, though, Dani had always failed to live up to her expectations. The irony of her mother preaching to her about living up to expectations wasn't lost on Dani. God knew her mother had reneged on her responsibility by spending her days drunk and ignoring her two girls. Dani hadn't been able to change that either.

She'd always felt like the only responsible adult in the family. It had been a sore point with Hannah. The sore point for Dani was that it didn't matter what trouble Hannah got into—she was the favored twin, and Dani never knew why. Now, she had nothing to live up to. Her mother and sister were dead, and her father might be; they hadn't heard from him in years. Dani's life, as she'd always known it, had died as well as she'd sat in that stairwell and listened to the gunshots.

The emptiness she felt when she thought about what her life would be going forward frightened her. There was nothing preventing her from leaving Colorado and creating a new life somewhere else. The problem was, she'd never given much thought to what she wanted. Now that she had to, she couldn't think of anything, and the emptiness terrified her.

A witness, he thought, as he picked up the glass and took a long pull. The ice barely took the edge off the vodka as it burned its way down into his stomach. If that wasn't shit for luck, he didn't know what was. How had he missed the person's presence, and what had they heard or seen?

He kicked himself for not doing a more thorough sweep of the place before he left, but he'd already spent too much time there. The house was small, and it hadn't occurred to him there might even be a basement. He'd discovered that a woman had hidden herself in the hall closet when he heard her scream after he shot Alphonse. He'd shot her as she bolted from the closet and ran into the living room. Just as well he'd taken care of her; she could ID him.

Over a second vodka, he realized his decision to remove Alphonse's body to throw in some confusion as to who was responsible for shooting whom had been stupid. Next time, he'd clear the place before he left and fuck confusing an investigation.

CHAPTER FIVE

CARL THOMPSON, THE PATHOLOGIST who'd done the autopsy, was a tall, thin man. Gowned and gloved and wearing a mask and eye protection over his glasses, he pointed to the entrance wound in the back of the woman's body. "Bullet entered here, with a slight downward trajectory, so the shooter was taller than she was. I can't say for sure, but using the trajectory of the bullet, I'd estimate the killer was at least five foot ten or slightly taller." He turned to his assistant. "Andy, help me turn her over."

They turned the corpse over, and Michaels and Sanders could see the exit wound was larger than the entry wound, not quite centered and angled slightly to the left of her chest cavity. "The bullet missed the scapula, which might have deflected it to something less lethal. As it was, it blew through the right ventricle of the heart, through the lung, and came out between the ribs. I assume, from the wounds, she was shot as she was trying to escape. It was over pretty quick." He turned toward Michaels and Sanders and leaned a hip against the table where the body lay.

"Based on her physical condition, needle marks, weight, and the condition of her skin and teeth, I'd say she was a long-term meth addict, but she could have been using other drugs as well.

The condition of the liver would also indicate a chronic alcohol problem. I've sent blood for toxicology, but I think that pretty much sums it up. Death may have been a mercy. She looks older, but her prints ID her as Hannah Calderwood, age twenty-nine. Her prints were in the system. She's got a long history of arrests."

"Okay, Carl, thanks. If anything else turns up, let us know." Michaels headed out of the morgue with Sanders on his heels. "Let's check her arrest jacket and see if she's got family. If so, get an address, and we'll do a notification. If she has family, maybe they'll have more background on the victim that'll point us to some suspects. Let's go update Jagerski and let her know where we're at."

When they got to Vice, Michaels went to talk to Kaye, and Sanders sat down at his computer. Before he searched for an address, he did a quick check of email to see if anything had turned up regarding the prints for the possible witness. At the end of a long list of new emails was one from the print section of the lab.

"Holy shit ..." Sanders said as Michaels walked up behind him.

"What? Did something come in?"

"Our witness is a twin sister, Danielle Calderwood."

"How'd her fingerprints end up in the system? Does she have a record, too?" Michaels asked.

"No, but she underwent a background check for her job, so she was fingerprinted."

"Did you get an address?"

"Hang on. Okay here we go," Charlie said, scribbling an address on a sticky note. He handed it to Michaels and started to get up.

"Look, you're better at this computer shit than I am. See what all you can find out about her. I'll go make the notification and bring her back, ostensibly so she can ID her sister. When I get her here we can have a chat about her being at the scene."

"You don't want me to come?"

"I want you to find something that we can leverage against her when we talk to her about being at a crime scene and not reporting it or sticking around. There has to be a reason she was there. See what background you can dig up on her." Michaels saw the look on Sanders's face. "What? You wanna go make the notification? Go. I'll see what I can find, I hate notifications anyway."

Sanders shrugged. "No, you take that. I'll see what I can find."

It was a nondescript apartment building about ten miles from the neighborhood where Hannah Calderwood had been killed. The grounds were mostly sidewalk and asphalt, with the exception of a tiny patch of grass near the front entrance, but the building was in decent repair. Apartment 2C. Michaels got out, walked up to the entrance, buzzed her apartment, waited, and buzzed it again. He buzzed the manager and got no response, so he buzzed the other apartments on that floor one after another until someone answered.

"Yeah?" a male voice said through the intercom.

"This is Detective Jack Michaels from the Denver Police Department. I'm trying to contact Danielle Calderwood in 2C but can't get an answer. Can you let me in so I can see if she's there?"

"How do I know you're a cop?"

Michaels blew out an exasperated breath. "Come down, and I'll show you my ID badge. This is important. I need to talk to her."

"Christ, what's she gotten involved in? Two cops were here earlier today, and now you want to talk to her. Be my guest," he said, and hit the buzzer.

Michaels opened the door, walked in, and started up the stairs. Standing at her apartment door, he knocked several times and got no answer. "Ms. Calderwood?" he called out, knocking on the door again. "I'm Detective Michaels, Denver police. I need to talk to you about your sister."

A guy from the apartment across the hall poked his head out. "Dude, stop knocking. She's obviously not there. I looked out back and her car's not in the parking lot. Give me your card and I'll give it to her when she gets back."

"D'you know where she went?"

"Didn't know she was gone, but all your pounding made me check for her car. I haven't seen her since early this morning when the cops showed up. She left shortly after that, and I haven't seen her since."

"Did she come back at some point?"

"I have no idea," he said, an annoyed look on his face. "I work at home. I've been busy. The only reason I know about the cops' visit is I was coming home from staying at my girlfriend's and walked past them in the hall. She didn't look happy, but then, neither did they."

With that, he walked back into his apartment and shut the door, leaving Michaels standing in the hallway.

"She's gone? You checked the apartment?" Kaye asked Michaels.

"Yeah. I was able to find the manager and convince him to open the door for a quick 'welfare check.' I couldn't really search the place—the manager was reluctant to let me even look but he finally opened the door and stood there while I had a quick look-see. She's gone—no toiletries, and her car is gone. Looks like she left in a hurry. The garbage hadn't been emptied, and she had perishables in her fridge. I asked around, and no one's seen her since this morning, when two cops showed up. We're looking into what that was all about now."

"Makes me wonder if she had something to do with the shooting. Why else would she take off and not call the cops when her sister was killed?"

"Anybody's guess at this point, but I think she must have seen or done something that made her run. I put a BOLO on her and her car when it was clear she was gone. If that doesn't net anything, then I'll do that Crime Stoppers thing and get pictures of her and her car out for public consumption. I'd like to try and find her without doing that. You know how those things draw all the nutjobs out of the woodwork, plus it might freak her out, and she'd totally disappear."

Kaye nodded. "Keep me posted," she said, but before she could walk back to her office Sanders walked up.

"So I talked to the officers involved," Sanders said. "They had come to arrest Hannah Calderwood for violation of her parole. She'd given her sister's apartment as her residence, but Danielle Calderwood claimed she hadn't seen her sister in more than a week and didn't know where she was living. My guess is she lied about that, and when they left, she drove over to the house to talk to her sister. In the process she got caught up in the shooting."

Kaye ran a hand through her hair and nodded. "Okay, that probably explains why she was there, but it doesn't explain why she lied to the officers who came looking for her sister or why she took off. That's suspicious. Keep digging. We need to find her and find out what her involvement was."

"Look, you've got no title. I can't trade the car for anything else, 'cause you've got no title. It isn't legal without a transfer of title," the manager of the used car lot in Silverthorne said.

"But—"

"No buts about it, lady. Either ya got a title, which means you've got the right to sell the damn car, or ya don't, in which case it may be yours, but you can't sell it and I can't buy it."

It hadn't occurred to Dani to retrieve the title to her car from her safe-deposit box. It hadn't occurred to her that she might need to. It hadn't occurred to her to do anything but flee, and she still wasn't sure if that'd been the right decision. The morning after the murder, she'd driven I-70 into the mountains west of Denver, not sure where she was going, just away from Denver. She drove until she'd reached Silverthorne, where she spent the night. So far, the phony credit card had been accepted.

By now she figured the police, and maybe the killer, had determined she was Hannah's next of kin and knew about her car, probably knew a lot about her. And probably wondered why she'd lied to the police officers who'd shown up to collect Hannah. The night before, she'd decided to try to find something less noticeable, something the police wouldn't know about. She was terrified that contacting them would result in her being in the spotlight and alerting the killer to who she was. They hadn't used a photo to identify her, yet, but she was sure they would eventually. Based on her actions, they probably thought she was the killer.

"Fine, never mind," she said to the used car dealer. She turned to go, and he caught her arm.

"Now slow down. I didn't say we couldn't make a deal, just that I can't officially trade you for your car. I got a couple vehicles I could sell you, and you could just leave your car here."

"But what would you do with my car?"

"Parts," he said, scratching at his chin and shrugged. "I can use it for parts."

That took her aback. She'd had the little red Fiesta for six years. She'd made the mistake of giving her a name—Berry—and the thought that he'd dismantle her and piece her out broke Dani's heart. But this wasn't normal life anymore. Berry was too visible, too identifiable, and the cops would know the make, model, and license plate of her car. She fought back her tears—*Jesus, tears over a damn car*, she thought—and nodded at the man.

"It's old, but it's solid, and I can give you the truck for five hundred bucks, no questions asked, if you leave your car with me."

"*What?* You can't expect me to leave my car and pay you five hundred bucks for one of your trucks. Why can't we just trade even?" she stammered.

The guy rocked back on his heels and leered at her. "Looks to me like you don't have a lot of bargaining room. We could always work out a deal."

"What kind of deal?"

He shrugged and gave her a sly smile. "A personal deal between us. You know, a favor from me in return for a favor from you."

"No thanks, I'll just pay you for it," she said, hoping that he'd still sell it to her.

"Your loss, but I won't pass on five hundred bucks. Let's go get it taken care of."

Dani knew she was getting screwed, but she had no choice, so she nodded, and they completed the deal. She'd used the forged driver's license she'd found in her sister's purse. The picture of her sister was decent enough that Dani could use it for ID. The truck would be registered in Beth Caldwell's name, and Dani paid cash for the truck. She hoped it wouldn't flag anything with the police.

"I'm sorry," she said, tearing up as she emptied Berry of her personal belongings. Dani took the insurance cards and the registration. No point in leaving them and having the creep discover her real name.

As it turned out, the bastard had truly screwed her over. The truck was as far from "solid" as they came.

CHAPTER SIX

IT'S WEIRD NEITHER BILLY ALPHONSE nor his body has turned up. That assumes the dead guy was Billy. We've found nothing on the missing twin sister's location either. D'you think Alphonse is dead or in hiding?" Sanders asked.

Michaels looked up from the file he'd been shuffling through. It had been a frustrating couple of days. No body of anyone, including Alphonse, had turned up. The BOLO on Danielle Calderwood had resulted in nothing. He wondered if she'd left the state and whether he should alert the highway patrol in neighboring states.

"He's dead, I'd lay money on it. We just haven't found his body yet. It'll turn up eventually. Either he'll float to the surface this spring when the weather warms up, or somebody will discover his body somewhere."

"I'd like to know why the shooter removed the body," Sanders said.

"It adds to the confusion about who did what and removes a source of evidence." Michaels leaned back in his desk chair and stretched. "I'd like to know what happened to the twin sister."

"No word on her car?" Sanders asked, shuffling through the file.

"Not yet. The BOLO hasn't turned up anything. I've got the IT guys monitoring her cell phone, but so far there's been no activity or ability to locate it. I put in a request for info about her on Crime Stoppers. They've got it up on their site, but I'm gonna talk to the media and see if that turns up anything on her or the car."

"The missing twin could've been the killer," Sanders said. "I wouldn't rule her out."

Michaels gazed at the ceiling, then looked at Sanders. "That seems unlikely. I find it hard to believe she'd kill her sister."

"Maybe, but family … the root of all evil."

"That's money, Sanders."

"And drugs bring in lots of it. Danielle Calderwood had to be involved to some extent—either she was there to bail her sister out or she was involved in the drug racket Alphonse ran in some way." Sanders chewed on his lower lip as he shuffled through papers on his desk. "Almost three days and we have nothing."

Michaels nodded. "Yeah, I think this is going to be one of those dead-end cases. Wanna place a bet on whether Alphonse's body turns up or not?"

Sanders looked up from his desk and frowned for a moment. "Okay, I'm in for twenty bucks. Does the bet have to be specific about where, or just that he's found?"

"Nah, just found. What side are you taking, body found or never found?"

"Never found."

"Deal."

Sanders nodded and returned to the documents he was adding to a murder book on one of their current cases. "Hold on," he said, looking up again. "How long does the bet last? I mean he could turn up ten years from now."

Michaels rubbed a finger across his lips. "Let's say six months.

By then the case will be stone cold, and I can't imagine Alphonse keeping that low a profile for that long unless he's dead."

Sanders nodded. "Deal."

CHAPTER SEVEN

DANI LEFT SILVERTHORNE LATE in the day and drove for as far as she could until sleep became a necessity. She hadn't been sleeping well, and the lack of sleep had finally caught up with her. She pulled into a rest area and parked near its exit. Stretching out on the bench seat, she pulled the unzipped sleeping bag she'd purchased in Silverthorne over her, and dropped off to sleep.

It was not quite three a.m., when she heard the sound of a car pulling up behind her truck. With a mixture of fear and apprehension, she sat up and saw that it was an SUV with a Mesa County Sheriff's decal on the door. The man who got out was in uniform.

It took a few minutes for him to exit the SUV. Maybe he was running her temporary license plate. She didn't think the Denver police would know about the truck or have flagged it, and she hoped that using the name Beth Caldwell from the forged ID would prevent that.

Please let this be something simple, she thought. She noticed that the officer rested one hand on the gun holstered at his waist and casually ran the fingers of his other hand along the side of the truck. She'd heard somewhere, that cops did that so their fingerprints were on a vehicle if something went wrong.

"Ma'am?" he said as he approached the driver's side. "Can you roll down your window?"

Dani cracked the window a couple of inches but didn't roll it all the way down. "Is there a problem, officer?"

"Deputy," he corrected her. "I'm just checking. Everything okay?"

"Yes. I … I stopped to rest for a few hours. It was a long day."

"You can't overnight here, ma'am. It's not safe, and it's not allowed. You're going to have to move along. There's a turnoff to a town about fifteen, twenty miles up the highway. It's pretty small, but you can probably find accommodations there. If not, you can at least park there overnight and be safe."

Dani sighed. "Okay, thanks."

"Sorry to make you move, but these rest stops aren't safe places for a woman on her own at night, or for anyone really. We've had reports of late-night assaults and robberies occurring in rest stops lately. If you can't afford a hotel," he said, giving the truck a quick once-over, "you'd be better off using a hotel or restaurant parking lot to overnight."

Dani nodded and tried to smile. "Thanks, deputy, I appreciate the heads-up."

He nodded. "Stay safe, ma'am."

She watched in her rearview mirror as he returned to his SUV and left. Perhaps the town he'd mentioned would be a good place to check out. At the very least, she could park for the rest of the night and hopefully get some sleep.

A good night's sleep had eluded her since the murder. Once exhaustion had sent her to sleep, she'd relive being caught in the dark of the stairwell—the scent of dust and the earthy, mildewed smell of the basement below filling her nose, the sound of the gunshots, the brief glimpse of the side of the killer's face.

The dreams never ended well. She'd see the man stop and cock his head toward the door she hid behind, turn, and walk toward it as she watched through the tiny open space between the door and its jamb. He'd jerk the door open, raise his gun, and point it at her. What woke her up before he could fire the gun was seeing that he had no face—like one of those store mannequins with no features painted on it. His lack of a face, more than the threat of being killed, was what always jolted her to consciousness, her heart pounding against her ribs as she gasped for breath.

At last, she saw a sign indicating that an upcoming road would take her to a town she'd never heard of. There was a highway sign announcing that the town offered food and gas, but no icon that would indicate a hotel. Hoping there was a grocery store where she could get supplies and perhaps somewhere to stay at least for a day or two, she took the turnoff.

She drove about fifteen miles down the exit road and turned down a two-lane road that a sign indicated led to the town. It did, eventually. The town was small. A main street and two side streets and a few isolated cabins barely visible off the road leading to the town. That was the extent of it. At a guess, Dani thought maybe two hundred people.

Dani parked in front of the grocery store and dozed. It most likely wouldn't open until eight or nine, and it was just going on four thirty. In addition to the grocery store, which indicated it had a pharmacy inside, there was a gas pump in front of an automotive garage, a bar, a building with a sign indicating it was a town hall, and a diner, but no hotels or motels. To her relief, however, there was no police department.

The sound of a car door closing woke her several hours later. She saw a man get out of the car and unlock the front door of the store. Dani waited a few minutes before getting out and going into the grocery. She took a small handbasket and grabbed a few necessities before heading to the checkout counter.

"This gonna do it for ya?" the fifty-something clerk asked. He had a belly that overhung his jeans belt, his hair was gray around the temples, and he wore glasses that continually slid down his nose.

"Yeah, I think so." Dani waited while he rang it up, and as she paid, she decided to at least ask. "Is there any place to stay in town, like a motel or something?"

The guy looked up and seemed surprised. "No, we don't get many folks needing a motel." He turned and reached behind him, offering her a three-by-five inch handwritten yellowed, card.

"Might talk to Irma Hotchkiss, see if she'd rent you her garage apartment for a few days. It's been empty since last year." He snorted. "If she doesn't take a dislike to you, she'll probably let you stay for a bit."

Dani nodded and took the card. "How do I get there?"

While she filled up with gas at the garage, she called Irma Hotchkiss and arranged to meet half an hour later. An older woman, Dani guessed perhaps sixty-five or so, answered her knock. Irma was friendly but all business. She'd surprised Dani by introducing her to a black Lab named Elmer, who she said she relied on to vouch for renters.

"Dogs know when people are bad. If Elmer likes you, then I'll rent you the room," she said, watching Dani and the dog interact. "Seems like he does, so I'll need the fifty in cash now. If you decide not to stay the week, then I'll refund some of it. You can use the washer and dryer in the garage if you need to. I'll be right back."

She left Dani standing in the kitchen petting Elmer, a bit bewildered and wondering how she'd passed the dog test considering all she had to hide. Fifty dollars a week was less than she'd paid for motel rooms for the night, and it was a temporary, isolated, off-the-road place to stay. When Irma returned, she carried a stack of clean sheets and towels. Without saying anything, she turned and headed out her back door and up the stairs that ran up the side of the garage.

"It's not much, but it's clean," she said, unlocking the door and handing Dani the key. The small efficiency apartment was minimally furnished. No attempts at decorating had been made. It was smaller but looked as barren as her apartment in Denver. "I dusted and vacuumed a week ago. You may want to open some windows to air the place out. Haven't had a renter in a while." Irma placed the sheets and towels on the double bed that sat in the corner of the room. "So," she said. "What brings you here? We don't get a lot of visitors."

"I stopped at a rest area. I was sleepy and I planned to rest for a couple hours, but a sheriff's deputy told me that the rest areas weren't safe and he suggested I come here. I ... I'm on my way to Utah. A relative lives there. I wasn't planning on stopping, but it'd be nice to take a break for a day or two."

Irma nodded, apparently satisfied with the answer. "I'll leave you to it. Let me know if you need anything."

It was a godsend, Dani thought looking around the tiny space as she heard Irma going down the stairs. The apartment was little more than a room with a bed. It had a rudimentary bath and an efficiency kitchen that held a two-burner plug-in unit and a toaster oven both of which sat on the counter, one on each side of the sink. A small under-counter fridge took up the lower cabinet. There was an odd assortment of dishes and cheap silverware. An ancient Mr. Coffee sat on the counter. There was a frying pan and a pot in one of the cupboards. Not a lot of amenities, but it was cheap.

Isolated as the town was, she could probably stay for a few

days, maybe longer. It'd get her off the highway and help avoid the highway patrol who at any moment might find out about the truck and be looking for her. After a shower and the possibility—remote as it was—of a good night's sleep, she'd feel almost human again, clean and safe, at least for a while. Hannah had told her to get a life, but she'd bet even Hannah hadn't imagined this.

"Have you been able to locate her phone?" Sanders asked as he and Michaels stood at the vending machine in the break room.

"It was on for a short stretch right after the killings, then nothing. I figure she ditched it and is using a burner. If she has a burner, IT would have to know the number or the name she bought it with so they could ID the provider and we could get a warrant for the phone records. Otherwise, there's no way to track it or know who she's called. This case is dead in the water. I doubt we'll ever know what happened to her or Alphonse. Sometimes I think drugs and prostitution should be legalized—let the addicts overdose and the pimps find something else to do. Of course I'd be out of a job, I guess."

"We'll always have jobs whether they legalize any of that or not. Somebody's always killing, or robbing, or cheating someone for some reason. And the dealers and pimps? They'd just find something else to sell."

Michaels laughed. "Yeah, that's true. Probably a good thing for us. Look, I gotta go. I'm doing that Crime Stoppers thing in about an hour."

"Think that'll generate any leads?"

Michaels shrugged. "Hell, who knows? They're going to broadcast it a couple times this week, so it might."

"We're asking anyone who's seen this woman to call the tip line listed at the bottom of the screen with any information," Michaels said on camera.

Behind the anchor desk where he was being interviewed, Danielle Calderwood's photo was prominently displayed. "We're also looking for her car, a red 2016 Ford Fiesta," He gave the Colorado license plate number. "Again, any information on Danielle Calderwood or her car, please call the Crime Stoppers tip line."

The reporter repeated the number and reminded viewers it was at the bottom of the screen. He thanked Michaels, the camera cut to the next story, and Michaels left the studio.

It was a long shot. Most tips that people called in amounted to nothing, but sometimes, something useful turned up. In the meantime, all they could do was try to find out where she was and hope it wasn't in a shallow grave somewhere.

CHAPTER EIGHT

GODDAMMED TRUCK, DANI THOUGHT as she turned the ignition key again and heard nothing. She'd about reached the limit of her frustration and fear, but she fought back the urge to burst into tears. She'd bought the truck only five days ago, but it probably shouldn't have come as a surprise that it had died. She hoped it was fixable, and if so, that she had the cash to fix it.

Now what? She seemed to be asking herself that question at every turn.

She'd made the mistake of driving for more than an hour and a half to Grand Junction to get some boots. The sneakers she'd been wearing when she'd left Denver weren't cut out for winter, and there had already been some brief dustings of snow the last couple of days. Her money was getting low, but she needed the boots. She'd also asked around about jobs. If she'd been able to find a job she planned to relocate there, but hadn't had any luck. The truck had died on the way back. If she'd found a job, she now had no way of getting there.

She checked the burner phone—no service, so she shut it down again. Once in a while, she'd turn the burner phone on to check the news sites; otherwise, she kept it turned off. There were portions of the road up the canyon that she'd discovered had black holes when it came to cell service, and, of course she was in one. She wasn't sure why she'd bothered to check. There was no one to call; it wasn't as if AAA would show up and get the truck started. It was unnerving, though, to be without phone service, even if there was no one to call.

Dani let out a frustrated scream and pounded on the steering wheel. Her life had gone to hell since the shooting. She hadn't figured out a way to earn a little money, and she couldn't relax or stop looking over her shoulder. The anxiety and the hyperawareness would probably never go away, not until the killer was dead or she was.

It had been a mistake to stop here. The tiny mountain town in the high country of Colorado had seemed like a perfect resting place. It wasn't a place the killer or the police would think to look—at least she hoped not—and she'd been so careful. The town had no police or sheriff of its own, which was good. It was a place to settle for a while, just a little while, so she could gather her strength and her wits and decide what to do next.

She felt cut loose since Hannah's murder, adrift—no job, no routine, no idea what to do, nowhere to go except away from Denver. Other than Hannah's chaos, her life had been routine and she needed that. Now even that was gone. She often woke up in the middle of the night thinking for a moment that she was in her apartment and life was as it always had been. Then she'd remember and be unable to sleep. The exhaustion weighed on her, and dreams about her sister haunted her. At times the insomnia receded, gifting her a precious three or four hours of uninterrupted sleep, then roared back, allowing only fleeting periods of sleep.

It was dark out, surprisingly so. The huge pines and the winter-bare aspens on either side of the road made it seem darker and more ominous. She turned the phone back on and rolled the window down with the hand crank—that alone should have warned her what a lousy deal she'd been forced to agree to. She held the phone out, hoping to pick up some service bars. If there were any, maybe she could call Irma. If there was cell reception, Irma would come and get her. But … no reception.

The older woman had latched onto Dani, as had her dog. Dani kept her story as close to the truth as possible, hoping to divert Irma's prying eyes from discovering who she really was. Irma fussed over her, pressing food on her, prying gently into who she was and why she was here. It didn't feel right lying to her, but she had no choice.

There wasn't much to tell. Friends were something that Dani had never made easily. She had a couple, mostly women she worked with. She enjoyed time spent with them but kept them at a distance to shield them from Hannah. Men were few and far between. Nowadays, she would see a guy a few times and then end it. There was no point in opening up to someone and having Hannah destroy it.

The burner phone remained useless, so she rolled the window up and tried to think what to do as she turned it off. She wasn't sure what the cops could do, but she figured phones—maybe even burner phones—could be tracked. The killer might not have her phone number, but the police most assuredly had her personal phone number, so she kept it turned off as well.

The darkness and silence settled around her. It had been hard getting used to the quiet and the blackness of the nights. The only night sounds she was used to hearing were traffic or someone else's music blasting, or an argument heard through thin apartment walls. Up here, it was deathly quiet except for the calls of animals and the wind. There was no traffic, no nightlife, no life at all really.

The town shut down around five or six in the evening, except for the bar, which stayed open until nine most nights. But even that was quiet—the occasional bit of music drifting on the air when someone exited the bar was the only sound she ever heard.

She reached for her coat on the seat next to her and shrugged into it. With the heater off, it was getting cold. Twisting, she reached behind the back of the bench seat and groped for the blanket that she kept there. It wouldn't be the first night she'd slept in the truck.

I guess I'll just stay here until morning and then walk to town and see if I can get the truck towed or … something, she thought.

She was uneasy sitting in a broken-down truck on the side of the road, but there was no way in hell she was getting out of the truck and walking alone in the dark at the mercy of who-knew-what. She'd heard what she thought might be a mountain lion's scream not far from the apartment a few nights ago.

Dani regretted storing her sleeping bag, bought the day she'd acquired this piece-of-shit truck, at the apartment. It was cold, and it would get colder as the night progressed. Mornings were becoming frostier every day, and temperatures never got much above the midtwenties. People in town said a big snowstorm was on its way; speculation was rife about when it would arrive.

I'll be fine with the coat and the blanket, she reassured herself. Staying with the truck was the safest option. *I'll be fine till morning.*

She jerked awake to the sound of tapping on the driver's side window and screamed. A flashlight caught her in the face as she sat up, a large figure looming behind it. The man standing outside the truck made a "calm down" motion with his hand and then one for her to roll the window down. She shook her head no.

"Miss? Just crack it a bit so I don't have to shout over the wind." He'd raised his voice, which was deep and a little husky. She could hear him well enough, and she wasn't rolling the window down.

She shook her head no again. "I can hear you just fine. What d'you want?"

He lowered the flashlight so it wasn't shining right in her eyes. The bright light had destroyed any night vision she might have had, and she couldn't see his face clearly, wouldn't be able to until the effects of the bright light dissipated. Had he done that intentionally? In the now-dark cab, she felt near her knee, her hand brushing the strap of her backpack. Pulling it up onto the seat, she carefully unzipped it and rested her hand inside it on the gun.

"I saw your truck at the side of the road. Didn't realize there was anyone in it until I shined the light in. Are you okay?"

"I'm fine," she replied hastily.

He frowned. "Did your truck break down?"

She frowned back, irritation welling up. "No, I just like sitting out here in the middle of nowhere, in the dark. Of course it broke down!" she snapped. She needed help, but his sudden appearance and his size had made her mouth go dry and her heart race.

He didn't respond to her sarcasm. "I don't live too far from here—the next turn in. Why don't you come back with me, and I can tow the truck to town in the morning?"

"Why can't you tow it now?"

He raised his eyebrows in surprise. "'Cause I don't have my tow chains or my emergency lights to hook up to the back of your truck, and I'm not going to try to tow your truck in the dark on this road."

"I'll just stay here. If you'd come back in the morning and tow it, I'd really appreciate it. It'd save me a walk. Come back in the morning when it's light out, when I can see you."

"You're going to stay in your truck all night?" He seemed taken aback.

"Yes," she said, trying to get a good look at his face. Not that seeing it would help her decide to trust him, but at least he would seem less threatening. He'd turned the flashlight down toward the ground, and he was hard to see except for where the headlights of his truck caught the side of his face.

He was tall—at least six feet—and his buttoned-up jacket, which filled the window, pulled tight over his broad chest. He outweighed her by close to a hundred pounds; she was staying with the truck.

He shrugged and flicked the flashlight over her coat and blanket. "Okay. If that's what you want. I'll see you in the morning." He turned and took a step toward his truck.

"Wait! What's your name?" she called out.

He turned back to her, and she caught a glimpse of his face in his truck's headlights. "Jess Walker. What's yours?"

"Beth ... Caldwell."

Holding up a hand in farewell when she didn't volunteer anything else, he said, "See you in the morning. Watch my taillights to see where I turn. If you decide I'm not Ted Bundy, you can walk up to my place. It's only about a quarter mile from here. I'll leave the porch light on, just in case."

And with that, he headed back to his truck. He limped, she noticed. It didn't slow him down, but it was a definite limp. She heard the engine roar to life and watched as he pulled out from behind her truck. She was surprised to see a plow blade attached to the front of his truck as he passed her and drove off up the hill.

Several hundred feet later, he turned right onto a gravel road, and his truck disappeared.

With the flashlight out of her eyes and his headlights illuminating him, she'd finally seen his full face. He wore a dark knitted beanie drawn down over his forehead, but dark hair showed at the back of his neck and he had a beard, not just scruff. He looked vaguely familiar. She thought he might be the guy who ran the bar, but she wasn't sure. *Normal-looking, handsome,* she thought. *But Ted Bundy had been a normal-looking, handsome guy, and so had Billy Alphonse. That's what most people said about killers after an arrest—he looked so normal.*

She rewrapped the blanket around her legs and feet and tugged her down coat around her and zipped it up, wishing she hadn't forgotten to wear her woolen beanie and keep her sleeping bag in the truck. It was going to be a long night.

CHAPTER NINE

J**ESS SET A MATCH** to the kindling in the woodstove and, once it was going strong, he left the door to it open so he could watch the flames. He'd been surprised to see the old truck sitting by the side of the road and even more surprised to find the woman who owned it asleep in the cab.

He grabbed a beer from the fridge in the tiny kitchen that occupied one corner of the cabin's large main room and settled in his recliner near the stove. Absently, he rubbed the top of his right thigh. Weather was coming in—the temperature was dropping steadily—and his leg made sure he knew it. Most of the time his limp was almost unnoticeable. He'd worked hard to get back to normal after the IED disaster, but when he was tired or the temperature dropped, like now, his limp became much more obvious. It didn't hamper him; it just hurt and made him favor it.

He frowned and rubbed his leg again, unsettled and uneasy. Against his better judgment, he'd left the woman in her truck. It was pretty obvious she wasn't going to come back to the cabin with him short of using force, which, based on her reaction to him, was what she feared he'd do. It was supposed to get into the low teens overnight, and snow was predicted. The weather forecasters, as usual, couldn't decide if it would be a normal snowstorm or a blizzard.

It was risky for her to stay in her truck with no working heater, but he wasn't going to try to convince her to come with him. In his experience, there was no point in arguing with a woman who'd made up her mind, even if her reasoning was questionable. He'd been taken for a lot of things in his life, but never a predator, which was what she seemed to think he was. As a woman alone, that wasn't necessarily a bad assumption, just wrong in his case.

Jess had caught glimpses of her in her truck recently but hadn't actually met her. The way she'd hesitated momentarily before saying her name made him wonder why. Either it wasn't her real name and she had to think about it before saying it, or she was just cautious. Irma's place was close enough that the woman could walk to whatever she needed in town. If he was any judge of trucks, she was probably going to be walking for a while. Her truck was a real piece of junk.

No one seemed to know much about her or why she'd chosen to come to a town that maps of the area often forgot to mention. Maybe it was just a randomly chosen, temporary stopping place. The gossip was she was renting the tiny studio above Irma Hotchkiss's garage before she resumed her trip to Utah to reunite with family. It made him wonder why she was still here. It made him wonder if she'd ended up in town out of necessity, not choice.

She kept to herself and rarely left the apartment, and that made her a hot topic. Tiny, with a heart-shaped face on which he'd never seen a smile, she'd caught his eye. She was pretty, despite her badly cut brown hair, but she looked lonely to him. It was hard to tell what she looked like under the clothes she wore. He'd seen her walking to the grocery store once, and it struck him that she was using clothes as camouflage. The loose-fitting jeans and the oversized shirts left him wondering what she was hiding under the clothes.

Polly Letofsky, the waitress at the Mountainside Café, where he ate a couple times a week when he got tired of his own cooking, was the town's source of all gossip and had regaled him with speculation about the woman. Polly hadn't been able to get much information about her and said the woman wasn't unfriendly, just not very social. With Polly, that usually meant she hadn't managed to get your entire life history out of you before you finished your first meal at the café.

The woman hadn't come to eat, Polly said; she'd come in asking about work. She'd been willing to do anything from dishwashing to cooking to cleaning the place after hours, but when she discovered there was no job available, she hadn't returned. That annoyed Polly. What kind of person, she'd asked Jess, didn't eat at the café once in a while? Someone short on money and wary of people, Jess had thought to himself, which was probably why she was still here.

The woman's unwillingness to be social and forthcoming, caused a spike in curiosity for most people, but Irma shared what Beth had told her and that went some way toward satisfying their interest. Irma was the town's barometer for acceptance; if Irma liked you then people assumed you were okay. Polly was tolerated at best. Irma and most of the women in town disliked her for the same reason most of the men liked her. The men liked to look and fantasize—a couple had done more than fantasize—and the women resented her. Polly thrived on all of it.

Jess could understand the woman's reticence to open up to people. He wasn't much for sharing either since he'd settled here two years ago. Bob Kirtcher, the bar's owner, had seen the bottom half of the Marine Corps tat on his arm one afternoon when he was unloading supplies from his truck and the short sleeve of his T-shirt had ridden up. It had taken months for people to stop the embarrassing "Thank you for your service" remarks after Bob had shared that Jess had been in the corps.

There were a couple of men in town who wanted to swap war stories, but he'd been vague and had shared only general information. He never talked about his injury, ever. It was a sore spot with him. The injury embarrassed him. People mentioned him being a wounded warrior when, as far as he was concerned, it was just a twist of fate that he wasn't a dead warrior. So he found ways to divert the conversation or just said it was bad luck and left it at that. People quit asking after a while. He shared enough information about himself that everyone in town thought they knew him. There was a lot they didn't know, and he liked it that way. Seemed like she did too.

If the woman needed a job, that was unfortunate. There weren't all that many jobs available in town. It was several hours away from any ski areas and at least an hour or more away from Grand Junction; it didn't attract tourists. Those who ended up here were rare and usually lost or needed gas. Jobs were scarce, and those that existed were taken. Most people drove into Grand Junction to work, which meant a lot of driving for a job. There were a couple of teenagers in town who did the odd jobs that existed, but no little kids or young families. Most young people moved away as soon as they could.

It had always puzzled him that Polly had stayed. According to what he'd heard, she'd arrived a couple of years ago with a boyfriend who left her stranded a week later. She could have moved on, and probably should have, considering the trouble she caused.

Since he was the only single man over twenty-one and under fifty in town, she'd tried to latch onto him as soon as her boyfriend disappeared, continually stopping and chatting with him if she saw him in town, and she always made a point of talking with him when he came to the diner. She'd slip him a of piece pie or add something she knew he liked to his plate.

Her behavior toward him was possessive—touching his arm, leaning into him while she talked, brushing a piece of hair off his forehead if she had the opportunity—as if her behavior could convince him to connect with her. He didn't like it, but was hesitant to make an issue of it. It was a small town; no point in making an enemy of someone you had to have close contact with. The problem was, not making an issue of it had led her to believe it was just a matter of time until he was hers.

He'd tended bar in the evenings since settling in the town, and he liked working there. It had a TV, which allowed him to keep up with what was going on in the state and elsewhere, and it was a good place to tap into the local gossip grapevine without having to listen to Polly. She made a point of stopping in two or three nights a week, but it was always busy, and he could avoid her most of the time. Access to a TV kept him from getting surprised by news or events. The job helped him fit in so people didn't view him as an outsider or spend a lot of time wondering why he chose to live here.

The woman, on the other hand, stuck out like a sore thumb. She arrived out of the blue, didn't fit in, didn't make any effort to fit in, and didn't seem to have a good reason to be here, which made him wonder where she'd come from and how she'd ended up here. It wasn't like Copper Mountain or Vail or Winter Park or Aspen or even Grand Junction. There wasn't much call to be here. Maybe that was *why* she was here.

He finished his beer, got up, and shut the grate on the stove, and went to bed. If his leg was any predictor, there'd be snow during the night and plowing to be done in the morning. He left the door of the cabin unlocked, just in case, but he doubted she'd show up. He hoped she didn't freeze to death.

CHAPTER TEN

DANI HAD FALLEN ASLEEP, but the colder it got, the more impossible staying asleep became. Her feet were blocks of ice, and even with her hands stuffed into gloves and clamped under her arms, her fingers were numb. She sat up from the bench seat, where she'd been sleeping fitfully, and saw that it had snowed several inches. She debated about going to the guy's cabin. It was risky, but she didn't think she could tolerate being this cold the rest of the night, and the snow didn't appear likely to stop anytime soon.

Dani gathered the small backpack she used for a purse these days, checked to make sure the handgun she carried in it was safely tucked into the interior pocket, and opened the door. A blast of cold and snow hit her. Reaching into the cab, she grabbed the blanket and wrapped it around her head and shoulders, closed the truck door, and began walking. She hoped his place wasn't far and that she'd recognize the turn off in the snow.

There was a porch light on when she finally saw the cabin. Was this the right place? He hadn't indicated that anyone else lived up the road he had turned onto, and she hadn't seen another cabin. It must be his place. Her heart was pounding as she stepped up onto the porch and glanced in the window. No lights were on, and all she could see were vague shapes of furniture. This could be a huge mistake, she thought with trepidation, but then freezing to death in the truck was the only other option.

Cautiously, she tapped on the door. Getting no response and remembering he'd said he'd leave the porch light on, she hoped he hadn't locked the door. She tried the handle, and the door opened. No squeaky hinges gave her away as she quietly stepped into the cabin's blessed warmth and closed the door behind her. She removed her gloves and made her way over to the woodstove holding her hands out, grateful for the warmth. When her fingers regained some sensation, Dani spread the blanket she'd been wrapped in on the floor near the woodstove so it could dry. One of the recliners in front of the stove had an old drab-green blanket lying on it. She wrapped the blanket around herself and dropped off to sleep, the backpack wedged between her side and the arm of the recliner, her arm threaded through one of its straps.

The smell of coffee woke her. She wondered for a moment why she was so stiff and why the bed was so lumpy before she remembered where she was and jerked upright.

"Morning. Want some coffee?"

She whipped her head toward the sound of his voice and saw him standing in the small kitchen area. She could see a closed door into another room, but the rest of the cabin was one large, open room. He had on a pair of well-worn jeans and a gray long-sleeved sweatshirt. Heavy socks covered his feet. How long had he been up and around while she slept? She glanced quickly at the backpack and was relieved that it looked undisturbed. It was the first night she'd been able to sleep for several uninterrupted hours since the murders, and it had left her groggy.

"What time is it?"

"About eight. You want some?" He held a cup of coffee up questioningly.

"No, I need to get back," she said, struggling up from the recliner and picking her backpack up.

"Neither of us is going anywhere."

Panic flared and sent her heart tripping. "I'm leaving. I'll walk to town if you won't take me."

"There's about ten inches of snow on the ground, and it's still coming down, so my guess is you won't get far. And your truck is stuck for the time being. I can't tow it in this weather."

She strode over to the window and glanced out. Appalled at how quickly the snow had piled up, she turned to him. "I didn't think it would snow this much."

"Snow's overdue. It just waited so it could dump a ton of it all at once. When it stops, I'll get the road plowed out and take you back to town."

Her hand tightened on the shoulder strap of the backpack, knuckles going white, her eyes darting around the room. She had no idea what to say or do. All she wanted was to get out of the cabin and get back to the garage apartment where she felt safe, but the snow had her trapped.

"You hungry?" he asked.

"No." The smell of the coffee enticed her, but she was reluctant to admit it.

He shrugged. "I'm going to make some breakfast. Let me know if you change your mind. Coffee's on the counter there. Milk and sugar are next to the pot, if you want them."

He didn't wait for a reply. He turned his back to her and began to beat what she assumed were eggs. Lifting his head a minute later and without looking in her direction, he said, "Bathroom's through that door, off my bedroom," and went back to beating whatever was in the bowl.

With relief, she walked to the door and stepped into his room, closing the door behind her. Isolated from the woodstove, it was colder in here. An electric space heater sat in one corner. The room, like the rest of the small cabin, was tidy—he'd even made the bed. There were no pictures or memorabilia, no carelessly tossed clothes, and no clutter. There were no feminine touches anywhere.

Out of curiosity, she opened the wooden cupboard that stood up against the far wall. It held men's clothing and not a lot of that. There were a few pairs of jeans, folded T-shirts, and a collection of heavy sweaters and sweatshirts. A drawer was filled with socks, undershirts, briefs, and thermal underwear. There was a small dark-blue box sitting on the upper shelf, which she opened to find a Purple Heart. Maybe that explained the limp.

Nature called, so she returned the box to its shelf, closed the cupboard, and went into the tiny bath. There was a sink with a small cupboard beneath it, a mirrored wall cabinet over it, a toilet, and a shower. She marveled that he was actually able to use the shower, as tall as he was. She peed and washed her hands, shocked at the water's coldness. After squirting a tiny blob of toothpaste on her finger and rubbing it over her teeth, she leaned down and rinsed her mouth from the stream of water that was cold enough to make her teeth ache.

When she returned to the living area, the warmth of the woodstove washed over her, and she felt warm enough to take her coat off. He—Jess she remembered him saying—was busy at the stove in the kitchen and the smell of bacon made her stomach growl.

"Get some coffee and have a seat," he said nodding his head

at the table and two chairs that sat against one wall. "This'll be ready shortly."

It puzzled her. He didn't argue, didn't dispute or contradict what she said. He hadn't tried to talk or force her into coming back here last night, he'd just given her an appraising stare and let her decide what to do. Most of the men she'd known insisted or bullied or manipulated women into doing what they wanted. She had to admit that most of the men she knew had been men Hannah had associated with. Jess was altogether different. She wasn't sure what that meant.

Her memories of what he had looked like in his truck's headlights last night had faded. He didn't look so intimidating now. He was handsome. His dark-brown hair was on the long side and damp from a shower, she guessed. It curled against his neck, and a lock or two dangled on his forehead and brushed over the tops of his ears. Didn't look like he'd seen a barber in a while. His beard was dark brown, too, as were his eyes. His beard was neatly trimmed, no ZZ Top look, which would have made her a little uneasy. The overhead kitchen light caught glints of bronze in his hair.

There was an inch of a scar on his right cheek that was visible above the carefully trimmed edge of his beard. If its whiteness was any indication, the injury had happened some time ago. Then there was the limp she'd noticed last night.

Based on the medal, the injuries were most likely military related, which wasn't all that reassuring. She'd heard that traumatic brain injuries, or PTSD, could render a person unpredictable. He seemed controlled and easygoing, not unpredictable; but she didn't know him or what he might be controlling.

"Thank you," she mumbled filling a cup with coffee and doctoring it with milk and sugar.

A few minutes later he put two plates on the table and sat down opposite her. She looked at the plate suspiciously.

"For fuck's sake," he said, scowling at her. "It isn't poisoned." He reached toward her plate and stabbed a forkful of eggs into his mouth. "If you want to wait to see if I keel over, go ahead, but your breakfast'll be cold."

She could feel the heat rise up her neck and flood her face. "I … I'm sorry. Thank you for this," she said and began to eat, keeping her head down, refusing to look at him.

They ate in silence.

CHAPTER ELEVEN

HE'D SEEN THE FURTIVE LOOKS she'd given him since waking up, and her hand shook when she reached for her coffee mug. She was on guard, hyperalert for no reason that he could think of, and that worried him. She'd slept with her arm tangled up in her backpack strap and had wedged it between herself and the arm of the recliner. God only knew what she had in the backpack, and that worried him most of all. She didn't look like a user; he didn't think her jitteriness was related to drugs, but you never knew these days.

She reminded him of Leah, a woman he'd served with who'd seen the man she loved blown to bits. Everyone thought she was handling it as well as could be expected until she'd killed herself. They'd missed the warning signs that, in hindsight, seemed obvious. Those faraway looks, the jumpiness, the rebuff of help, the irritability, the difficulty sleeping, and the almost nightly dreams she'd had should have warned them all was not well. He shook his head and stood up abruptly, startling the woman who sat across from him. He took his plate to the small sink and began to run hot water into it.

Not now, he thought as he filled the sink with water and dishwashing soap. *Put it away.* But he couldn't stop the video that played in his head, couldn't stop the memory of finding his friend with a vicious wound that ran halfway up the inside of her arm, or the smell of blood, or the warm stickiness that covered his hands as he'd tried to stop the blood pulsing from her arm, or the futility of it all. Most of all, he'd never forgotten the peaceful smile she had given him before she'd died when she'd looked behind him and said, "Bobby," the name of her lover, as if he were standing behind Jess waiting for her.

"Ev … everything okay?" the woman asked hesitantly.

"Fine." He turned and indicated her plate. "Done?"

She nodded. He gathered her plate and utensils and turned back to the sink.

Jess tried to distract himself, shut off the memories, and focus on his current houseguest. Something serious had happened, which might explain her reluctance to give him her name or to come back to the cabin with him last night. Her wariness and twitchy behavior made him wonder just how serious whatever had happened was. It made him cautious. He'd moved here to get away from Denver and the insanity and drama of his family, and he damn well didn't want to deal with someone else's problems. It'd be best to get her back to town as soon as possible and wash his hands of her.

"Radio says the snow will last until tomorrow midday. When it stops, I'll plow out to the road and see if towing your truck is possible. If not, I can drive you into town and drop you off wherever you like. I'll see if I can round up some guys to help dig your truck out."

She watched him with an anxious frown on her face. "I guess I'm stuck here."

He raised his eyebrows at her. "Better than freezing to death in your truck."

"I can't pay you for any of this," she said.

"I don't recall asking you to."

He poured himself another cup of coffee, raising the pot in a "want some?" gesture. She shook her head no, so he replaced the pot. He took his mug and walked into the living area, and set it on the small end table by the recliner opposite the one she'd slept in.

"You're welcome to use the shower, if you want," he said, unlatching the door on the woodstove and adding a log.

"No, I'm fine," she said, that wary look back in her eyes.

He turned toward her, his brows drawing together in a deep frown, the scar making him look fierce. "Let's get something straight. I'm not into raping women or spying on them in the shower or drugging their food and holding them prisoner for some warped reason."

Her eyes went wide and her face paled, which pissed him off even more.

"I'm offering you a place to stay until the storm is over—*that's all*. When it stops and I get things plowed out, I'll take you back to town and you never have to see me again. So relax and stop acting like you're one step away from being assaulted."

She said nothing, but her body was tense, her gaze anxious, and it angered him. He turned and walked to the door. Sitting on the bench next to it, he shoved his feet into a pair of insulated boots and pulled on a coat, a wool cap, and gloves. When he opened the door, a flurry of snow blew in before he pulled it shut after him.

She didn't need to be afraid of him, although he could see she was. He wished to hell he'd stayed in Grand Junction last night or that he hadn't found her truck. He should have just driven by it and ignored it, but it was odd seeing the truck sitting there with no lights and he'd stopped to find out why. Since then, he'd been attracted, intrigued, and frustrated by her.

That'll teach me to be nosy, he thought as he collected firewood at the side of the cabin.

The dull color of her brown hair looked like it was a dye job, one she'd done herself, but it curled in a way that made him think it was natural. People always seemed surprised by the acuteness of his observations, but three tours of duty in a country where most of the population hated you and was trying to kill you made being observant a necessity.

He wondered what her normal hair color was, the brown didn't seem to match her complexion. If he had to guess, based on her eyebrows and pale complexion, she was probably blonde. Her eyes were large and a surprising shade of green that reminded him of the water in the Caribbean—but from what he'd seen, they were always on alert and periodically, depending on what he'd said or done, went wide in fear or apprehension.

She was pretty … when she didn't look scared, he thought. Her eyes had drawn him in and her mouth looked infinitely kissable. If they'd met in a more social context, he would have flirted with her to see where it would take him. That wasn't going to happen now. His curiosity had been triggered, and he knew, for him, that was the first step down the rabbit hole. He wanted to know who the hell she really was and who or what had terrified her.

After they'd eaten, feeling awkward about her reactions to his hospitality, Dani had washed the breakfast dishes while he was out getting more wood. He bumped the front door open carrying an armful of wood and dumping it next to the hearth where the woodstove stood. Without a word he turned and went back outside returning a few minutes later with another armful.

Sitting on the bench and removing his outerwear and without looking at her, he said, "You didn't need to do that. I planned on cleaning up after I took care of the wood."

She shrugged, using the towel in her hand to dry the plates as she watched him tug his boots off. "I appreciate you letting me stay here. It's the least I could do." Then she gave into her curiosity. "What happened to your leg?"

He looked up, surprised. "I was in the wrong place at the wrong time."

"Is that how you got the scar on your face?"

"You ask a lot of questions for someone who hasn't volunteered anything about herself, including why you're here in a town almost no one chooses to come to, or why you're so jumpy." He watched her for a moment, maybe wondering if she'd tell him anything.

When she didn't, he went over to the pile of wood and began stacking it neatly by the hearth without saying anything further. While he stacked the wood, she took a better look at the interior of the cabin. An old, plaid-covered recliner that sat in front of and slightly to the left of the woodstove and an identical one, the one she'd spent the night in, sat opposite. Small end tables sat next to each.

Two small bookcases flanked the original stone fireplace where the woodstove now sat. The shelves were filled with books. There was no trophy animal head over the mantle, which surprised her, seeing as there was a rack near the door where a rifle stood. In a corner behind where the recliners sat was a desk but no computer, no phone. Instead, there was what looked to her like some kind of radio communication equipment. Maybe a CB or a radio of some sort? She'd never seen either, but this looked professional.

"You don't have a TV or a phone," she said without thinking.

He glanced up from stacking the wood. "Nope."

"Why?"

He returned to stacking wood, and without stopping what he was doing, he replied, "I have a cell phone, but cell service is random out here. It's 'cause of the mountains and the locations of the cell towers. The cabin's not close enough to town for getting a landline—too expensive—and there are too many big trees around for a cable dish. I'm not big on TV anyway."

"What do you do if there's an emergency?"

"I've got the radio and a satellite phone if I get into trouble," he said, indicating an oddly shaped object that looked like an oversized remote control lying on the desk. "And I can use my cell if I'm in town or somewhere with reception."

"I've never seen a satellite phone. Does it work like a regular phone or a cell phone?"

"Sort of. It works off a satellite rather than a cell tower." He gave her an appraising stare. "Want me to show you how to use it? In case you feel the need."

She could feel the heat rise in her face. He finished stacking the wood and stood up. "You're free to go anytime you want, snow or not. I won't stop you, but it's pretty miserable out there." He pointed to the desk. "The owner's manual is in the desk drawer. Feel free to read it."

She didn't reply.

After he finished stacking the last of the wood, Jess sat in one recliner and began reading the book that he'd left on the end table—or at least he tried to, his leg was aching like an abscessed tooth. The weather was playing hell with it.

Periodically, he still dreamed about the trip outside the secured Afghan base that had left two other soldiers dead. The trip had gone badly wrong and ended with him—by some bizarre twist of fate, the only survivor—lying by an IED-wrecked Humvee with a shattered femur, bleeding badly from the open wound that had exposed one end of the broken bone. The medevac crew got to him in time, but it had been close. Too close, and way too late for the two guys who'd been with him. Fortunately, the dreams had lessened over time, but they never went away entirely. He'd had one last night. The ache in his leg had brought it all back. It usually did.

He'd taken some ibuprofen last night, then again this morning, but so far it had only taken the edge off the pain. The orthopedic surgeon who'd put his femur back together had given him narcotics post-op. Once home, he'd been given a prescription for a narcotic pain med by the Veteran's Affairs doc. Jess knew some soldiers who'd become quickly addicted to painkillers after an injury, so he was wary of taking them. He'd filled the script because he'd learned in Afghanistan that you never knew what you might need in an emergency.

He'd considered taking one last night. He remembered the hazy, mellow feeling the IV pain meds had given him in the hospital. The allure of the drugs and the memory of his pain fading and the dreamless sleep engulfing him was hard to resist. When his leg was acting up and the dreams returned, a small part of his brain wanted those pills badly. Taking them was a temptation at times like this.

The woman finally stopped pacing and sat down in the other recliner. It didn't take long for her to drop off to sleep. She couldn't have gotten much sleep in her truck. The recliner was an improvement over sleeping in her truck, but not by much. At least it was warm in here. He watched her. Even asleep, she kept her backpack close. It rested between her hip and the arm of the recliner at the moment, and she had linked one arm through its strap. Yeah, there was something important in there all right. Drugs? A gun? Something that would no doubt cause a lot of trouble. Of that, he was sure.

He thought about it and decided now probably wasn't the best time to try to see what it was. Maybe during the night. He got up to add more wood to the stove, and the creak of the floor as he put his weight on the floorboards startled her awake. Light sleeper, so it was a good thing he hadn't tried to get a look inside the bag.

"Sorry, just adding wood."

She rubbed her eyes like a kid waking up. It softened her face, banishing, for a moment, the anxiety that seemed to be a permanent fixture. She eased the footrest of the recliner down. Standing up, she moved to the window and looked out. "Still snowing," she said.

"Yep, probably will till tomorrow morning. At least that's what the weather service said when I checked it yesterday."

"I wish I'd known."

"Up here in the winter, it's best to check the weather service before you head out. Or have a vehicle that isn't likely to break down." He looked at her and quirked up the side of his mouth.

"I wouldn't have driven anywhere, but I needed a pair of winter boots." She sighed. "I'm not used to … The truck was all I could afford. I thought it'd be fine."

"Well, I doubt you'll be going anywhere for a while."

"Because of the snow or the truck?"

Jess shrugged. "Both probably. Why'd it stop?"

"I don't know … I pulled to the side of the road because it was acting funny, and it just conked out. It's done that a time or two lately, but it always started. Last night it wouldn't turn over. It just made a clicking sound."

"Not out of gas are you?"

"No," she replied, frowning at him indignantly. "That's not the noise a car makes when it's out of gas."

"Know about cars, do you?"

"I know enough to keep them filled up with gas. I'm not an idiot."

"Just asking—no offense intended. If you're lucky, all you need is a new battery. If not, it could be your starter or your alternator. That old a truck, hell, it could be all of them." Jess rubbed his thumb, index, and middle fingers together. "That can be expensive."

She frowned, and her shoulders drooped. "Then just leave it where it is and drop me in town. I can't afford to fix it."

"Nah, I'll tow it into town. Pretty sure Ray at the garage won't care if you leave it there until you can fix it."

She looked truly confused. "Why are you being so helpful? You don't know me, I don't know you, I can't pay you … I don't get it."

"Never heard of paying it forward, I guess."

"No. All I know is payback." Her eyes flared, and then she frowned.

Evidently she'd said more than she intended. He stared at her, wondering what "payback" meant, but she clammed up, crossing her arms over her midriff. Figuring it was the end of the conversation, Jess returned to his book. She paced in front of the window until she retrieved her coat from the hook by the door and put it on.

"I'm going outside for a bit. I need some air."

"Don't wander too far. I'm not going to search for you if you get lost," he said without looking up.

"Paying it forward only goes so far, I guess."

"I don't have much patience for people who don't use their heads. It's cold and the snow is deep. The woods surrounding the cabin can be treacherous when you can *see* the ground, but it's worse when it's covered in snow. If you choose to wander off, then you're on your own."

"At least that's familiar," she muttered and opened the door.

CHAPTER TWELVE

THE WIND OUTSIDE WAS BITTER and made the snowfall a virtual whiteout. Dani could no longer see the road that she had walked the night before because of the drifts. The only indication that it was there were the trees that bordered each side of it. What a mess, she thought. No truck, no way to leave, no job, and no sister. Her life had morphed from having a job that gave her a sense of order—figures didn't lie—into chaos. She'd always enjoyed the calm, orderly, if boring, life she led and deeply resented the intrusions of her out-of-control twin and the chaos she brought. Now she lived that chaos and uncertainty 24/7.

Hannah's face, the face Dani had known all her life, the face that had once looked so much like her own, was fading. In its place, all she saw now was Hannah lying in a pool of blood. Despite of all the chaos Hannah had brought into their lives, it was as if half of Dani was gone—the wild, irresponsible, reckless, self-destructive, terrifying half. Dani was both relieved and bereft.

Amputees had phantom limb pain, the sense that a part of you was there in spite of the fact that it wasn't, in spite of the pain it still caused you. Her phantom limb was Hannah—there, but not there, and painful. And the thing about phantom pain was how badly you wanted it to go away.

In the depths of her grief, she felt relief, relief that she no longer had to deal with Hannah, and it shamed her. As always though, Dani had to clean up the mess. She was so god-awfully tired of running and trying to hide. Tired of lying, tired of jumping at every little noise, tired of not being able to trust or talk to anyone, and tired of arguing with herself about whether to stop running and go to the police or just keep running.

She didn't know what to make of Jess Walker. His size was intimidating—he was six feet if he was an inch—he was broad shouldered, and from what she could tell through a sweatshirt, he was fit. If he chose to do any of the things he'd mentioned, she'd be unable to prevent him unless she got to her gun first. The gun gave her a sense of security, which was ludicrous because she didn't have a clue how to use it other than to throw it at someone.

Jess had tried to reassure her—perhaps he knew his size would make her wary—and her reaction to him had angered him. He seemed okay, and nothing felt off about him, nothing she could detect at any rate. It was just … she was tired and scared and didn't have it in her to trust anyone, not even someone who believed in paying it forward.

A gust of wind buffeted her. Standing on the porch with the snow swirling around her, Dani thought about what she was up against. There was no way the killer would be arrested and punished for what he'd done. Aside from the fact that she couldn't identify him, the police would see Hannah as just another addict who'd been killed in the company of her supplier, someone who was simply collateral damage in the drug trade. Their goal was to catch the big fish. It was unlikely they'd waste time on Hannah. No doubt, with Alphonse's body gone, they were probably trying to figure out who, besides her sister, had been killed. But they were looking for her. They knew she'd been there, thought she could ID the killer, and they knew she'd lied about where Hannah was.

Alphonse *had* killed her sister, if not literally, then certainly by association. He'd attracted her, charmed her, like most sociopaths could, and hooked her on more potent drugs. She was so dependent on him for drugs that no matter what Dani had said or how much she pleaded, Hannah refused to leave him. For once, Hannah had told her the truth—she liked her life, as dismal as it seemed to Dani. The final blow had been Hannah telling her to get another life and leave her alone before hustling her into the stairway where what life Dani had fell apart.

The backpack she'd taken held Hannah's wallet, a gun, two fully loaded clips, and the original $500 in cash she'd added to the $400 that she'd emptied out of her account. She had wasted $500 on that piece-of-shit truck. She'd planned to use the credit card until it was denied, but the remaining money had dwindled. She had panicked and hadn't thought things through before she'd fled Denver, and she wished she'd had the sense to use her credit card to get a cash advance. She couldn't use it now for fear the police were monitoring it. As a result, she only had $240 left. She needed a job and hadn't been able to find one. Now the damn truck was done for. God, she missed her car.

Dani leaned up against the cabin wall and sobbed. Maybe she should just walk into the woods. She'd heard that dying of hypothermia wasn't a bad way to go, and it would be over, but she couldn't make herself walk off the porch. There was a strong part of her that, even in the depths of her despair and grief, kept her from trying anything.

What drove her, was the need to see Hannah's killer punished. She might not live to see it happen, but it wouldn't be because of suicide.

CHAPTER THIRTEEN

T HERE'S SOMETHING GOING DOWN, I just can't figure out what. Yet," Michaels said as he sat in Kaye Jagerski's office. "Somebody's cleaning house, but the question is, who and why? We can't find Alphonse's body, but if he's alive, he hasn't shown his face. He could be taking out competitors, but no one is talking, and there are a lot of worried people out there."

"No witnesses?"

"Just Calderwood at Alphonse's place. Whoever's doing this takes out everyone at the scene. Although, after the last one, if anyone witnessed anything, they probably wouldn't talk."

Kaye agreed. "Messy. Whoever it is, is thorough, I'll say that."

"Yep, two dealers taken out in their squat and another two in back of a known sales spot. Somebody was serious—shot all of them in the chest, then in the head. I'm thinking it was Alphonse. Probably used a suppressor. Nobody heard any shots, and the houses and businesses are pretty close together in both neighborhoods.

"All we've got so far is that the gun that was used was a Glock 9mm, but those are everywhere. All the bullets are similarly marked, but we have no gun. No guns at Alphonse's that match and none in the other victims' places. Plenty of guns, just none that match. It's probably untraceable, but fingerprints would be nice." Michaels ran his hands through his hair and blew out a breath in frustration, then laughed derisively. "And of course Benny decided to eat soap, so no fingerprints there."

"Don't you think it's odd that Benny Tulio was killed? According to his file, there was no connection between him and the other inmates in the shower that night, and he was just a foot soldier. He was in constant trouble with the law, but it was fairly small stuff other than a couple assaults." Kaye shrugged. "What he was arrested for this time was far more serious, but it was his usual stupidity. I had planned to interview him, but I didn't figure he'd have anything important to give me. It's not like he was the brains of any operation."

"I don't think it's odd, necessarily. People like Benny make enemies. Jail isn't a safe place," Jack said with a grin. "It's full of criminals."

Kaye rolled her eyes and laughed. "Yeah, so I hear. But seriously, Jack, it *is* odd. It's his first night at the DDC—he hasn't been there long enough to get into it with anyone. And, aside from there being no connection to Benny, none of those in the shower had been to a bail hearing yet. Why kill him there and risk the chance for bail? Why not wait until you've been sentenced and do him at the prison?"

"None of those guys were going to get bail. They all have records a mile long. Two of them had been picked up for parole violations, so it's back to jail to serve their sentence, and the other one was headed for the county jail until his trial."

"Still, think about it. They just made life harder for themselves. Even if no one can prove they did anything, the fact that they were in the shower with him makes it highly unlikely the one awaiting trial will get any leniency at sentencing. Any good prosecutor is going to capitalize on this incident to paint them as high risk and ask for the maximum sentence at trial." Kaye sat back in her chair and frowned.

"True, but the other two were going back to prison regardless, so they had nothing to lose."

"There's no connection, at least that I can find, between Benny and the inmates who were in the showers with him."

"There doesn't need to be a connection to an inmate, it could be that whoever is his boss decided he was expendable. There could be a payoff for the inmates—taking care of family or providing protection in prison, something like that. Same goes for the guards."

"So far, they check out okay. But then they would, right?" she continued. "If they had criminal histories, they wouldn't have been hired. Doesn't mean they don't do favors on the side, under the radar. All they had to do in this case was look the other away and claim to know nothing."

Jack nodded. "Someone on the outside wanted Benny shut up permanently. He's been in more than his share of trouble. Maybe whoever he was working for got tired of dealing with him. This last stunt was just plain stupid and cost his boss a lot of money. That alone probably signed his death warrant. To be honest, I can't imagine what, if anything, he had to talk about."

"What if it was simply a message? You know, 'If you're dumb enough to get yourself arrested, and you cost me product, you'll be eliminated.' Maybe it was to set an example and keep the troops in line."

"That makes sense—his boss probably decided he was too much trouble to have around. Nobody knows for sure who he was working for, but it could have been Alphonse. That's the theory at the moment." Jack shook his head. "Alphonse could have engineered Benny's death, but it seems like unnecessary overkill to me. He can't have been privy to anything big, but Benny's death happened before Alphonse disappeared, so it could be him. The other deaths can't definitively be pinned on Alphonse 'cause we can't find him. I think someone else is running the show or staging a coup."

"If it were me, and someone pulled a stunt like Benny did—just out of jail, speeding, high as a kite, and then he goes for a gun? I'd be pissed. He cost the boss—whoever that is—a hefty amount of product, and the jerk is back in jail getting the famed "three hots and a cot." I'd make an example of him."

"And they say women are the weaker sex." Jack laughed.

Kaye ignored his comment. "Wouldn't you do that? The guys at the top of these businesses, for lack of a better term, have to rely on fear to stay on top of things. If underlings think they can skim profits or product or screw around and cost the head guy money, that's not good for business. Benny was expendable, and his death would send a clear message—cost me money, you pay with your life." Kaye shrugged. "It makes sense to me. I doubt Benny could have told anyone much, but if he wanted a deal, he could have identified who he was working for. That'd be enough to go to the trouble of offing him."

"Yeah, it makes sense. Problem is proving it or finding out who did it. No one, and I mean no one, is talking."

"Guess it worked then, didn't it?"

"Yeah, it did."

Jack stood and stretched. "Well, back to the salt mine. I'll keep you posted, L.T."

❧

Jess had stopped on the way into town to check her truck. It was almost buried in snow. He said he'd come back and dig it out, but it'd be later, after he'd cleared the town's two streets and a few driveways. Dani told him, again, to leave the truck where it was when he dropped her off at Irma's. It would be less work and trouble to leave the truck where it was. She couldn't pay to get it fixed, but he seemed intent on taking it to the garage in town.

They had spent the night before quietly. He'd made some chili and cornbread for dinner and they'd sat in front of the wood-stove with beers, Jess reading and Dani enjoying the comfortable, relaxed atmosphere. He'd offered her his bedroom but she'd declined. With a shrug, and a "suit yourself," he'd disappeared into the bedroom, reappeared with a pillow and two blankets, placed them on the recliner, and wished her a good night. No argument, no discussion. He baffled her. He was the first man she'd ever known who didn't push, cajole, or outright demand her cooperation. She wondered as she fell asleep if he was actually as uncomplicated as he seemed, and what it might be like to be involved with a man like that.

One of Dani's friends had told her that her picker was broken—in other words, Dani didn't pick men well. It was her explanation for Dani never having any long-term boyfriends. Despite his easygoing ways and how different he was from the men she'd known, Dani was worried about what Jess would want in return for his help. In her experience, people always had agendas, and no one did anything for free. That suspicion had always played a large part in ending her relationships. And, she supposed, choosing emotionally unavailable men ensured relationships didn't last

Her sleep was restless, and she dreamed of Billy Alphonse and her sister. Dreamed of the way he'd bullied Hannah into doing what he wanted, dreamed of the stairway, the fear of being found, and finding Hannah in a pool of blood. She let out a keening moan. "No! Oh God … I'm sorry, Hannah, I'm sorry," she cried.

"Hey … hey … come on now, wake up, it's just a dream."

Dani startled awake and found Jess kneeling next to the recliner, his hands on her shoulders talking to her like she was a frightened animal.

"I'm sorry …" She took a deep breath and ran a hand over her eyes.

"I thought I heard something and came to check it out. You were crying and apologizing to someone in your sleep. Are you okay?"

Dani nodded as Jess took his hands off her shoulders, and she sat up. "It was a bad dream. I'm sorry to wake you."

Jess pushed himself up, hands on the arm of the recliner, and stood tentatively on his right leg. There were lines of pain around his eyes. "I have them, too, from time to time. Can I get you something? Water maybe?"

"No, I'm fine," she replied with a weak smile. "I'll be fine." He wore long underwear and a thermal top. Both left little to the imagination and Dani looked down at her hands to avoid staring.

"Okay, then." He paused, combed the fingers of one hand through his beard, and frowned. "Sure you don't want the bed rather than this old recliner?"

She smiled and shook her head. "I'm fine here."

"You keep saying that. Makes me think you're not, but I'll let you get back to sleep." He took a few steps, and the limp was very evident.

"Does the cold bother your leg?" she asked.

"A lot of things bother it. Sleep well," he said as he entered the bedroom and closed the door.

Jess swallowed four ibuprofen in the bathroom and returned to bed. The room was cool even with the space heater on, and the down comforter was welcome warmth as he pulled it up around himself. He lay in the dark and thought about what he'd heard. She'd said the name Hannah more than once between the keening moans that had woken him. Who was the Hannah she was crying over? Whatever had happened, it didn't bode well for the real Hannah as far as Jess was concerned.

He rolled onto his side and burrowed under the comforter. Closing his eyes, he waited for the ibuprofen to ease the ache in his leg and thought, *Time enough tomorrow to worry about who she is.*

CHAPTER FOURTEEN

IN THE TINY APARTMENT over Irma's garage, Dani counted her remaining money again, as if hoping it had somehow increased. Two hundred and forty bucks. That would barely pay the rent, let alone feed her, until she could figure out what to do about the truck. There were no big-box or chain grocery stores she could walk to where she could purchase boxes of ramen noodles, instant soup packages, or dry cereal cheaply. There was only one grocery store, prices were high, and she had no way to drive anywhere to find less expensive items.

She ran a hand through her hair and sighed in frustration. It had been a stupid idea to stop here, but the run-in with the sheriff's deputy at the rest stop had spooked her. She'd only intended to stay a few days, but she'd become comfortable. It felt safe to stay because of the isolation of the town, and the appeal of not being on the road had kept her longer than she'd planned. Now, it looked as if she was stuck here.

Jess would probably drive her to the nearest town that had a bus depot, if she asked. God only knew where that was—maybe Grand Junction? But once she got there, where would she go with no money? She had to find a job of some kind. Maybe Irma knew someone who needed help, or maybe she needed help with something. Thinking it was at least worth a try, she walked carefully down the snow-covered stairs that ran along the outside of the garage and knocked on Irma's back door.

"There you are. I was beginning to worry about you," Irma said, holding the back door open and motioning Dani into the kitchen. "I haven't seen you since the storm began. Were you stranded somewhere?"

"My truck broke down."

"Good heavens, tell me you weren't stuck in that old rattletrap the entire time."

"No. I broke down near Jess Walker's cabin. He let me stay there."

Irma was a large woman with graying hair in a short no-nonsense haircut and a face that looked like she'd seen her share of difficulties. Her hands were large, the knuckles slightly swollen, and big ropey veins were prominent on the backs of her hands. She smiled and made an appreciative humming sound. "That is one handsome man. Lucky you. What're you going to do about the truck?"

"Nothing. I can't afford to fix it. Jess said he'd tow it to the garage in town, but I told him to leave it where it was. I don't think he will."

"He's a bullheaded man if I ever saw one. Does what he wants, but then that's what most men do. At least he's pleasant about it." She indicated a chair by the kitchen table. "Sit down and chat for a spell. Would you like some coffee or something else?"

"No, ma'am, but thanks." She watched Irma bustle around the kitchen and return with a plate of cookies and two cups of coffee and ease into the chair across from Dani. Apparently, she either hadn't heard or was ignoring Dani's refusal. Maybe she was as bullheaded as Jess Walker. *At least she's pleasant about it*, Dani thought and smiled to herself.

"You're way too thin, young lady. Have some cookies."

Dani took one and ate it, trying to figure out how to bring up the subject. At last, she blurted, "My truck is out of commission, and I need a job. I have no idea how to find one here." She felt the heat climb up her neck onto her face. "I hadn't planned on staying here more than a few days. Now with my truck, I can't go anywhere and I need to make some money. Is there … is there anything I can do around here to help offset the rent? I have enough money to pay for another week or two, but …" But what? She let the sentence drop off.

"What about your family in Utah? Can't they arrange a plane ticket or wire you some money?"

"I … I can't ask. I don't know them well, and they don't really know I'm coming …"

"I see." Irma took a sip of her coffee. "You could walk Elmer. I don't like walking him when the weather gets bad. My arthritis acts up, but dogs, they don't care what the weather is as long as they can go out. You could shovel the walkway and grocery shop for me. That'd take care of the rent."

"That hardly seems enough to compensate for the rent."

"Honey, that fifty bucks a week isn't what I live on. Most of the time, I don't even rent the place. That sign in the grocery was left over from the summer when we get occasional backpackers and such around here.

"I got my social security and my husband's railroad pension, so the convenience of having someone else do those things is valuable. 'Sides, I'd have to pay the Thompson kid to walk Elmer twice a day this winter, and Devon and Elmer don't always get along. He seems to like you though." Irma pushed another cookie Dani's way. "I'm fixing to visit my sister in Denver over the weekend, and I'd be grateful if you'd take care of Elmer. I was planning on taking him with me, but Vivian doesn't like dogs, so it'd be better to leave him here."

Relief washed over Dani. "Of course, I'd be happy to."

It wasn't much, but at least the rent would be covered, and Irma was always pushing food off on her. Maybe between that and dry or canned food, she'd get by until something else turned up or she could find a way to leave that didn't rely on the truck.

"Thank you so much."

Irma waved a dismissive hand at her. "Elmer could use a walk now if you've got the time. He hasn't been happy since the storm blew in. I usually take him around the town twice a day, but with this snow I've just been letting him out in the backyard when he needs to go. So, he'll be happy to get out. Walk him where you can—just don't let him do his business on the sidewalk. People get annoyed with that."

Dani went out to the garage for the snow shovel and cleared the walk, the stairs to her apartment, and the driveway. When she returned, Irma got up and retrieved a leash, walked into her living room, rousted her aging Lab from his doggy bed and walked him into the kitchen. He approached Dani, tail gently wagging, and sniffed cautiously at her hand before giving it a lick.

"Are you sure he's up to this with all the snow?"

"He'll be fine once he gets going."

The dog was fine and actually rolled in the snow several times, seeming to delight in it. Most of the sidewalks near Irma's had been cleared of snow so Dani was able to walk him up to the town's main road. On her way back, she saw Jess in his truck plowing the roadway. He intrigued her. She was pretty sure he wouldn't tell her any more than he had about his injuries, but having seen the Purple Heart, if it was his, he'd been injured while serving.

It might not be his medal, she thought; it could have belonged to someone else in the family. She hadn't taken it out and looked to see if the recipient was identified. Jess had a practical no-nonsense way about him, though, and he carried himself with the same posture and economy of movement that she'd seen in former military men. The constant monitoring of his environment added to the impression. If she had to bet, it was his medal.

Maybe I could have explained what happened to me, what the dream was about, she thought. *Maybe he'd know what to do.* She didn't trust anyone enough to talk about it, though. Other than Elaine, she never shared her personal life with anyone, and she couldn't share what had happened in Denver with anyone in this tiny, isolated, mountain town. If she could find out more about Jess, it might help to have him on her side. Maybe he would help her figure out what to do or, at the very least, help her stay hidden.

Dani walked back into town that afternoon and prowled the grocery store aisles. There weren't any instant ramen noodles to be had, but she stocked up on canned food, pasta and jarred sauce, crackers, some prepackaged cheese, and some frozen dinners. That, and the cookies Irma had pressed on her when she'd returned Elmer, would get her by for a while.

Stuffing some of the heavier items in her backpack, she began the trudge back to the apartment carrying a plastic bag filled with the rest of what she'd bought. She saw that her truck now sat in the fenced yard belonging to the garage. There were a couple snow-covered trailers and one RV in the lot, so perhaps the garage owner rented space for people to store vehicles they only used sporadically. She couldn't afford to pay for truck repairs or for its storage, and once again, she wished Jess had left the truck where it had broken down. But he hadn't, and now it was one more mess she had no idea how to deal with.

Annoyed, she walked past the gas pump and entered the garage's office. A large man with thinning gray hair and black grease well worked into his hands, stood up to greet her from behind a desk.

"I'm Ray Decker. You must be Beth; Jess said the truck was yours. I'll check it out tomorrow and see what the problem is. If you'll leave a phone number, I'll call you."

"Thank you, but as I told him, I can't afford to fix it. I tried to convince him to leave it at the side of the road where it broke down, but he insisted on towing it here. I … I can't afford to pay for parking it in your lot either. I'm looking for work, so maybe at some point I can get it fixed …"

The man raised his hands and patted the air. "Hold on, hold on. Jess paid the fee. It's only twenty bucks a month. I'll take a look at it and give you an estimate. When you can afford it, let me know and I'll fix it."

She nodded. "Thank you. I'll check back with you in a day or two. I don't use my phone. The reception's so unpredictable here, I just keep it off." She couldn't afford to fix the damn truck anyway, so it hardly mattered. "I … I don't know when I'll be able to fix it."

"That's okay. Just let me know when you're ready."

Dani fumed on the way back to the apartment. He'd towed the truck to Ray's, even though he knew she couldn't afford to fix it, and he'd paid the storage fee for her. She was indebted to him for the time spent at the cabin and now the lot fee, which made her wonder, again, what he'd want in return. People never really paid things forward; they did what they wanted or what they hoped would gain them something. What did he hope to gain, and would she be willing to provide it?

She had nearly reached Irma's when she saw his truck and flagged him down. He stopped and lowered the window, but before he could say anything Dani began to speak.

"I see you towed my truck to Ray's and paid the storage fee. I asked you to leave the truck where it was, but you ignored me. I can't afford to fix the damn thing, and I can't afford to pay for long-term storage." She pulled her backpack around, retrieved her wallet and fished out a twenty-dollar bill—twenty dollars she could ill afford to part with. "Here's the twenty dollars. Thanks for causing one more problem for me."

Jess looked nonplussed and didn't take the bill. "It's not safe to leave the truck where it was and as for the twenty, I don't expect payment, so keep your money."

"You don't want my money, then what do you want in return?"

He frowned and shook his head. "I don't *want* anything." He saw the puzzled look on her face and snatched the bill out of her outstretched hand. "You're a piece of work, you know that? If you don't want the truck in Ray's garage, I'll tow it and leave it out in front of Irma's. Let me know what you decide. The twenty takes care of the month so you've got time to figure out what you want to do." He put the truck in gear and drove off.

He must want something, Dani thought as she turned toward Irma's.

"So what did you find out about our new resident?" Polly asked when Jess came in for dinner before heading to the bar.

"What?"

Polly set a plate of roast chicken, green beans, and mashed potatoes in front of him and leaned against the counter next to him, arms folded across her chest. "Well, she stayed at your place through the storm. Surely you must know more about her now."

"How d'you know she was at my place?"

"Ray Decker came in for lunch, said you towed her truck into town, that she'd broken down near your place."

"Jesus, this place rivals the CIA," Jess said. He scowled and shook his head, still angry about the truck and the twenty bucks. "All I know is her truck's a piece of shit and she can't afford to fix it."

"Seriously? You didn't talk while she was there? How can you not know anything more than that?"

"'Cause I don't make it my job to butt into other people's business." Jess bent his head to his dinner, refusing to look up or discuss anything further. Polly huffed off to the kitchen and, for once, left him alone.

She was easy on the eyes, red haired and well endowed, and most men in town enjoyed looking, but she liked to talk too much and would divulge anything she'd heard to anyone who asked, regardless of whether it was true or not. As far as Jess was concerned, there was an undercurrent of nastiness in her that repelled him.

There weren't any other eligible women in town, so he kept his distance from Polly, which wasn't easy. He couldn't imagine starting anything with her in the first place, even casual sex. He didn't want to get involved with her and have to move if he broke it off. It was clear that, if that happened, one of them would have to move and it would most likely be him.

He liked the town because it was so small, but that was also one of its drawbacks. If he wanted sex, he had to find it elsewhere, and it only lasted for a night or two. On rare occasions, he'd hit it off with a woman and the connection lasted longer. His work hours and the distance to wherever she lived usually ended things after a few weeks. Having his liaisons outside of town worked and didn't cause complications. *Son, when it comes to women, if you're not serious, don't mess in your own backyard.* His father had made that point more than once, and it seemed like good advice. Probably the only good advice he'd given Jess.

What he knew about Beth wasn't much more than those in town knew, but he had no intention of sharing it with anyone. One thing he did know was that she didn't trust him. That kind of suspicion and distrust didn't just appear overnight. Whatever her experiences were, they hadn't been good ones. He planned to keep an eye on her and try to figure out what she was caught up in. Based on the dream she'd had and her unwillingness to let her backpack out of her sight, he was pretty sure it was serious.

He'd thought about seeing what he could find out from sources he had outside of town. The more he thought about it, though, the more he leaned toward doing nothing, for now. Unless something changed, or something worrisome arose, he'd keep his mouth shut and his eyes open.

CHAPTER FIFTEEN

NOTHING. NONE OF THE FEELERS *he'd put out had produced any information. She was in the wind, and he couldn't decide whether that was a good thing or if she was still a threat. He supposed the longer it went without her turning up, the better. It was possible she hadn't seen anything and took off to avoid police scrutiny. That little voice in his head that he'd always listened to, and regretted it when he hadn't, kept telling him that regardless of what she did or didn't know, she was a risk that was best eliminated. He would eliminate her. If he could just find her.*

Jess had figured the bar would be slow because of the weather, but based on the current crowd, when people wanted a drink, they'd walk if they couldn't drive. Despite, or maybe because of, the snow, there were about fifteen people in the bar drinking and talking. That was good for business, but it failed to keep his mind off Beth Caldwell or the run-in with her earlier.

Calling her cynical didn't quite describe it. She was wary and suspicious and trusted no one, apparently, not even someone trying to help her. Not for the first time, Jess wondered what the hell had happened to her to have caused that. He'd known a few people he'd served with who were like that. When they would share, and that was a rarity, it seemed they'd all had pretty rocky childhoods or had fallen on hard times before enlisting. Being wary and suspicious was warranted in Afghanistan, or any war zone you were sent to, but for some it extended far beyond that. Whatever had happened to Beth Caldwell must have been traumatic. Jess hoped it hadn't rendered her unstable as well.

Aside from being curious about her, he was attracted to her. She was pretty in spite of the hair color. She was the kind of woman he'd always been attracted to—tiny, slimly built, and eyes you could get lost in. It would probably be best if she did leave, but he didn't want her to, at least not until he figured out the puzzle that surrounded her.

The more rational part of him wanted her to go. He'd considered offering to pay for the repairs to her truck thinking perhaps it would encourage her to move on. Based on the interaction over the twenty-buck storage fee, she'd have a meltdown if he did that. He sighed. Being attracted to her was courting trouble. Best to leave her to her own devices. Anyone in town, including him, would be happy to drop her in Grand Junction, where she could catch the train or a bus and be on her way. That is, if she asked, and that seemed unlikely.

Jess put her out of his mind and retrieved a beer for Ray who sat at the end of the bar holding his empty beer bottle in the air. Most of the regulars used the bar as their after-work home away from home. Aside from the few people who had jobs in town, most had to drive to Grand Junction for work. After a long drive home and some dinner, a little time at the bar was a good way to relax. Some of the married men brought their wives occasionally, but most of them just came to drink and trash-talk sports teams or whatever happened to be on the TV.

After enough to drink, some couples even got up and tried to dance to the tunes from an old jukebox that played 45s. Bob Kirtcher had found it years ago and spent a fair amount of time tinkering with it to keep it running and trying to find 45 rpm vinyl records to put in it. They weren't easy to find. As a result, the selection rarely changed and relied heavily on tunes from the fifties and sixties.

Bob had taken his wife and flown to Arizona to stay with relatives until after New Year's. That didn't sound like fun to Jess, but it was the first real vacation the couple had been able to take since opening the bar. Bob had broached the subject with Jess during the summer and had been pleased when Jess agreed to handle the bar until he got back. He'd given Jess a crash course on troubleshooting the jukebox, but Jess was praying the old machine held out until Bob got back. If not, he planned to let it sit until Bob returned. Jess wasn't afraid of much, but he was afraid to touch the jukebox.

At the moment, Jamie Stanton and his newly twenty-one-year-old girlfriend, Kelly Price, were celebrating her birthday. Hard. They were currently locked in an embrace on the small dance floor, swaying in an aimless, rotating circle, her arms around his neck, his hands welded to her butt cheeks, lips locked together. Jess wasn't sure they were ever going to come up for air. He planned to confiscate Jamie's truck keys as soon as they sat back down, which looked like it might be a while. A cold walk home might help sober both of them up.

He'd turned to gather some glasses from the under-counter shelves behind him and the TV mounted on the wall caught his eye. A photo appeared on the screen, and his heart rate doubled.

It was her, he was sure of it, despite the long blonde waves that fell around her face in the photo on the screen and the lack of a Ford Fiesta. Danielle Calderwood, also known by the nickname Dani, was wanted for questioning in a drug-related murder and was thought to be driving a red 2016 Ford Fiesta.

He'd been right about her name and that she was in trouble. Jess reached for the remote and clicked the TV to another station broadcasting a basketball game. He didn't need anyone else discovering she was living in their midst. At least not until he figured out what to do. It might be a futile hope, but if he switched channels maybe no one had seen it, and if they had, chances were that with the alcohol on board, they wouldn't remember it.

"Thanks, Jess, I was just about to ask if you'd find something else to watch. Hate the news these days," Ray said from the other end of the bar.

Ray hadn't seen much of Beth—Danielle—since her arrival, as far as Jess knew, but the Fiesta might have caught Ray's eye, being a car enthusiast. At least that wasn't what she'd been driving when she arrived in town. It was going to be a long night. Only seven p.m. and already it looked as if most were settled in for the evening. He gave Ray his beer, wondering what the hell Danielle Calderwood had done.

CHAPTER SIXTEEN

JAGERSKI, MICHAELS, AND SANDERS sat around the conference table in Vice.

"So what'd the guy tell you?" Kaye asked.

"He says she showed up in Silverthorne wanting to trade for a car in exchange for the one she was driving," Jack said. "Problem was, she had no title or proof of ownership. He says she finally paid cash for an old pickup and left the car she arrived in at his lot. He says he'd been busy and intended to contact us because he figured the car was stolen, but the TV spot reminded him."

Jack laughed. "My guess is he planned to strip it and sell it for parts, then changed his tune when he saw the broadcast. We've impounded the car and it's hers. He gave me the temp tag info for the truck, but we're seven days out from the murder and she hasn't been seen or heard from since she showed up at the car lot the day after the killing. She's probably in another state by now.

"There've been no sightings of her or the pickup or Alphonse, but a couple informants I deal with say they hear somebody's looking for her. Nobody's actually seen Alphonse, though, so no telling if he's after her and has his crew looking for her, or he's just lying low, or he's dead."

"You think she's still alive?" Sanders asked.

"At that point, she was. The guy said she was alone, and that's pretty much all we know."

"And no scuttlebutt on Alphonse? No gossip, no rumors?" Kaye asked.

"Not a word."

Charlie Sanders drummed his fingers on the table. "He's dead. I'd bet money on it." His face reddened and Kaye wondered if they'd started a pool on where or when the body would turn up.

"The only question is whether she's the killer or a witness. Either way, she needs to be found," Kaye said.

"I cancelled the BOLO on the Fiesta and put out one on the truck and the temp tag, so maybe something will turn up. It's a long shot, but … it's something."

"Okay," said Kaye. "Let's move on to the Oswald surveillance. What've we got so far?"

"You nearly finished here, boss?" Michaels asked Kaye from the open doorway of her small office.

She looked up surprised at his appearance. "Almost. Why?"

"I thought we could grab some dinner. I'm starving and some company would be nice."

Kaye thought about it and wasn't sure whether this was a simple get-some-dinner-and-talk shop invitation or something more like a date. She'd never dated anyone from work. She'd thought about asking Blake Halloran, a homicide detective, out a number of times, but she'd missed her chance. Probably just as well. If a work relationship ended, it created all sorts of problems.

"What did you have in mind?"

"I thought we could head down to LoDo and check out this new restaurant I've heard about."

"I'll follow you there."

"Parking's a bitch down there. Let's take my car, and I'll bring you back here when we're done.

Kaye agreed and they headed out. He'd always reminded her of Tom Hiddleston. He had the same high forehead and the big blue eyes as Hiddleston. His brown hair was carelessly brushed back from his forehead and it curled if he went too long between haircuts, which he tended to forget. He was compactly built and wiry, and at five foot ten, he didn't make for a physically imposing presence. For a Vice cop, that worked well and had helped him work undercover—he'd perfected the strung-out junkie look. He could also look intense and formidable—someone you wouldn't want to cross—when he narrowed his eyes and the double creases appeared between his brows. His lips were a bit on the thin side, but with a grin or when animated he was pretty damn attractive.

Kaye had known him for the five years he'd been in Vice. He'd transferred into Vice from Sex Crimes, where no one stayed for long. The work had a way of turning officers into burned-out, angry, sometimes unpredictable people. Vice wasn't much better. The ugly, unrelenting work seemed to bring out the worst in everyone eventually. That hadn't happened with Jack, or if it had, he was able to hide it better than most.

The restaurant was a tapas wine bar near Thirtieth and Larimer in the River North area of Denver. The area had gone from a neglected industrial area to a thriving, hip place to live for people who liked urban life. Small bars and restaurants were prevalent, Coors Field was nearby and the light rail trains that ran from the suburbs into Denver all converged at Union Station. Most of the area was walkable if you lived there.

Kaye had thought about buying a condo in the area, but the prices were absurd. Rents were just as insane. She had her grandmother to thank for leaving her a small two-bedroom house, which was close to the University of Denver. The area would have been totally out of her reach had she needed to buy it, but three years ago her grandmother had died and left it to her with no mortgage and a basement apartment she rented through Airbnb. All she had to do was pay the exorbitant property taxes and heating bill.

They sat at the bar and drank while waiting for a table. The restaurant was busy and there would be about a half-hour wait.

"I didn't realize it'd be so busy on a weeknight. Hope you're not as hungry as I am," Jack said with a grin.

"Are you going to make it?"

"Yeah I'll survive. I hear it's worth the wait." He looked around at the people sitting in the bar area.

"You look tired," she said.

He ran a hand over his face. "You know how it goes—lotta work, lotta cases, and little progress, especially with finding Calderwood." Jack sipped his old-fashioned. "With the BOLO on the truck and the updated Crime Stoppers info, maybe we'll get some action. Anything turn up on Tulio's murder?"

Kaye gave him a jaundiced look. "No one will admit to anything, but a warrant to check the guards' phones netted a call to Baxter from a burner phone the night of Tulio's arrest. Pretty sure he's the one who arranged the shower incident. Martinez's phone came up clean, although he had to be in on it. There's just no evidence to prove any of it.

"Baxter's on suspension and is under investigation by Internal Affairs. Arresting or prosecuting him would be impossible. He didn't kill the guy, and there's no hard proof he set it up. He won't talk and the burner phone is long gone. I'm guessing he'll be fired and lose his pension. Martinez is suspended and IA is taking a deep dive on him as well to see if there's anything to incriminate him. Chances are he'll be fired as well, if for no other reason than leaving prisoners unmonitored."

Kaye huffed out a breath in exasperation. "You know as well as I do, someone else will take their places. They aren't paid enough and some of them find a way to moonlight."

"None of us are paid what we should be paid for what we have to do," Jack said.

Kaye looked up as she saw the hostess approach them. "Looks like we may get dinner tonight after all."

Jess ran the last two die-hard customers out of the bar at nine p.m., turned the front lights out, and went about his usual closing routine before he sat down at the desk in Bob's small office and booted up the computer. It was nearing midnight before he shut it down, locked up, and went out to get in his truck.

He started the engine and sat for a moment to let the truck warm up a bit. He knew now why she was so wary of people, even someone who had tried to help her. Looking up the street, he was surprised to see Beth—Dani—walking Irma's old dog. He watched her, mentally sorting the information he'd been able to glean from news reports about the crime and the questions about her role in it. Speculation at the moment still raged about whether the drug dealer was dead or alive, and the police weren't giving their opinion on the matter. The police were calling Danielle Calderwood a person of interest; that was never good.

Jess watched her stop for the dog to sniff around the base of a tree. She stood silently, head down, her hands shoved into her coat pockets and waited for the dog to do his business. A knit cap covered most of her hair. Jess tried to imagine her with the long wavy blonde hair from the photos. It would be a huge improvement, he thought.

She had this air of loneliness about her and a formidable barrier that kept people at arm's length. Jess understood the need for barriers. He'd discovered that up here, letting people in—maybe not all the way in but at least part way in—wasn't such a bad thing. After pulling out of the bar's parking lot, he drove down the street and pulled up next to her. At the sound of his truck engine, she whipped around to stare and then frowned.

Lowering the passenger window, he said, "I'm sorry about our conversation earlier. I should have asked you before taking the truck to Ray's. I didn't think my paying the twenty bucks would be a problem."

She hesitated, evidently weighing her words. "Thank you for that. I'm a little short on money, so the idea of having to pay him kinda freaked me out. I … I don't like to owe people."

Jess nodded. "Kinda late for a dog walk, isn't it?" he asked, hoping to steer the conversation to more neutral ground.

"Irma is visiting her sister in Denver. She asked me to take care of Elmer, so he's living in the apartment with me. It's easier that way, but he seems to have a sixth sense for when I wake up. That's his cue to want to go out, and he never wants to just go pee in the backyard. Silly old fart actually brings me his leash. So, we go for a walk."

Jess laughed, then grew serious. "Not sleeping well?"

Her brows drew together, and then she shrugged. "I have nights, like the other night. My guess is you do, too."

He nodded. Yeah, he had nights like he'd witnessed her experience at the cabin. Knowing what he now knew about her, he imagined her nights were far more frequent than his had become. "Is he done?"

Dani looked down at the dog, who sat patiently at her side. "Looks like all he's going to do is water the tree."

"Want a lift back to the apartment?"

"It's not far."

"It's cold and dark. Let me drop you off."

She gave him a quick nod and opened the door, pulling the seat forward so Elmer could jump into the small back-seat area. He didn't quite make it, and she had to boost his butt up until he could gain some purchase with his hind legs. Climbing into the front seat, she blew out a breath. "Thanks. Elmer moves kinda slow these days."

They rode in silence until Jess pulled up in front of Irma's house and stopped. As Dani went to open the door, Jess laid a hand on her arm. He felt her go rigid, and he quickly removed his hand. "Sorry. I know you don't like owing anyone, but if you need anything, let me know. There are no expectations on my part."

She stared at him with a puzzled look on her face before opening the door and stepping down from the truck. "What d'you mean 'need anything'?"

"You know, a ride or something since your truck's out of commission."

Dani unlatched the front seat and motioned for Elmer to get out. "Thanks, I'm fine."

"I have transportation, and you don't. I'm here if you need—"

"I'm fine," she said, then softened a bit. "I appreciate the offer, but I'm fine."

Jess watched as she closed the door and made her way toward the garage. He doubted that. She was broke and without transportation, the focus of a police investigation, and, if he was alive, the focus of a particularly vicious drug dealer or the killer. She was a piece of work all right. He watched her slowly climb the stairs with the old dog and waited until the lights went on in the upstairs window before he drove off.

CHAPTER SEVENTEEN

SOMETHING HAD HAPPENED, DANI THOUGHT. Jess had gone from, "I'm offering you a place to stay until the storm is over—that's all," to telling her he'd help her if she needed it. Courtesy to a stranded stranger was one thing, but this abrupt change worried her, especially after their exchange earlier in the day. The few people in town that she'd made any ongoing contact with seemed nice. Maybe he didn't want anything from her. It could be he just felt bad about her truck and her lack of a job.

She wasn't sure how good she was at reading people; she'd never known any nice guys, and that included her father. What kind of man ran off and left his two young daughters with a drunk incapable or unwilling to take care of them? Despite her uncertainty, Jess seemed steady and ... safe? She remembered his touch when he'd woken her from the dream about her sister. It had been comforting and grounding, but just now, his hand on her arm had taken her by surprise. He didn't strike her as a touchy-feely kind of guy. It hadn't felt aggressive, but it had alarmed her, and her first thought had been, *Here it comes. Now he'll tell me what he wants*, but he hadn't asked for anything. Why had he offered to help her? She wasn't sure if she could trust him—or anyone—and if it came down to it, she wasn't sure who she would ask for help.

How likely was it anyone had heard anything about what had actually happened or her role in it? She'd been here for nearly a week, and it had been ten days since the murders. No one had said anything to her, but something had changed for Jess, and she wasn't sure what had caused the change. If he knew about her, would he help her or turn her in?

Dani sighed and shifted under the covers, trying to find a comfortable spot. Last night, after one of her dreams and his required walk, Elmer had taken up residence next to her on the double bed, which he now seemed to consider was his right. The walk had helped calm her, and having him next to her was a new experience. It was cold, he was a warm body, and she hadn't the heart to make the old dog sleep on the floor. She reached out and stroked his head and heard his tail thump softly. His presence was a surprising comfort; he seemed to sense her need for it. If only she could stop worrying and sleep like Elmer, it would be such a relief.

It was going to be a long night. If she did nothing else well, she knew how to worry.

Jess sat with a glass of Maker's Mark in his hand and stared at the woodstove, enjoying its warmth. It was nearly three a.m. Unable to sleep, he'd taken up his familiar place in the recliner and thought about what he'd learned. It was hard to tell from the broadcast about the tip line whether the police wanted to find her because she was a witness or because they thought she was the killer.

He'd trolled the last two week's online news sitting in Bob's office at the bar and finally found the brief announcement about the killing. The unflattering mug shot of the drug dealer didn't look like anyone he'd ever seen, but the mug shot of Hannah Calderwood shocked him. The article said they were identical twins, and if you looked closely, there was still some resemblance between them, but Hannah was thinner and harder looking than Dani. He liked the nickname Dani; it fit her better than Beth.

Damn, he thought, *maybe that was why she was crying on the porch during the snowstorm.* He doubted she'd seen the broadcast earlier tonight. If she had, he figured she'd have disappeared. Somehow. It's what he would have done, but he had transportation.

Impulsively, he'd offered to help her, and she'd shut him down, nicely but firmly, despite being without her truck or a job. Despite, in his estimation, needing someone on her side. If he was any judge of character, he doubted she'd killed anyone, certainly not her sister, but her level of distrust told him there was something serious about whatever her involvement was. Best keep it to himself and hope no one else in town put two and two together. And best talk to Ray to see if her truck was repairable. As places went, the town was a good spot to lie low, so she'd picked well; her luck and ability to leave just hadn't held.

Far more unsettling was how he felt toward her. He'd caught brief glimpses of her since she'd shown up in town, but having her at the cabin had sealed it. She had taken up residence in his thoughts ever since. His attraction to her wasn't smart, now that he knew what was going on with her, but it was understandable. Those eyes, he thought, like the Caribbean Sea; they mesmerized him. His sudden need to protect her baffled him, but he wasn't sure he'd ever scale the wall she'd built around herself.

"That old beater is done for," Ray said, one grease-stained hand on his hip and the other massaging the back of his neck, leaving a faint smudge of black on it. He and Jess stood in the garage bay and looked at Dani's truck. "I don't know what she paid for it, the temp tag will expire in another month, but I can promise you it'll cost more to fix it than it's worth. 'Course, it is her only set of wheels, so I could give her the repairs half-price. That don't account for the parts, though."

"How much would that be?" Jess asked.

Ray shot his eyebrows up and then pulled them into a frown and pursed his lips for a moment. "Well ... at a guess, probably a thousand for everything, parts and labor. Depends if I can get a couple of the parts for that old a truck."

Jess blew out a frustrated breath. "I'm pretty sure she hasn't got that kind of money."

"What d'ya think she'll want to do with it?"

"I dunno. I'll have to talk to her. If she can't repair it maybe she could sign it over to you for a couple hundred and you could use the parts."

"I probably could, but then she's got no transport."

"Yeah, I know." Jess frowned. "Just let it sit for now, and I'll keep you posted."

"She reminds me of somebody, I just can't remember who."

Jess had worried about whether Ray had paid much attention to the broadcast on the bar's TV. Sounded like the photo of Dani might have registered on some level. All he hoped was that Ray didn't figure out who she reminded him of.

"I'm probably wrong. Beth's a pretty little thing—skittish, but pretty." Ray said giving Jess an appraising look.

"I suppose," Jess said, as he left the shop. He'd noticed, but there was no point in giving the gossips anything to talk about or acting too curious about why Ray thought he knew her. The sooner Ray got that idea out of his head, the better. What worried him was whether others in town had seen the broadcast. *Time will tell*, he thought.

The knock startled Dani, Elmer raised his head gave a soft *woof*, and lowered it to his paws. *Some guard dog you are*, she thought. No one visited her, and Irma wouldn't be back from Denver for another two days. Getting up from the tiny table that sat near what passed for a kitchen, she walked quietly to the door, pushed aside the curtains that blocked the door's window, and peered out. Jess Walker stood on the other side glancing around as he waited for a response to his knock.

"Got a minute?" he asked when she opened the door.

"Yeah."

She invited him in. He pulled the knitted beanie off his head, leaving his hair in disarray, and stuffed the hat in one coat pocket and his gloves in the other. As he stepped into the apartment, his presence brought home how small the space was; he seemed to fill the room. Dani stared at him waiting for him to say something.

"I talked to Ray Decker a little while ago …"

"Let me guess, the truck will be sitting there indefinitely, right?"

He frowned. "Depends, I guess. He thinks he could get it running for about a thousand."

"*Dollars?*" she exclaimed, taken aback. He nodded. She walked over and dropped into the chair she'd been sitting in. "Well, I haven't got the money to fix it, and as it stands, I won't be earning any anytime soon." She closed her eyes and ran a hand through her hair. "What a mess," she said in a barely audible voice.

Jess sat in the other chair. "I had a thought about that, if you're interested." She shrugged slightly, which he took as consent to continue. "I work at the bar in the evenings, from about five to nine every night. Friday and Saturday, it's open until ten. Sundays and Mondays, the place is closed. Bob, the owner, is out of town until the end of January and left me in charge. I could use some help. When Bob's here, we split the work. With him gone, when it gets busy, there's no one to keep up with the tables or bring in supplies from the storeroom or keep up with dishwashing chores. It'd be minimum wage but ..."

"Why are you doing this?" she asked, looking as if she was on the verge of crying.

"Jesus, woman. I need some help, you need a job—there's no fucking hidden agenda. What's the matter with you?" He hadn't meant to say the last bit, but he couldn't figure her out.

"I'm not like you. I'm not used to people helping."

"Well take it or leave it. I wouldn't want to force you to deal with someone who was trying to help—"

"I'll take it," Dani said, cutting him off before he retracted the offer. She paused. "But ... Irma won't be back for another two days. I can't leave Elmer cooped up for that long."

Hearing his name, Elmer got up, walked over, sat next to Jess, and leaned up against his leg. Jess reached a hand down and scratched behind the dog's ears. Elmer closed his eyes and thumped his tail in approval. "Bring him with you. As long as he stays in Bob's office it'll be fine."

"When?"

"Meet me there at four today, and I'll go over where things are and what I need help with. You any good at cooking?"

"Um … basic stuff, I guess."

"Good. We keep it simple—mostly burgers and fries, a couple other things that go in the fryer or the microwave—but with Bob gone, I had to quit offering the food. Folks'll be happy if it's available again."

She looked a little less certain now about agreeing to the job.

Jess shook his head. "Don't worry, it's not rocket science."

"Thank you. I really need the job. I guess I should let Ray know I can't pay to get the truck fixed. I don't know what to do with it."

"It can stay where it's at. The month's paid for. I told Ray to sit on the repairs until he heard something from you. No point in talking to him until you're ready to do them." Jess wanted her to stay away from Ray on the off chance his sense of knowing her had come from seeing the Crime Stoppers broadcast.

"I only intended to stay here for a few days, a week at the most, and then be on my way, but now I'm stuck."

"It's a good place to be stuck."

At least he hoped it was.

CHAPTER EIGHTEEN

YOU GOT RID OF THE UNIFORMS monitoring the tip line." Jack stood in Kaye's office doorway, an angry scowl on his face.

"I did. It's a waste of manpower." Kaye sat back and watched him, then gave him a frustrated eye roll. "Jack, you said yourself there haven't been any viable tips since the car dealer contacted us. If someone sees or hears anything about Calderwood or Alphonse, they can call the general Crime Stoppers line, and they'll contact us. I let Crime Stoppers know and gave them the updated truck info to post on their site."

He watched Kaye go back to what she'd been doing. He slammed his hand on the door jamb and got some satisfaction in seeing her startle, but it was short lived.

"Do you have a problem with my decision, Detective Michaels?"

"You should have talked to me first. You don't just dismantle part of an investigation without talking to the detective handling it."

Kaye gave him a steady, intense stare. "I run this department. I'm well aware of what's going on with the case and that there haven't been any viable tips since the car dealer called. It's not helping, and it's tying up personnel who could be better used for other work. I'd have told you personally, but I couldn't *find you* to tell you." She paused, then said, "Just because we had dinner the other night, don't overstep here." Her stare and the steel in her voice warned him to back off.

"I'll remember that, *Lieutenant*," he said and stalked off.

The dinner was a mistake, but what happened afterwards was worse, Kaye thought. She should have known better, but it had been a relief having dinner with him, talking about work and not having a date be appalled or uncomfortable and then never call back. Unfortunately, it had ended in sex at his place.

It began in his car. Both of them had enjoyed a few drinks, and when they reached his car, he kissed her. They nearly had sex right there but came to their senses, and he drove to his apartment. It was in the River North area, which surprised her.

"Nice place," Kaye remarked as they entered his apartment.

Jack nodded. "I came into some insurance money a few years ago when my dad passed. That always helps."

"Evidently," she said.

They were so busy tearing each other's clothes off, that she forgot about the apartment. She woke up a little after three a.m., and knew it had been a mistake. Jack was a skilled and attentive lover, but he was a subordinate in her department, which was frowned on for good reason. Kaye quietly dressed, used her car ride app, and left without waking him.

The following day at work, she'd told him privately that it was a one-off event, a mistake on her part that couldn't continue. He'd said he didn't figure it would be anything else and not to worry about it. He took the comment calmly, but she saw the look in his eyes. It made her wonder if he really was okay with it. Her lapse in judgment had created a problem. Now, running her hands through her dark, curly hair and sighing, she went back to the paperwork she'd been dealing with, hoping the issue would resolve itself with enough time and wouldn't result in difficulties working with him or a complaint against her.

$\sim$

"Jagerski shut down the tip line," Michaels said to Sanders as they sat in the break room in Homicide.

"I figured she would. There haven't been any tips worth investigating since the car dealer called in. Probably was a good decision, since it doesn't seem to be helping. People can call Crime Stoppers, and they'll let us know if anything happens."

"It just pisses me off that she didn't talk to us before she made the decision. The uniforms monitoring the line know what to ask and how to sort through legit tips and nonsense. I think it was worth keeping for a while longer, maybe running another public announcement."

Sanders shrugged. "I don't think it's worth it. People have the attention spans of gnats these days. If it doesn't directly affect them, they don't pay much heed to it."

Michaels frowned. "Yeah, you're probably right. It's frustrating. We've got nothing, not even a body, and nobody is talking."

Kaye had a point, but it still rankled him. He often wondered if having women on the force was worth it. They were just too unpredictable. He'd thought, mistakenly, that she would be more amenable to him after the other night or that he could put a little pressure on her when needed, but he'd found out quickly that wasn't going to work.

"Any hits on Calderwood's phone?" Sanders asked.

"No. Either she tossed it or she's keeping it turned off." Jack finished his coffee and stood up. "The case is as cold as it is outside.

It'd be nice to find her to see what she knows and put her in a safe house, but either she's dead or she's good at hiding."

"Something may turn up. Alphonse's body may even turn up," Sanders said standing up and tossing his plastic water bottle in the recycle bin.

"You seem pretty sure he's dead."

"I think it's highly likely. He was never the type to run silent about anything. Not a peep or a sighting since the murder. That tells me he's dead."

"It would be no big loss if he is," Jack said.

The bar was dark and quiet inside. A faint scent of beer hung in the air as Dani and Elmer followed Jess in. He flipped on a couple light switches that lit up the main area and walked back toward the room behind the bar as Dani followed.

Entering the kitchen, Jess flipped the light on and pointed to a small room off to the side.

"That's the office where Elmer can hang out."

Dani walked Elmer in and lay the dog's bed she'd brought with her on the floor by the door. "Stay, Elmer," she said as the old dog walked over, turned around several times, and lay down. "I don't know how well he minds, especially if there's food around, but hopefully he'll stay put."

"We don't get many health inspectors up here, but try to keep him in the office. I don't think it's a good idea for people to know he's here. Next thing you know, they'll all be bringing their dogs with them."

Walking over to the grill and deep fryer, he pointed to several switches on the control panel. "These are the switches that turn the grill and fryer on. Don't worry about cooking for now. Let's give it a few days so you get the hang of the place. On Sunday, when the bar's closed, I can show you what's needed without a house full of customers. It's burgers, fries, wings, and nachos, nothing too complicated. Most of it's in the freezer."

Jess walked over to a storage closet and pulled about a dozen small bowls out of a cupboard and set them on the counter. "Right now, these need to be filled with the snack mix and set out on the bar and the tables," he said, pointing to the large bag of mixed crackers, pretzels, and nuts. "Check that the napkin dispensers on the bar and the tables are full, and we'll be ready to open at five."

Dani nodded, but her mind was reeling. It all felt so normal and yet so utterly surreal—hiding from a killer and the police while Jess oriented her to a job. Overwhelmed, she followed his movements, watching as he opened more cupboards, pointed at things, pulled supplies out, and showed her how to operate various appliances in what seemed like an endless one-sided conversation.

He closed the last cupboard and turned to her. "By the look on your face, I've totally overloaded you." He pulled on an earlobe and raised his eyebrows. "Didn't mean to, but honestly it's all pretty simple and common sense. All you have to do tonight is take drink orders and deliver them to the tables, clean up when people leave, and load and run the dishwasher. I can hold off on telling people about the food until you've had a few days to get used to things."

Dani nodded again. "That would help, I think. Thank you for this. I couldn't find any other work and with the truck disabled ..."

Jess waved a dismissive hand. "I'm gonna pay you in cash. That'll keep it simple." It'd also keep her off the official books, Jess thought.

"I really appreciate it. Stopping here was impulsive. I was tired, and I was getting short on money. I just wanted to rest here for a few days and move on, find a job in Grand Junction or somewhere to earn a little money, and keep going. But the truck screwed that up."

"If you were going to get stranded this is probably the best place to be. Most people here, with a couple exceptions, are nice. And Irma likes you, which is rare." He'd almost slipped and said it was a place few knew about and would be safe for her to stay.

He watched her for a few moments, glanced at his large, military-style watch, and pushed away from the cabinet. "Showtime's in half an hour. Let's take care of those snack bowls."

CHAPTER NINETEEN

WE'RE GOING TO PUT THE ALPHONSE MURDER and those of his associates on the back burner for now. We'll touch base regularly and if anything turns up, it will become a priority." Kaye shuffled through a stack of papers on the conference room table. "By turn up, I'm thinking Alphonse's or Calderwood's body, or if she's still alive, we find out where she is. Have any of you made any headway on either of those?"

"I've been asking around, talked to a couple of my confidential informants and no one knows anything concrete, but pretty much everyone thinks Alphonse is dead. I think that's most likely true. Even if he was the shooter, he'd have been back in the game a long time ago," Michaels said. "I've got a meet with one of the undercover guys in a day or two. I'll find out what he knows."

"Be nice to have a body, but I think you're right," Kaye said.

"Yeah, well, that's unlikely. If we find a body, his prints and his DNA are in the database. It's been long enough, though, there may be nothing left to print, and all his body would prove is he wasn't the shooter. It might give us slugs we could connect to the gun if we find it. Big if, in my opinion."

"Any news on Calderwood?" Kaye asked.

"Man, that chick's gone to ground. No tips, no sightings of her or the truck, and no phone activity. She's either dead or damn good at disappearing. I'm going to follow up with people she knows and those she worked with again, see if she's contacted any of them, see if I can find out more about her. I may be able to figure out where she is." Michaels frowned and rubbed his neck.

"Okay then, let's let this ride until we have something to go on. Keep your feelers out, check with the Crime Stoppers bunch periodically, and see what pops up."

"I've been pinging it regularly, but I can't find the phone if she's got it turned off. I don't think she's using it at all," Ben the IT tech said.

"Jagerski's already shut down the tip line monitoring, and my guess is she'll shut this down, too."

"That makes sense." Ben replied. "Nothing's turned up."

Michaels nodded and left. There was no point in beating his head against a brick wall.

Immediately following the murders, he'd canvassed the people in Calderwood's apartment building and discovered none of them knew her well. The manager verified that she'd lived there about two years but said he hadn't had much interaction with her and she'd caused no problems. Residents knew her by sight or because they'd had polite social conversations with her in passing, but no one was close to her. The warrant to search the apartment had turned up nothing helpful.

As far as he could tell when he searched her apartment, she'd taken next to nothing with her other than some clothes. Michaels wasn't even sure about that because he had no idea what had been there to begin with. There were only two people who could have told him what was missing—one had disappeared and the other was dead. He'd confiscated a photo album and a box of letters and cards he'd found, but been unable to find a laptop. Either she'd taken it with her or she didn't own one. Based on her salary and the meager possessions found in the furnished apartment, he doubted she'd owned a laptop. More than likely, she used her phone for email and texts and went to a library to print something out. She didn't have any social media accounts that he'd been able to find.

Her phone records over the last six months showed calls and texts to her work, to two female friends associated with her job, and to another number, which, based on the frequency of calls from and to the number, he assumed was her sister's phone. There'd been no phones corresponding to that number in the house where her sister had been shot, and Michaels figured Danielle had taken the phone with her. He'd had that number traced, and it was a burner that was no longer in service. There were occasional calls to a number in Nebraska, which belonged to an old friend.

"Dani has always spent the majority of her time keeping an eye on her sister and bailing her out, which is a full-time project," Elaine Foster said when he called her. "She actually moved to Denver about two years ago because Hannah had ended up in Denver and had been arrested. She tried her best to get Hannah clean and keep her away from Alphonse—even offered to find and pay for her treatment, although I have no idea how Dani would have afforded that, but it was pointless. Hannah wasn't going into treatment, and she wouldn't leave Alphonse. He was her supplier, and at least in Hannah's mind, he was her boyfriend."

"But you don't think he was?"

"He was a drug dealer. Based on what Dani told me about them, Hannah was a customer who provided sex in exchange for drugs and happened to live with him. But it was typical of Hannah to create her own fantasy world."

"Why was Danielle so caught up in it?"

"Ever heard of enablers? Dani was so caught up in trying to save Hannah that she couldn't walk away. It wasn't all her fault. She grew up taking care of Hannah. Their dad disappeared, ran off with another woman, and her mom never was much of a mother. Dani was the only adult in the entire family, so she learned early on that if she didn't take care of things, nothing got done. She felt responsible for her mother and her sister. It's totally messed up her life. I don't think she's had a long-term boyfriend in ages, and the one she had several years ago left because of Hannah. It was just as well. Her taste in men was always questionable.

"She would call me periodically and we'd cover the same ground—the latest crap Hannah had pulled, why Dani needed to accept that Hannah wouldn't change until she wanted to, why Dani needed to walk away. It was pointless. She was never going to walk away."

"If she contacts you, please find out where she is and call me. She's not safe out there alone. We'd like to put her in protective custody until we find the killer."

"I'll let you know if she does, but I haven't heard from her for about a month. We kinda got into it during our last conversation. I couldn't keep saying the same things to her over and over and listen to tales of Hannah's self-destruction. I told her to let Hannah do what she was going to do anyway and get a life." There was silence on the line for a bit before Michaels heard her take a deep breath and blow it out. "Maybe now that Hannah's dead, Dani can move on. I hope you find her."

"We hope so too."

Michaels called the old boyfriend after getting his number

from Elaine Foster, but he wasn't any more helpful than she had been.

"I haven't seen or heard from Dani in … ummm … must be close to four years now. I doubt she'd call me; she knows she won't get any sympathy from me about her sister. Actually, as callous as it sounds, Hannah's death is probably a good thing."

"That's why you broke up?"

"Yeah. Dani's sister? That was one fucked-up woman. We all grew up in the same area and Hannah was crazy. Always in trouble, sleeping around, always the first one to get into a new drug or go out drinking. That was well before she was of age, but she had people who'd buy the alcohol for her and of course she had suppliers for the drugs.

"They had a tough time growing up. Elaine probably filled you in on that. Her mother was as messed up as Hannah. I never understood how Dani turned out halfway normal." He paused. "I got involved with Dani before she followed Hannah to Colorado. When Hannah took off, I was glad. Dani had finished her degree and had a good job as an accountant. I figured we could be done with Hannah, that I could have Dani to myself, have a normal life. I shoulda known better, but … you know how that goes— you always think people will change, then they don't. I don't like playing second fiddle to anyone, but definitely not a druggie. It wasn't worth it."

"Okay, well if for some reason she contacts you or you find out she's been in touch with someone she knows, please call me."

Jack had paged through the photo album multiple times, hoping to get some clue to where she might have gone. He hoped there'd be pictures of vacation spots or relatives that she might have fled to, but he couldn't find any. The album surprised him; most people's photos lived on their phones these days. Hard copies of photos were rare, but these looked at least a few decades old or more. There were no identifying names or places written on the backs of the photos. Michaels assumed they were photos of her parents, but there was no way to identify locations or people in the photos.

Dani's neighbor across the hall, Dave Parnell, the guy Michaels had talked to the day of the murder, knew her slightly better than most. "I don't know her real well. She gave me her card and told me she'd be happy to help me with my taxes. I think she handed the cards out to the people on this floor. I don't know how many took her up on the offer. I think she was doing it to supplement her salary. I had her do them for me last year and she did a great job."

He leaned against the doorjamb of his apartment and said, "Other than that, we'd talk a bit if we ran into each other on the stairs or by the mailboxes, but we didn't hang out together. She dated sporadically. I'd see her with a guy for a few dates, then he'd be gone. I don't think she was into long-term relationships. All I know about her sister is that she'd show up periodically drunk or high and get into it with Dani for one reason or another. I have no idea where she's at or where she might go, but if I hear anything, I'll let you know."

Cassie Baker had a young kid perched on her hip when she opened the door to Michaels's knock. "Well, I know who she is, but I really don't know her."

"Any information could help. Did she have visitors or friends that you know of?"

"The only person who came to visit was her sister, as far as I know. Occasionally there were dates who picked her up or dropped her off, but none of them were … permanent. I don't remember ever seeing any of them leave in the morning. If you know what I mean." She blushed. "My husband saw Dani and her sister arguing outside Dani's apartment once and told me to stay away from both of them. He said the sister looked like an addict, and if Dani associated with her, he didn't want me or our son Trevor having anything to do with them.

"Her sister didn't visit often, but they never seemed like friendly visits," she continued. "I'd hear them arguing. One argument spilled out into the hallway, and it was over the people her sister hung out with, her drug use, and money that her sister had stolen from Dani. Turns out my husband was right. Other than seeing her around or running into her in the laundry room, I sort of knew her, but I wasn't close to her."

Michaels gave her the spiel about calling if she heard anything and moved on to the manager of the small accounting office where Dani was employed.

"She's worked here almost two years. She called and explained she had a personal emergency to deal with before she stopped coming to work, but I never imagined it was as serious as you say. I didn't know she had a sister. Do you have any news? Is she okay?"

"At this point we don't know where she is. Can you tell me about her? Who are her friends? Does she have a boyfriend?"

"Dani's a quiet one. I'm pretty sure there's no boyfriend. I never heard her talk about one. She never mentioned having a sister. She's friends with Kayley, our secretary. Kayley tried to set her up once or twice, but she wasn't interested."

"Set her up with a guy?" Michaels asked. "Maybe she didn't swing that way. Are you sure she liked guys?" Michaels knew from her neighbors' comments that she wasn't gay, but he'd asked. People often saw different sides to a person.

The woman looked taken aback. "She never gave me the impression she didn't like men. I just assumed … I never asked. But maybe that's why she turned the offer down … it never crossed my mind at the time." She straightened her shoulders suddenly and slipped back into her office manager role. "Her sexual orientation is none of my business, and it isn't relevant to her job. In any event, her personal life wasn't something she talked about."

"I'd like to talk to Kayley if she's in the office today."

"I'll ask her to step into my office."

As the woman reached for the desk phone, Michaels asked, "Has she taken any time off, like for trips or a vacation?"

"No. She never took any extended time off, just a day here or there if she was ill or had something she had to do during business hours."

"And she never talked about places she liked to go or places where extended family or friends might live?"

"No, she wasn't chatty, especially about herself. She put Elaine Foster as an emergency contact. Seemed odd that she'd put someone who lived out of state as an emergency contact. I asked if she would rather list someone here in town, but Dani said no. Her parents are dead—at least that's what she said when I asked about emergency contacts. I don't think there were any other family members, and now, knowing about her sister, I can see why she wouldn't list her as an emergency contact. Dani has been here longer than most, but I don't try to be friends. It makes it hard when you have to deal with them as a boss."

"I understand. If you'd ask Kayley to step in here, I'd appreciate it. If for some reason Danielle calls here, try to find out where she is and let me know. We need to find her."

After getting no new information from Kayley other than annoyance about Danielle's refusal of "a great guy" setup and how she knew her socially but not well, Michaels left shaking his head in frustration. Danielle Calderwood seemed to have lived in an impenetrable bubble of isolation. It was entirely possible that the only people who actually knew her were her friend Elaine Foster and her dead sister. Unless something broke or she contacted the police, they might never find her.

CHAPTER TWENTY

THE EVENING DIDN'T GIVE HER TIME to think about anything other than taking drink orders, carrying drinks to tables, cleaning tables off when customers left, and keeping up with dishwashing and snack bowls. Once food service was back on, Dani would spend her time in the kitchen, cooking and keeping the dishwasher going. Jess would handle orders and delivery of drinks and food.

It was a busy night, which didn't allow for a lot of conversation with customers, and Dani was grateful. She'd never had a job with this much customer contact, and her responses to their banter were awkward. Sitting in a cubicle quietly working on accounts was more her style. She saw the surprise and watchful curiosity from customers when they first arrived. But after a drink or two, that was forgotten.

Dani noticed the waitress from the diner, whose name she thought was Polly, come in about seven and take a seat at the bar, making several attempts to strike up a conversation with Jess. Dani had seen her with Jess around town, talking, laughing, and touching him, so clearly there was something between them. While she was busy in the kitchen with the dishwasher, the woman's voice surprised her.

"So you're working here now. Are you and Jess an item?" Polly stood in the kitchen's entry off the hall leading to the restrooms and leaned against the doorframe. She didn't look happy.

Dani closed the door of the dishwasher. "An item? What do you mean?"

The woman laughed. "An item, a bedmate, fuck buddies—you know."

Dani felt her face heat with embarrassment. "Of course not. He offered me a job, that's all."

"Hmm. Two days at his cabin and now working with him at the bar. Doesn't look like just a job to me."

"You must have an active imagination," Dani said and turned her back on the woman.

"Just so you know, he's mine, so stay away."

Dani said nothing as she turned the dishwasher on and busied herself with wiping down the countertop. It was a moment before she heard Polly leave. She stayed in the kitchen for a bit until she could get her face under control, but the woman watched her each time she entered the bar area.

At nine, Jess hustled the remaining customers out and locked the front door. They'd fallen into a good rhythm with each other the first hour or so after the bar opened, and it continued now as they began clearing tables and cleaning without talking. Elmer had been well-behaved and had stayed in the office except for brief bathroom breaks in the vacant lot outside the back door. Excluding the encounter with Polly, it had been the first normal evening Dani had experienced since her sister's death.

"You did a great job," Jess said as he came into the kitchen and watched her as she loaded the dishwasher.

Dani gave him a slight smile. "Thanks. It's like you said, not rocket science." Jess finished mopping the floor and put the mop and bucket away. Dani closed the dishwasher, and leaning against the counter above it, she said, "Do you like being around so many people every night?"

"Yeah, I know them; they're friends. It's not like a big city." He scrutinized her for a moment, then said, "I saw Polly talking to you earlier. You seemed upset afterward. What'd she say to you?"

Again, Dani felt the heat rise in her face. "She wanted to know if we were an 'item.' She knows I was at your cabin during the storm, and because I'm working here evidently she thinks we've … um … slept together."

Jess was a bit taken aback. "Don't pay her any mind."

"She seems a bit proprietary toward you." When Jess didn't respond, she continued. "She said you were hers. Are you?"

"My advice is to stay away from her."

That hadn't answered the question. Dani decided to change the subject, not wanting to delve deeper into the subject of Polly. Polly was great looking, and it was hard to imagine a man refusing her if she offered. "Can I ask you a personal question?"

Jess turned away from the storage closet toward her and raised his eyebrows. "I thought that qualified as one. What else d'you want to know?"

"What happened to your leg and face?"

He frowned. "Afghanistan happened. An IED blew up the Humvee I was in. I got thrown out of it and survived. Two other guys didn't. I ended up with a badly fractured femur. The docs debated about amputating my leg at one point. Shrapnel did the damage to my face and some to my chest." He ran a hand absently over the right side of his chest. Shocked that he'd actually answered the question about his injuries when that had always been off limits, he waited to see if she had other questions. "Ask away. If there's something I can't or don't want to tell you, I'll let you know."

"Have you always lived here? In this town?"

"No, I ended up here a couple years ago. After I came home, Denver was just too noisy and crowded and ..." he shrugged. "And impossible."

"Family?"

"A younger sister. My dad passed a few years ago, and my sister lives in Denver near my mom."

"D'you see them or do they visit?"

"No, not since I moved up here. Not much here to visit."

"You're here."

Jess snorted an angry laugh. "That's not a big draw. We don't see eye to eye, and they don't like it up here. I haven't been to Denver since I moved here, so we don't see each other."

"You don't think it's worth the effort to stay in contact with them?"

"I've found that some people never change and trying to change them is wasted effort. Sometimes it's best to walk away and get on with your life."

Jess walked into the bar area and opened the register, removed the cash and the credit card receipts, and returned to the office. Dani was silent, thinking about what he'd said. It was true. Her efforts on Hannah's part were definitely wasted effort. Jess counted out bills, handed her evening's pay to her, and deposited the rest of the money and receipts in the safe. Locking it, he stood and turned to her. "Tell me a little about you."

Dani ran a hand through her hair and sighed. "Not much to

tell. I grew up in Nebraska. My parents have passed—well my mother has. I don't know what happened to my dad. We lost touch years ago. And … I don't see my sister anymore." *Stick as close to the truth as possible*, Dani thought.

"Where's your sister?"

"I don't know." She frowned. She didn't know where Hannah was and didn't want to think about where she might be. "We … we're like night and day. I guess that's the problem. I love her but I've never really understood her. She wa—is, an addict. She could be dead for all I know."

It was the first time Dani had actually talked to anyone about her sister, and the force of it hit her. She began to sob, tears tracking down her cheeks as she wiped them away with her hands and tried to cover her face.

"Hey," Jess said, putting a hand on her shoulder. Then, because she looked so lost and unhappy, he pulled her into his arms and stroked her back. God she felt good in his arms. "I'm sorry, I shouldn't have asked. I didn't mean to make you cry."

Elmer got up and walked over to Dani and leaned against her. Dani stepped out of Jess's arms, and shook her head. "Not your fault. You didn't know. It's just hard talking about her," she said as she wiped at her eyes and face with the backs of her hands. It had felt good to be comforted; it had rarely happened to her.

Jess walked to the kitchen door. "Follow me. I think we could both use a drink."

At the bar he poured himself a Maker's Mark and raised the bottle inquiringly at Dani. "I'm not a big hard liquor drinker," she said, pulling a napkin out of the dispenser on the bar and wiping her nose. "How about a glass of the house red?" Watching her mother get drunk on gin every night had soured Dani on hard liquor.

They sat at the bar in the dim light and sipped their drinks. Elmer lay at her feet. "So, were you a career military guy?" Dani asked at last, hoping to divert the conversation away from her.

"It kinda worked out that way, although that wasn't my intention. I graduated from college with an engineering degree. I'd mostly gotten the degree because it's what my dad did." He shrugged. "I didn't have a clue what I wanted to do. I let a friend of mine talk me into enlisting. The Marine recruiter had a great sales pitch, *Semper fi* and all that. Seemed like a good idea until we hit basic."

Jess laughed and shook his head. "I've never regretted a decision as badly as I did that one, basic training was hell. But I discovered the life suited me. I did three tours in Afghanistan. It was a risky job, but I thrived on the work and the risk, before this happened," he said, rubbing his hand on his leg.

"How'd you end up here?"

"After my leg was repaired, I was discharged and sent home. A job as a regular engineer didn't appeal, I'm not sure it ever had. I thought for a while about becoming a cop, but the rehab on my leg was brutal. I might have been able to meet the physical requirements. I can walk and run now. It just hurts when the weather's cold; makes me limp. Mentally, though, I figured out pretty quickly I wasn't up for it. I'd lost my taste for risk and death and chaos." He took a drink.

"I did my rehab at the VA for a year, but Denver made me twitchy and hypervigilant. It was like ... I couldn't breathe. It was too noisy and too crowded, so I loaded up my truck and headed into the mountains. I lived in several places before I found this place and stayed. I can breathe here."

Dani nodded. "It's peaceful. The people I've met seem nice." She sipped her wine then said, "I'm sorry for being so suspicious of you. It's … really hard for me to … well let's just say that in my experience people always want *something*. There's no free lunch. My dad always used to say that. I guess I took it to heart."

Jess nodded and didn't reply. They sat in silence, seemingly all talked out, as they finished their drinks. At last Jess stood up, walked around the bar and deposited their glasses in the small sink under the bar.

"You must be tired. I'll drive you home. Come on old man," he said to Elmer. "Let's take you home too."

CHAPTER TWENTY-ONE

THE JOB WAS A HUGE RELIEF. It made life seem almost normal again. Irma had returned from Denver, and although Elmer was ecstatic to see her, he still chose to spend a few nights a week at the bar with Dani, and on those nights, he slept on the bed with her.

"You sure made a friend of Elmer," Irma said when Dani arrived to walk him. "I've never seen him take to anyone like he's taken to you."

Dani smiled and scratched Elmer behind his ears in his favorite spot. "He's a sweetie. I enjoy his company."

Irma laughed. "I'd be jealous, but it helps to know I can trust you to take care of him."

"Happy to. Maybe you can visit your sister more or take a fun trip."

"Oh, I'm not up for trips, but seeing my sister more often would be nice. I've thought about moving to Denver. We're both getting older, and it's so isolated here. Haven't decided yet." She pushed the plate of cookies at Dani. "How's the job working out at the bar?"

"Good. It's easy work, and people are nice around here."

"Can't be a misery working with Jess Walker either," Irma said with a coy smile.

"He's been very kind, offering me the job and all. He didn't have to."

"Have you decided not to continue on to Utah?"

"No, but I have no way to get there. The truck's fixable—I just can't afford to fix it." Dani bit into a cookie. "If I can save up enough to pay for a bus ticket or catch the train in Grand Junction, I could get to Utah that way. If I can save enough, maybe Ray can fix the truck. Right now, I'm just glad to have the job."

"Jess might be pretty disappointed if you moved on."

Dani coughed as she swallowed the bite of cookie wrong. Talking a sip of coffee, she said, "I'm sure he could find another person to help at the bar."

Irma laughed and shook her head. "Honey, that wasn't what I was talking about. I've seen a few of the looks he's given you."

Dani didn't know how Jess felt, she thought, walking up the stairs to her apartment. She hadn't given him much reason to like her; she'd been suspicious and prickly with him, although that was changing. He could be hard to read, and she hadn't figured out what his relationship with Polly was.

He was a handsome guy, but it was as if he didn't realize it. Most good-looking guys she'd known knew it and used it to get what they wanted. Jess was different. He was intelligent and had a wry sense of humor. Easygoing and thoughtful—safe was the word that always came to mind when she thought about him.

At the end of the evening, Jess would count out her wages, then suggest they sit at the bar and have a drink before he drove her home. By then, her feet hurt from standing all evening and her lower back ached. She'd also reached a saturation level for having to interact with people and sitting at the bar with the lights on low talking to Jess was a relief. The glass of wine relaxed her and allowed her to sleep once she got back to the apartment.

Jess never asked about her family again, and she chose not to inquire further about his. He talked about the places he'd seen while in the military, and she talked about school and the various jobs she'd had. They joked about the jukebox and talked about the music they liked when not forced to listen to 1950's and 1960's rock. It was talk that skirted anything serious, but she was beginning to feel comfortable with him.

He didn't pry, which struck Dani as odd. It was as if he didn't want to know about her. When Hannah was alive, that lack of prying would have been welcome. It would have been a relief to know that there would be no questions, nothing she'd have to explain or make excuses for or lie about. Now … it felt different. Their lack of any meaningful conversations left her wanting, although she wasn't sure what she wanted from Jess.

She'd never thought about what she wanted, she had allowed other people to dictate her life. She made decisions based on who needed or wanted something from her or what needed to be done. Facing a life without parents or her sister meant the choices were hers now. When she thought of that, among the vague ideas of safety and peace that popped up, Jess figured into those choices more and more often.

Rather than thinking of it as simply a job that brought in a wage, Jess now looked forward to going to the bar. He'd always enjoyed the conversation with patrons. With a couple of exceptions, people in the town were good company. Dani, though, had added a flavor to his life that had been missing for far too long.

A brush against him behind the bar as she collected glasses to be washed made him a bit light-headed with the thrill of the close contact. Seeing her bending over to retrieve plates or clean a table brought a tightness to his groin. To keep from making a fool of himself, he'd make a few casual comments to customers sitting at the bar to distract himself. When his and Dani's hands brushed as she handed him plastic baskets filled with food, it rattled him, and with each encounter, he wanted more. If his dreams were any indication, he wanted a lot more.

She had relaxed around him, and he'd felt that wall of hers begin to lower. Being around her was easy and comfortable. She could be subtly funny, he discovered, and he found himself laughing more, like he'd laughed with friends when he was deployed. All that was missing was the danger. He had to be careful, had to remind himself that the danger was missing for him, but not for her.

After he'd learned her real name and the nickname they'd mentioned in the Crime Stoppers broadcast, he thought of her as Dani. He liked that name more than Beth. Calling her Beth didn't feel right. Once or twice, he'd nearly slipped before he managed to correct himself with an almost unnoticeable hesitation. For the most part, he tried not to call her by name at all. He'd caught a few puzzled glances from her, an occasional frown, but she didn't question him about it.

They had a good rhythm between them. As more people realized he'd retuned to providing food, she spent most of her time in the kitchen, filling orders and handling the cleanup, while Jess handled the bar side of things. He missed having her out front, watching her smile as she delivered drinks to patrons or chatted with him. But it was a good thing she spent most of her time in the kitchen. It kept him from being distracted by her bending over to clean off tables or brushing up against him or touching his back as she moved behind him in the narrow space behind the bar.

Having her mostly in the kitchen had taken some worry off Jess's mind. People in town knew her and seemed to accept her presence in the bar as normal, but Jess worried that someone might figure out who she was. He hadn't seen any further Crime Stoppers bits about her, and no one had mentioned seeing the one he'd caught. Ray hadn't said anything further about her reminding him of someone, which was a relief. The best part of that broadcast was they'd mentioned a car and not the truck, which might keep people from putting two and two together if they had seen the broadcast. He kept the TV in the bar turned strictly to sports stations. Still, having her in the kitchen out of sight was good. No point in asking for trouble.

It had been nearly two weeks since he'd seen the news bulletin when he slipped up. Irma asked if he would take a look at Dani's sink, which was leaking. The town had no plumber or other handyman. People usually took care of problems themselves, but they knew Jess was good at fixing things. They either fixed whatever was broken themselves or asked Jess for help. Over time, he'd become the town's jack-of-all-trades.

He was lying on his back, head and shoulders barely squeezed into the small cupboard under the sink, working on putting the pipe back together. Fumbling his hand around outside the cupboard trying to locate the pipe sealant, he called out, "Can you hand me the container that says pipe sealant?"

There was no reply. Maybe she was in the bathroom. He listened and heard her footsteps and without thinking, he said, "Dani, can you hand me—" *Shit, shit, shit!*

He heard a sharp intake of breath as he squirmed out from under the sink and sat up, banging his forehead on the cupboard frame, watching as she stumbled away from him, her eyes wide with fear.

"How d'you know my name?" she said in a strangled voice. "*How d'you know my name?*" she said more insistently when he didn't reply but stood up.

She began backing away from him toward the corner, where her backpack lay on top of the bed. He'd never had a chance to discover what was in it, but he figured he was going to find out if he didn't do something fast. He lunged toward her and grabbed her arms as she let out a scream and began to fight him. He turned her quickly and pulled her back against his chest, securing her with his arms clamped across her chest so she couldn't move. Well, couldn't move too much. She was struggling and landed several good kicks to his shins.

"Stop for Christ's sake and listen to me!" he shouted.

She didn't stop struggling and gasped out, "How do you know my name?"

"Stop fucking kicking me!" he shouted and squeezed his arms tighter until he felt her stop struggling a bit.

"I ... can't ... breathe ..."

Jess eased his hold cautiously, prepared for her to lash out again. When she didn't, he said, "I heard a news bulletin asking for information about you the night I offered you a ride back here, the night you were walking Elmer. You don't look much like the photo they showed, not with the hair color and the cut, but I'm good with faces and ... I knew it was you."

"Did you *call them*? Did you *tell them I was here*?" She stopped struggling. He'd heard the despair in her voice.

"No, Jesus, I wouldn't do that to you." He let go of her, and she dropped down onto the end of the bed. "Dani, I'm not going to hurt you or turn you in. I didn't call the tip line. I wasn't going to say anything. I just … slipped up and said your name. I wasn't going to say anything to anyone."

As a caution, he leaned over and moved her backpack out of reach. He could feel something heavy shifting in it. Probably a gun. *Christ*, he thought, *what have I gotten myself into?*

"Doesn't matter. Someone here will have seen it. They'll figure it out and call the cops."

"If no one has by now, that's not likely."

She let out a moan and said, "You don't know that, and I have no way to leave. I might as well call and tell the cops where I am and get it over with."

Jess knelt on the floor in front of her, grimacing as his leg strenuously protested the move. "Why'd you run in the first place?"

"I was scared. I was there, I heard what happened, I'm a witness. The cops and the killer may not have known about me at first, but if the cops are asking for information about me, if they showed my photo, they know I was there, and *if they do*, then the killer does too. If I'd stuck around, I'd be a dead woman, just like … like … like my sister."

The sob escaped her before she could prevent it. She slapped a hand over her mouth and squeezed her eyes shut.

Jess placed a hand on her shoulder and gave it a squeeze. "It's okay. You can trust me."

It was as if her mind was in a loop as she said again, "Someone will have seen the broadcast and when they realize it's me, they'll turn me in."

"I've checked online, and the Crime Stoppers segment hasn't aired again since that night, and no one's said anything about it. Believe me I'd have heard about it at the bar, especially with you working there." Jess had tolerated kneeling on the floor for as long as he could. He pushed up from the floor and sat next to Dani on the bed stretching his leg out. "I don't understand why you ran. If you know who did it, the police could offer you protective custody until he's caught. Maybe you *should* contact them."

She shook her head no. "I can't. I was there and ran. I cut and colored my hair and I called 911 but didn't identify myself. That looks guilty as hell. But the biggest problem is all I saw was the back of a dark-haired man. I only got a glimpse of the side of his face, and I heard his voice. I can't ID him, but he doesn't know that, and neither do the police.

"He took the dealer's body with him and cleaned up after himself, so my guess is the police don't even know for sure that the dealer's dead. The killer knows who I am, thanks to that broadcast, but he could be *anybody*. He could talk to me face-to-face, and I don't know that I'd recognize him."

Jess rubbed a hand over his mouth. "I could drive you somewhere and …" He didn't want to, didn't want her out of his life, but maybe it was safer for her to leave.

Dani cut him off. "Where the hell would I go? When you hired me, I had exactly a hundred and fifty bucks left after buying food. I have a little more now but not enough to fix the truck, so I have no transportation. I don't even know where to buy a bus ticket … and when I get to wherever a couple hundred bucks will take me, then what?"

"I thought I heard Irma say you had relatives in Utah."

"I don't. I told her that to help explain why I was here. I told her I'd been driving for days and wanted to stop and regroup, rest. I hadn't been driving for days, but I was tired and panicked and the town was so isolated I thought I could safely stay for a little while. There's no one in Utah or anywhere else. I'm it. I have nowhere to go and no one who can help me."

She stood up and paced away from him staring bleakly around the small apartment. At last, she let her head drop into her hands, her hair falling forward and hiding her face. "I don't know what to do anymore."

"Stay here. It's safer than being out there alone."

She shrugged in defeat. "I don't really have much choice, do I?"

CHAPTER TWENTY-TWO

IT GALLED POLLY THAT BETH CALDWELL had caught Jess's attention. Beth seemed to have him in some sort of thrall. Polly loved that word. She'd read it in one of her paranormal romance novels. She'd had to look it up, but it fit. Beth had cast some sort of spell over Jess. Polly had tried her best to be wherever he was and talk with him, but he barely said two words to her; in fact, she seemed to irritate him when she tried to get him to talk to her.

And now? Now the bitch was working at the bar, spending every night except Sundays and Mondays at the bar with him. Cooking, no less. Food hadn't been available since Bob Kirtcher had left on vacation, and that had brought more customers back to the bar. Customers who ought to be eating at the diner and tipping her. Polly had half a mind to call Bob and tell him Jess had hired the woman, but she and Bob hadn't always gotten along, so she hadn't done that.

Beth had said nothing was going on between her and Jess, but Polly had made a point of being at the bar several nights a week, and Polly had seen the looks he'd given Beth when she wasn't looking. If nothing was going on, she was pretty sure Jess Walker wanted there to be. Polly couldn't figure out what the attraction was. At a minimum, Beth could use a haircut and a professional dye job. It looked like she'd done both herself. And she was so quiet, hardly talked at all—other than to Jess. More than once when Beth was walking Irma's dog, Polly had seen him stop his truck, get out, and walk with her for a bit. Talking and laughing with her.

There were a lot of things that galled Polly about Beth Caldwell. She'd won over Irma, who as far as Polly was concerned, was a crotchety old bitch. No matter how friendly Polly had been toward her, Irma had never warmed up to her and treated her like a nuisance. Beth had taken Devon Thompson's job as dog walker and snow shoveler. Polly didn't like Devon; she really didn't like most people in town except Jess and some of the other men who flirted with her. But Devon had had the job first and didn't deserve to have it taken away and given to a stranger. How was Irma going to find someone who'd walk her old dog when Beth took off? If she took off. That was what Polly was most worried about.

Jess was the only eligible bachelor in town. There were a couple married men who'd enjoyed dalliances with her. She preferred that term—also learned in her romance novels—but there was no future there. If Jess was falling for Beth Caldwell, that would ruin Polly's chances. There had to be some way for Polly to get rid of her before she got permanent claws into Jess.

They sat in their usual spots at the bar after they'd finished closing down for the night, Jess sipping on Maker's Mark, Dani enjoying her glass of red wine. Neither had said much about the previous day's revelations and the silence was heavy.

"I think if you're gonna carry a weapon, you need to know how to use it."

"What?" Dani asked, surprised at the non sequitur and alarmed that Jess knew, or guessed, that she had a gun.

"Pretty sure that was a gun I felt in your backpack. Am I right?" Dani nodded reluctantly. "Do you know how to use it?"

She sighed and took a mouthful of wine. "No. It's not my gun. It was with cash in the backpack that I took when I left the house where the murders took place."

"It's your gun now. The problem with that is you don't know how to use it, which makes it a weapon that's highly likely to be taken from you and used on you." Jess let that thought sit for several minutes while he sipped his drink. "If you're going to keep it, then you need to know how to use it; otherwise you shouldn't be carrying it."

"Can you teach me?"

Jess nodded. "Considering how you got it, the gun's probably stolen, but there's nothing that can be done about that. Can't get you a legit gun, 'cause you can't afford to undergo a background check right now, so ..." He let the sentence die.

"It's a mess isn't it?"

Jess snorted a laugh. "Well, darlin', it isn't pretty, that's for sure, but at the very least you need to know how to use it. That, I can help with."

Dani nodded and tried to ignore that flutter of happiness she'd felt when he'd called her darlin'. She knew it was a figure of speech, not something he actually meant, but hearing it had made her wish it was.

"When could we start the lessons?" she asked to distract herself.

"We can shoot our hearts out at my place tomorrow, and no one will care. I'm far enough from the town proper it won't bother anyone, even on a Sunday. It'd save time and a trip into town if you'd stay at my place tonight. You okay with that?"

"Yeah."

"Let's get going, then. I'll swing by your place, and you can pick up what you need."

Dani threw a change of clothes, her toothbrush and her hair brush into her backpack and grabbed her rolled-up sleeping bag. Another night spent in one of the recliners, unable to turn onto her side because of the angle of the recliner, wasn't something she wanted to repeat. In her sleeping bag on the floor, she would at least be able to stretch out and change positions to get comfortable.

Jess raised his eyebrows when she returned to the truck and he noticed the sleeping bag. "You can have the bed. I'll sleep in the recliner."

"You'd never get comfortable with your ..." She stopped, embarrassed to have made a reference to his leg. She'd seen how his limp would go from barely noticeable to blatantly obvious, but she'd been reluctant to question him about it or even comment.

He shook his head, the irritation plain on his face. "I've slept in worse. My leg hurts this time of year whether I sleep in the bed or one of the recliners, but suit yourself."

They rode in silence until they were outside of town. "Will it get better?" she blurted.

"My leg was totally fucked up. I refused to let them amputate it, so they did the best they could to put it back together. But this is it." He was frowning, and Dani wished she hadn't said anything.

"Can't they do something for the pain?" she asked, deciding to risk talking about it.

"All they can do for the pain—aside from me going to a pain clinic for an evaluation and trying some of the new therapies—is give me narcotics, which is a road I don't want to travel. I've seen too many people get hooked and ruin their lives. As long as I keep moving, it does fine. I've gotten used to the way it feels. You learn to live with it."

"But should you? Maybe a pain clinic could help."

"I'd have to go to Denver and spend time there, and I don't want to do it. In the summer it doesn't bother me at all. It's the cold that does it. So I just deal with it."

Impulsively, she reached over and laid her hand on his thigh. "I'm sorry. I shouldn't have asked, and I'm sorry that happened to you."

He pushed her hand away and said in a low, angry voice, "I don't need or want your pity."

"It wasn't pity. What happened to you … I'm sorry that it happened."

"That makes two of us," Jess said, his voice softening a little. He said nothing further until they reached the cabin.

God, he wished she hadn't put her hand on his thigh. The place she'd rested it was still warm and still arousing. Interest had perked up below his belt, and he quickly routed his thoughts elsewhere. His feelings for her had grown until he found himself eagerly looking forward to the evenings at the bar and especially their late-night talks over drinks. Gradually, she'd opened up to him, and he'd learned more about her and her family. It surprised him that she'd turned into the woman she was.

He knew she was grieving. If Elmer came to the bar, she'd often come in from letting him wander the back lot until he found a spot to pee with tears hastily wiped from her cheeks as she entered the back door. She'd latched onto the dog, and the dog obviously felt the same toward her. He comforted her, and Jess was glad, although he'd wished more than once he could take the dog's place.

He was worried about her, about what to do, about how to protect her. Although, she probably didn't need his protection; she'd done pretty damn well so far. The truck breaking down was the first major hitch in her game plan. He kept thinking he should take her to Denver where they could talk to the police, convince them she knew nothing that would help ID the murderer, and ask them to stop looking for her. Remembering the corruption of officials on both sides that he'd seen on his tours of duty and the way information had of leaking out and coming back to bite you in the ass, made him change his mind.

Lie low, keep your eyes and ears open, and hope that the police give up and stop looking for her, he told himself and hoped it was the right decision.

CHAPTER TWENTY-THREE

ARRIVING AT THE CABIN, Jess turned to her. "I'm serious about the bed. You're welcome to it. Half the time, I fall asleep in the recliner anyway."

"I … I wouldn't feel right chasing you out of your own bed."

"Well, we could share it, in the interest of comfort," Jess saw the look on her face and the flush that crept up her neck and laughed. "It was a joke, Dani. Although, I'm not opposed to sharing a bed with you. It could be a lot of fun." When she didn't respond to his comment, he nodded. "It's late. You want the bed or the sleeping bag?"

"Sleeping bag."

He shrugged, retrieved a pillow from his bedroom, and handed it to her. "I'll be right back." He retrieved a foam bed roll from the storage shed at the side of the cabin and returned with it under his arm. "Put your sleeping bag on this. It'll be more comfortable."

"Thank you."

Jess nodded and disappeared into his bedroom. He stood in the dark at the small window that looked out on the back of the property, thinking about Dani in the other room. The moonlight barely penetrated the trees, which looked like ghostly snow-shrouded guardians, silently watching and protecting the cabin. It was how he'd felt since he'd returned to the States—a ghost alone and separate from those around him, standing and watching. He wondered if he could be less of a ghost with Dani.

❧

"Michaels!" Kaye shouted from her office doorway. Hearing no response, Kaye walked out into the main room and glanced around. Michaels wasn't there, but Sanders sat at his desk staring intently at something on his computer screen.

"Sanders, where's Michaels?"

Sanders looked up, confused, as if he'd been pulled from a trance. "No idea, boss. I got back from lunch about half an hour ago, and I haven't seen him."

"Get your coat then and come with me." Kaye retrieved her coat and they headed to the parking garage.

"What's up?" Sanders asked as he struggled into his coat and tried to keep up with Jagerski.

"Got a call from the Arapahoe County Sheriff's Office. Dog walker found a body at Cherry Creek Reservoir. The body's not in the best shape, but they found a wallet with ID for Alphonse in a pants pocket." Kaye unlocked her car and as they were getting in, she asked, "Where the hell did Michaels disappear to?"

Sanders shrugged as he buckled his seat belt. "Ya got me. He left before I went to lunch and didn't say where he was going, just that he'd be back in a bit."

Kaye shook her head as she drove off. "Text him and let him know what's going on. He's been disappearing a lot lately. Is something going on with him?"

"He's been doing a lot of interviews with people who know Danielle Calderwood."

"On his own?"

"Yeah. There's a ton of other work that needs doing, so both of us do stuff on our own. Is that a problem, boss?"

"As long as it gets done, I'm good. He should keep you in the loop about where he's going, though." She drove for another ten minutes. "Has he responded?"

"No, not yet."

"Text him again."

Silence descended. As Kaye drove, she thought about Michaels. Since the confrontation about the tip line, their interactions had returned to a stilted normal. The easy conversations and banter had disappeared. Sex and coworkers never mixed well, and she was angry with herself for allowing it to happen.

Live and learn, Kaye thought, and she wondered where the hell Michaels was.

The body was not anywhere a passerby would have seen it, and were it not for a dog who escaped its leash and had taken off after a rabbit with its owner in hot pursuit, there was no telling how long it would have gone undiscovered. Denver had had a brief span of above average temperatures, which was not uncommon, and the snow had receded from the body. But animals had found it long before the snow receded, and over time, had done what animals did. A hand was missing. The body was lying face up, but the right arm and hand were partially concealed beneath it. The eyes were gone, most likely due to crows or other birds. Rats or other small predators had gone after the ears and soft parts of the face. Larger animals had gone to town on the chest and belly.

"Jesus," Sanders exclaimed, quickly turning and walking several feet away.

"Not much left, but we found a wallet that had Billy Alphonse's driver's license in it, and he was flagged for your homicide," said the sheriff's office investigator. "We can have the body transported to the Denver ME's facility when we're done processing the scene. The right hand is still intact. Maybe your ME can get a decent fingerprint off one of the fingers. If not, then there's always DNA to confirm the ID."

Kaye nodded. "Thanks, that'd be great. You'll send me the photos and your report?"

"Of course. Glad to hand this one off to you guys. It's been a busy month for us."

"Anything you need us to stick around for?"

"No, I wanted you to see the body before it was transported. We're done with photos. Once the body's gone, our techs will process this area for evidence."

"He's kind of a mess, so ask them to be on the lookout for bullets that may have been spread around by the predation."

"Will do. I'll get the reports and photos and evidence over to you as soon as possible."

"Thanks, I appreciate it," Kaye said. "We'll get out of your way."

Back in the car, as Kaye drove out of the park, she looked over at Sanders. "No shame in being grossed out. Thanks for walking away. Better to do that than puke on a crime scene."

"I wasn't going to puke," he replied with just a hint of annoyance in his voice. "I just needed a minute. I've seen a lot of bodies but never one left out in the wild for long enough to look like that. It just threw me."

"Well, now you've seen one. Be glad it's not the middle of July. Next time you'll know what to expect. It's less shocking if you have an idea what you're walking into."

Sanders nodded and said nothing further.

When you were a woman on the force, Kaye thought, you learned pretty damn fast to hide your revulsion and tackle the horror without flinching. If you didn't, you'd suffer the derision of your male colleagues, most of whom had thrown up at their first crime scene but would rarely admit it.

"Where have you two been?" Michaels asked when he saw Jagerski and Sanders walk into the department.

"Doing *your* job. Where've you been?" Kaye said.

"Out following a lead on a case. What d'you mean doing my job?"

"They found Alphonse, or what's left of him."

"No shit? Whcre'd they find him?"

"Off the beaten path at Cherry Creek Reservoir."

"How'd they ID him?"

"Wallet ID. One hand may be intact enough to get a print. If not, DNA will confirm it. He'll be transported to the ME here. The Arapahoe County Sheriff's Office is processing the scene. They called and Charlie and I went out to see it."

"Man, I'm sorry I missed that."

"Me too," Kaye said with an edge to her voice. "Keep your partner apprised of where you're going and when you'll be back. And answer your fucking text messages in the future."

She walked away from them and into her office, closing the door a bit too loudly.

It was all over the news that a badly decomposed body had been discovered at Cherry Creek Reservoir and preliminary identification indicated it was that of drug dealer Billy Alphonse. Well, he thought, it wouldn't help them much, other than to confirm that it was Billy who had been popped. They'd probably retrieve bullets, but they had no gun, so until they did—and he had no plans to help them with that—it got them nowhere.

Still no word about Danielle Calderwood, and that kept him up at night. He'd seen no evidence of a witness at the house and had heard nothing. More importantly, he had no idea what she'd seen or heard. He needed to find and eliminate her, and that was proving impossible.

CHAPTER TWENTY-FOUR

DANI SAT OPPOSITE JESS at his small kitchen table and watched with fascination as he broke down the gun quickly and efficiently, explaining as he went what each piece was and its function. He cleaned it and reassembled the gun, showing Dani how to load the clip, how to insert and remove it, and where the safety was. He handled the gun with the ease of long familiarity.

"Okay, you take it apart and reassemble it."

"Me?"

"You." He held the gun out to her. "If you plan to use a gun, you need to know how it's put together, not just how to shoot it. Take your time. This part isn't as important right now as getting you used to shooting it, but it's a good place to start. It'll give you a little more confidence handling it if it's not mysterious."

It took her a while, but Dani managed to disassemble and reassemble the gun with a few pointers from Jess.

"Not bad for a first timer," he said with a grin. "Now, the fun part. Follow me."

One hundred yards to the side of the cabin in a clearing surrounded by bare aspens and pine trees, whose boughs were heavy with snow, Jess showed Dani the area he'd set up for target practice. Several straw bales were stacked on top of each other. An old paper target with a human form on it had come loose on one side and looked bedraggled from being left out in the snow. Jess removed the old target, stuffed it in a nearby barrel he apparently used for trash, and replaced it with a new one.

"You practice shooting?"

"Yeah."

"With all your military experience, why would you need to practice?"

Jess frowned at her as he checked the gun. "Doesn't matter how much experience you have; you need to practice. Otherwise, you shouldn't have a gun. People usually buy guns for protection. In situations where you need to protect yourself, you have to rely on muscle memory, not trying to think through each step. Using a gun in those situations requires you to be on autopilot, and that comes with practice."

Jess saw the look of uncertainty on her face. "Look, Dani, either you learn how to use it, or you leave it with me. Walking around with a gun you're not familiar with and have never shot is a recipe for disaster."

Dani nodded, but she looked as if she was having second thoughts.

Being unfamiliar with the gun, and based on who'd owned it, Jess worried that the gun had somehow been altered or damaged. He hadn't seen any evidence of that while cleaning it, but he wanted to shoot it first. He took a pair of headphone-like ear protectors, tucked her hair behind her ears, and slid them on her head. He cradled her head as he adjusted the headphones over her ears. Her hair was soft, as were her cheeks, and he nearly dipped down and kissed her. Letting go, and forcing the impulse out of his mind, he handed her eye protection glasses and put his glasses and ear protection on.

"Okay," he said raising his voice so she could hear him. "Stand behind me back about ten feet and stay there until I'm done. I'll go over everything with you once I'm sure the damn thing works properly."

Dani stationed herself where he'd indicated and watched. He dipped his head once in a nod then turned to face the target and pulled his headphones on. Assuming a wide stance and crouching a bit, he racked the slide, aimed, and fired several times in succession. Satisfied after firing several more rounds, he turned and motioned her forward.

"It works well. That's a relief. Let's get started."

Dani picked up on his instructions quickly, learning not to close her eyes before firing or flinch when the gun ejected a cartridge. She wasn't a bad shot, but her aim was unpredictable, and she needed to practice. Jess enjoyed watching her shoot, but what he most enjoyed was standing behind her and wrapping his arms around her to correct her hold on the gun or to show her how to correct her aim. The chance to pull her in and kiss her had been nearly irresistible. He thought he felt her shiver once when he held his face near hers and spoke next to her ear.

"Cold?" he asked. They'd been out for about half an hour, and temperatures were in the low teens, but he wondered if it was the cold or his closeness that had caused the shiver.

She shrugged. "A little bit."

"Then let's stop for now. We can come back later and have another go before I take you home."

"Home," she said softly. "It's funny. I haven't really given my apartment a thought until just now. I wonder what's happened to my belongings, the stuff I left behind."

"They might still be there, don't you think?" Jess asked as they walked back to the cabin.

She raised one shoulder and let it drop. "Maybe. My next check was scheduled to auto deposit, so money was in my checking account to pay for another month's rent. I'd scheduled the payment online, but not after that. I don't suppose there's any point in worrying about it. I can't go back."

"You're a witness to a major crime. The police may have stored your belongings somewhere."

"There wasn't all that much anyway," she said, interrupting him. "It's funny, I'm more attached to where I'm living now than to my apartment in Denver."

"Places have a way of becoming home without you realizing it."

"I suppose. My apartment wasn't really a home, just a familiar place. Actually the apartment over Irma's garage is more of a home. Where's the home you miss?" she asked, shifting the conversation away from her.

"This place has become home, but before that, it was the base camp where I was stationed before the accident. Not because of the accommodations." He laughed. "They were pretty rough. It was more because of the people I hung out with. They were home, I guess."

"Do you still hear from them?"

He shook his head as he held the cabin door open for her. "No. Four of them never made it back, and the rest don't know where I am."

"Why not?"

"Because I don't want their pity. I don't want the memories either, and there's nothing else for us to talk about."

He announced his intention to take her home after they'd eaten dinner, and she surprised him by asking to stay another night.

"I don't want to go home to an empty apartment tonight—if that's okay with you. If you need some time to yourself though …"

"You're welcome to stay."

"I'm sorry to—"

"It's okay. I enjoy your company." There were a number of other things he'd enjoy with her if he could figure out whether she'd welcome his ideas.

She gave him a tentative smile. "Thanks." Reverting to a practical tone of voice she said, "I'll help with dinner."

Jess raised his eyebrows. "I don't have burgers, fries, nachos, or wings. Are you any good at cooking anything else?"

"That depends. What d'you have?"

"Mostly leftovers at the moment, I wasn't planning on a houseguest."

"I should probably go—"

"I'm kidding. Well not about the leftovers, but … I'd like you to stay."

"Okay, let's heat up the leftovers."

A couple of beers and two baked potatoes smothered in left-over chili made for a filling dinner. Sitting in front of the wood-stove with another beer was comfortable, the conversation easy, and it made Dani wonder if a long-term relationship like this was possible.

"This is nice."

"It's pretty basic. No frills that's for sure."

"That's what makes it nice. Quiet and snug in the company of a friend. It's a new experience for me."

"No fond memories of past friends or your family?"

"No, not really. There was nothing quiet or snug about any of them."

"Really? No boyfriends? I find that hard to believe, having seen your 'before' photos."

She took a deep breath, exhaling it in a huff. "Hannah ended my last serious relationship, so I kept it to dates here and there, nothing long term. My … obsession … with trying to keep her out of trouble meant that most guys got sick of dates being cancelled because I had to bail her out or pick her up at the hospital, or because she was coming down off a drug binge at my place, or she'd shown up unannounced and high and looking for a fight. I had one guy tell me he was attracted to me because my hair made me look like a fairy princess. That lasted a few weeks. He learned the hard way that looks can be deceiving.

"I have friends. They're mostly just social, but I have a friend who's stuck around longer than anyone else. We got into it over Hannah. Listening to the same problems and seeing no change in me was getting to her and it had become embarrassing for me to talk to her. I wanted to cut Hannah off—I just couldn't figure out how. I haven't spoken to her in quite a while."

"That doesn't sound like a friend to me."

"She was right, though. I should have walked away from Hannah years ago. She was addicted to drugs, and I was addicted to trying to save her."

"Why'd you do it?"

Dani shrugged. "It was habit. I was older by five minutes, and my mother thought it was my duty to watch over my 'little sister.' Somebody had to, God knows my mother never did. She was an alcoholic, and then my dad disappeared. The problem was, Hannah didn't want me taking care of her. She was going to live her life as she pleased, regardless of how destructive her choices were, and I couldn't walk away and leave her to her fate. It's like you said, though, sometimes it's best to walk away. I just couldn't do it."

"Why were you at the house that day?"

Dani rolled her eyes. "More of the same. Two police officers showed up at my apartment looking for Hannah. She'd missed the last two appointments with her parole officer, and unbeknownst to me, she'd listed my address as where she was living. They were there to arrest her. I told them she didn't live with me, and that I didn't know where she was. I should have just told them where she was and let her take the consequences. She might be alive if I had.

"After they left, I drove over to Billy Alphonse's house to drag her to the parole officer. She refused to go, and we were arguing when she saw something—the killer I now know—outside the front window and hustled me into the basement stairwell."

Dani paused, took another deep breath, and exhaled. "I had gotten to the point where I didn't love her anymore. I fantasized about moving away and not letting her know where I was, changing my phone number. I was sure she had stopped loving me, but maybe not. She saved my life, after all."

Jess saw a tear roll down her cheek. He reached across the space between recliners, took her hand, and gave it a squeeze. "Families are inexplicable, and relationships get very tangled."

They were silent for a bit and Jess released her hand reluctantly. They drank their beers, and at last Dani asked, "What about your family? Based on what you've said, things are not great there."

Jess snorted. "No, they aren't. Neither of my folks were happy when I enlisted. According to them, I was ruining my life, wasting the chance for a good job that my bright shiny new degree would have guaranteed. And doing three tours? They thought I was doing it to piss them off."

He took a drink and shrugged. "Maybe I was. When I returned with this," he said, laying his hand on his thigh, "that only gave them more ammunition. According to them, the Marines had destroyed my life and now … now that I was *crippled*," he said, angrily grinding the word out, "what was I going to do? That was a favorite refrain."

Dani watched as he stared off into space and absently rubbed his thigh. "When my dad died, I was nearly through with my rehab and sick to death of hearing the same old, same old, so I took off. Mom hasn't forgiven me, and it's better for me to stay away and not get into it with her."

"We sure didn't win the family lottery, did we?"

Jess laughed. "No, ma'am, we did not. But then, not many do."

Dani liked to see him laugh, he didn't do it often enough. He was more likely to give her a quick smile, but when he laughed it lit up his eyes and made him look less fierce. He was a good man, one who'd been through hell, yet he'd returned with that goodness intact. She smiled back at him.

The fire in the stove had died down, and Jess rose to add more wood. When he sat back down, he asked, "Have you thought about what you'll do?"

Dani shook her head. "No. I hope I can stay off the police's radar. As long as they can't find me then the killer most likely can't. Other than that, I don't have a lot of options without the truck. Up to now, I've stuck my head in the sand and not paid attention to the news. I've been afraid to turn my phone on long enough to check the news. Which is stupid, considering the mess I'm in.

"I haven't thought through any of this," Dani continued. "I've just been winging it. I think, at some point, they have to either find the killer or drop the investigation. When that happens, if I can blend in somewhere—here maybe—then I can live my life without worrying about them."

"That might take a while."

Dani nodded.

"So far, it's working," Jess said. "I'll keep my eyes and ears open. If you have to move, then I'll take you somewhere safe."

"I wonder where that'd be."

"We'll think of something if we have to."

CHAPTER TWENTY-FIVE

DANI LAY ON THE FLOOR in her sleeping bag, hoping, but failing, to fall asleep. The conversation with Jess had stirred up too much. It had brought back in full force the loneliness she'd endured for the last several years.

Her sister was gone, and Dani was grieving Hannah's life, lost long before she'd been murdered. In spite of the danger Hannah had exposed her to, Dani had found respite and friendship in this unlikely little town. She'd finally found someone who knew her, knew almost everything about her, and liked her. Maybe he liked her as more than a friend.

She'd seen some looks on his face lately that had left her a little breathless. The touch of his fingers as they'd tucked her hair behind her ears and then adjusted the headphones had made her long for him to kiss her. The feel of him wrapped around her when they were practicing with the gun had been so distracting that she'd said she was cold so they could return to the house. The grip of his hand and the squeeze he'd given it earlier, had made her heart melt.

The fire in the woodstove popped, startling her. She rolled over and looked at the closed bedroom door. Was he having a hard time sleeping too? At last, she crawled out of her sleeping bag and walked to the door. She stood there for several minutes, hesitant to cross the threshold into his room, trying to decide how much of a mistake she would be making if she'd misread the situation. Cautiously she leaned in and raised her hand to the doorknob, but before she could turn it, the door opened, and she let out a startled cry. He caught her as she took a stumbling step toward him.

"You scared me."

"Did you need the bathroom?" he asked puzzled.

"No … Why are you up?"

"I wanted … a glass of water."

"Oh …"

"If you didn't need the bathroom …" He hesitated, looking at her face in the moonlight streaming through the window. He still held her shoulders in his hands, and his gaze seared her as she leaned into him. Taking her look as encouragement, he pulled her in, kissed her hard, and backed into his room pulling her with him. "I lied. I didn't want a glass of water. I was going to see if you were awake. If this isn't what you were looking for, this is your chance to say no. If you're going to, then do it now," he said, his voice low and rough.

She reached up and cupped his cheek, his beard soft beneath her hand, kissing him hesitantly. "I don't want to say no."

He quickly pulled his thermal crewneck over his head and pulled her T-shirt off as they walked to the bed. She slipped her pajama bottoms off and reached for his thermal leggings, freeing him and sliding them down his thighs so he could step out of them. He sat on the bed and pulled her toward him nuzzling her belly. She ran her hands over his head, tangling them in his hair, enjoying the feel of his beard on her skin.

"Your beard's softer than I thought it would be," she said,

tipping his chin up, kissing him, and resting her hands on his broad, warm shoulders.

He leaned in and kissed the hollow of her neck, cupping her breasts in his hands, shaping them and flicking his thumbs over her nipples. "Glad you like it." He stretched out on the bed and patted it. "Come here," he said, giving her a hungry look as she lay down next to him. He ran his hands over her body. "God, woman, you're beautiful."

"I'm not—"

"Hush. Learn to take a compliment. You're perfect."

He leaned in and traced his lips down her neck and over her breasts. Feeling his hand slide down her belly and between her legs, she arched toward him as he stroked her. She grasped his hips and tugged on them pulling him between her legs, seeing him close his eyes and sigh.

"I'm gonna apologize for how quick this first time will be. I've been dreaming about this for a very long time." He rolled onto his side and pulled a condom out of his bedside table, quickly tearing the package open and rolling it on. "I'm not going to last long, but we have all night, and I promise to make it up to you."

He grasped her hands and held them above her head as he pushed into her slowly making sure she was ready. "Ah, Jesus," he groaned as Dani wrapped her legs around him and pulled him into her. He began to move fast and hard and—he'd been right—it didn't take much time at all until he lay spent on top of her. She ran her hands up and down his back, enjoying the weight of him and the feel of his heartbeat against her chest.

"Give me a minute, then I have plans," he said rolling to her side and disposing of the condom.

She smiled in the dark. "I love a man with plans."

Jess woke slowly as he became aware of the light from the window. For a brief moment, until he felt her lying spooned against him, he thought that last night had been a dream. He'd had many of them in recent days and he fully expected to wake up in bed alone. He nuzzled his face against her hair and breathed in the faint scent of her shampoo. He hoped one day to see her curls in their natural color, which was beginning to show at the roots, but even the flat brown of the dye she'd used couldn't diminish the appeal of them. He dipped his head and placed a kiss on her bare shoulder and felt himself harden as he ran his hands down her flank.

She sighed and pressed against him. "Good morning," she said drowsily, turning over and into his arms. Jess smiled. "I love it when you smile. You ought to do it more often."

"I have a good reason to do it now," he said, pressing himself against her belly.

She looked embarrassed. "I don't think I can, Jess. I'm … it's been a very long time. I'm a little sore. I'm sorry."

"How about I kiss it and make it better?" he asked with a grin.

She blushed and smiled back at him. "That might help." The flush of her face grew more intense.

"It's worth a try," he said, moving down the bed and taking his job seriously as she wrapped her legs around his shoulders. The contrast between her hesitant, wary, withdrawn public front and her openness and sensuality with him had amazed him. She was a baffling mix of sensuality and innocence, and it delighted him.

He was gentle and and focused on giving her as much pleasure as possible. When she came, it was nearly impossible for him to resist rising up and entering her, but he didn't want their lovemaking to cause her any discomfort. Instead, he kissed his way up her body and rested his head between her small, firm, perfect breasts. She was flushed and a little breathless, and he could hear her heart beating rapidly. As her heartbeat settled, she reached for him, and rolled him onto his back.

"Your turn," she said, stroking him.

"You don't have to, Dani."

"I want to," she replied.

She kissed her way down his belly and kissed the top of his thigh. He went still, waiting for her to be as put off by the scars as he was, as women often were.

"These don't bother me," she said, running her hand over the scars on his leg pressing a kiss to them. He relaxed as she stroked him and moaned as she took him into her mouth, sliding up and down the length of him, and running her tongue around the tip of his erection before taking him back into her mouth. As the tension built for him, he grasped her head and held on, until at last he let go. His breath came fast, and he closed his eyes against the pleasure that washed over him.

"Where have you been all my life?" he whispered.

"I've been thinking the same thing all night."

He pulled her up to him, cradled her in his arms, and kissed the top of her head. "Maybe this is the home we've both been searching for."

"Maybe it is."

She ran her hands over his chest and the spray of scars across it. They had been invisible in the dark the previous night. Now she could see them clearly. Some were flat, slick slices, and several were raised knots of scar tissue that hid in his chest hair. Jess let her run her fingers over them until he reached up and stilled her hand with his.

"I'm sorry. Are they sensitive to the touch?"

He shook his head. "Not anymore. I just don't want you to … focus on them. They're ugly, like my leg."

The scars on his leg were formidable. A long scar ran down the top of his thigh starting several inches below his groin and stopping before it reached his knee. Other, smaller scars clustered around it. Looking at his leg made it hard to dismiss the seriousness of the injury, and she knew it bothered him for her to see them.

"We all have scars, Jess. Some are just more visible than others. The scars don't make you ugly, not to me."

He stroked her hair. "All that sex has ruined your eyesight, darlin'."

"Aren't you lucky, then?"

Jess laughed out loud at that. "Yes, I am. I am one lucky bastard."

CHAPTER TWENTY-SIX

I **CAN'T GIVE YOU DETAILS** like I could if the corpse was fresh, but here's what I know," Carl Thompson said. He stood next to the stainless-steel table where what was left of Billy Alphonse lay and crossed his arms on his chest.

Kaye had accompanied Michaels and Sanders to the morgue out of curiosity and to make sure Michaels showed up. In addition to the usual smells of a decomposing body, a scent overlaid it that reminded her of the wet, decayed leaves and murky water that was always present at the bottom of her parents in-ground swimming pool in the spring, and her mask did nothing to relieve that. The body was even less appealing lying on the table nude. There wasn't much left of Billy Alphonse. In spite of the intervening snows, animals had found a way to unearth it and feed off it.

"First off, I was able to rehydrate the index finger and get a print," Carl said, pointing to a glass specimen jar filled with some sort of fluid in which a severed finger floated. Sanders looked a little green. "I'm told by our fingerprint folks that the print matches Alphonse's, but we'll run DNA comparisons just to be thorough since a visual ID is pretty hard to do in his current state. Based on the bullet I found lodged in his spine and the level of its location, it most likely transected the aorta and ended up in the spinal column.

"The abdominal and chest cavities don't have a lot of tissue left because of the predation, so I have no soft tissue to corroborate that determination, but it's the most likely scenario. That's the only wound I can be sure of based on the condition of the body. All I can say for sure is, he was shot once, and it did the trick. It would have been enough to kill him. And because of the predation, I can't tell you much else."

Carl pointed to two evidence bags lying on the counter. "The bullet I found here looks like the same type and caliber of the bullet retrieved from the woman found at the scene of the crime. Ballistics will have to confirm that, and I'm having them see if they also match bullets retrieved from the bodies of the drug dealers who were killed around the same time. My guess is they will. There's no gun to match them to, but if we ever get a gun, it'll be easy to determine if it was the murder weapon."

Carl looked at the ceiling, as if gathering his thoughts. "I can't give you a time of death other than to say that the condition of the body is consistent with the date of his disappearance and when the woman was killed at the same location. I can say that his current state, based on location and temperatures, would support that time frame. What lividity I can see would indicate that he was left lying on his side for a time before he was dumped at the site where his body was found. Obviously, the dump site was not where he was killed."

"Thanks, Carl," Kaye said, preempting Michaels. "Send the autopsy report to Jack when it's done and let me know if anything else turns up."

As they left the autopsy suite, disposed of their gowns, gloves, and masks, and headed down the hall to the exit, Michaels said,

"So are you gonna follow me around from now on to make sure I fall in line?"

Kaye turned around to face him. "Detective Michaels, you were nowhere to be found when the call came in about the body and didn't answer the text messages Sanders sent. Your partner and I went to the scene. Because of that, I wanted to hear what Thompson had to say, and I wanted to make sure *you showed up*." Kaye took a breath and tried to still the anger that had welled up at his comment.

"I don't micromanage my crew for the most part, but you've been unreliable of late. You showed up today. Don't bail on your responsibilities in the future, and we'll be fine." She turned and walked off, leaving Michaels and Sanders standing in the hallway watching her departure.

"Must be that time of the month," Michaels said, making no attempt not to be overheard.

"For Christ's sake, Michaels, do you have a death wish?" Sanders hissed, throwing an apprehensive glance at Jagerski's retreating figure.

"No, I just don't like bitches."

Sanders shook his head and, as he walked toward the exit, heard Michaels say, "You owe me twenty, Charlie."

"What?"

"Alphonse turned up. You owe me twenty."

Sanders scowled and pulled out his wallet. "Here," he said, handing Michaels the twenty before he turned and walked through the exit doors

Coming out of the grocery store, Polly watched Jess's truck pull up at the curb in front of Irma's house. She saw Jess lean toward

Beth and give her a kiss before she got out. At the stairway to the garage apartment, Beth turned and waved at Jess, giving him the first actual smile Polly had ever seen her give to anyone.

"That sneaky little bitch," she said under her breath.

Since Beth had started working at the bar, Jess had chauffeured her around when she needed it. Polly had been watching both of them. Up to now, she'd seen Jess simply drop Beth off after the bar had closed. Saturday night, though, Jess had stopped at Beth's place and waited until she'd returned with her backpack and a sleeping bag. Polly hadn't seen either of them for two days, and now the kiss.

Polly hadn't come up with any ideas about how to get Beth to move on. If Beth's truck still worked, she might have left on her own. Polly might have been able to persuade her to leave, warned her about how snowed in and boring the place got as winter progressed, how if she didn't get on her way soon, she'd be stuck here until spring. But without the truck, Beth was going nowhere.

Polly had made repeated attempts to break through Jess's aloofness, but nothing she did seemed to get his attention. He noticed her and spoke to her, but not in the way she'd hoped for. Now that Beth was working with him at the bar, he didn't seem to see Polly at all.

She should have moved on when Greg had disappeared, but she was in much the same boat as Beth; Greg had taken off in his car, and she didn't have the money to buy a replacement. This town had turned into the end of the line for her and Beth.

CHAPTER TWENTY-SEVEN

VICE COPS WERE PRETTY BLASÉ about the clothes they wore. None suited up. If they were undercover, most wore clothes that wouldn't look out of place if they were standing on a street corner buying or selling drugs or worming their way into an illegal operation. There was a cockiness about them, and something about the risk of undercover work fueled them. A few were so deep undercover, they were rarely seen unless "arrested" or brought in for "questioning" so they could report in. Some were so deep under that it seemed as if they'd become one with the people they were supposedly investigating.

Sanders had been assigned tech stuff and spent most of his time at his desk following cyber leads and money laundering trails, going through bank and phone records, handling tech equipment on stakeouts, following up on trafficking leads, and doing other activities that required high-tech skills. He stuck with slacks and dress shirts with a tie handy if it was needed. If you weren't undercover or in uniform, there was an unspoken dress code.

Michaels had transitioned from being undercover for several years to coordinating ops with those in the field. He dressed in jeans, some in better shape than others. His one concession to leaving the undercover life was wearing decent shirts and a jacket; no tie ever appeared. The jacket came off when he entered the department and hung on the back of his desk chair unless required.

"Charlie, you going on a date after your shift?" Michaels had asked him shortly after they'd been assigned as partners.

"No, why?"

"You're pretty dressed up, my man—tie, suit jacket. I figured you were trying to impress someone. Jagerski, maybe?"

Sanders frowned, fingering his tie. "You could stand to clean up, maybe look like a detective once in a while."

Michaels laughed. "I've been undercover too long. I still deal with dirtballs, so I don't see the need to dress up—for anyone."

Sanders kept his opinion about Michaels's clothing choices to himself after that. He didn't like being partnered with Michaels. He was mercurial—one minute friendly and buddy-buddy, aloof and irritable the next. It wasn't a partnership like he'd had with other cops. Michaels operated solo most of the time, rarely sharing information unless asked. Charlie couldn't find fault with his work or its results, but most of the time he had no idea where Michaels was and often didn't find out until after Michaels had finished whatever he was doing. Even Jagerski's warnings had rolled off Michaels's back and had very little effect on his behavior.

There was a recent, puzzling tension between Jagerski and Michaels; Charlie could feel it every time they were together, and it worried him. He'd wondered briefly whether they'd slept together and it hadn't gone well. He decided it was unlikely, not because of Michaels, but because he found it hard to believe Jagerski would allow it.

Michaels was good, Charlie thought, but a little unconventional in how he worked things. Too unconventional. Most days, Charlie was content to sit at his computer and work, but he didn't fit. More and more, he thought about transferring to another department. Maybe Fraud would be a better fit.

Dani counted out the bills she'd been hoarding. Between Irma comping her rent in exchange for her help and her job at the bar, she'd managed to save about $300. She'd scrimped on food, eating a simple breakfast and eating dinner courtesy of the bar. Jess had told her it was included. She doubted that would have been the case for someone other than her, but she'd taken advantage of it. She'd gotten awfully tired of burgers, fries, wings, and nachos. In fact, she'd probably never eat them again by choice, but beggars couldn't be choosers.

Sundays and Mondays were a welcome relief, a time when Jess and Dani could let down their public boss and employee act. It meant a home-cooked meal and being able to relax. She hadn't gotten used to being with a man who made no demands on her other than wanting her company, wanting her, and requiring her to practice firing her gun. They'd gone on some hikes when the weather allowed, and once, he'd driven into Glenwood, where they'd enjoyed the hot springs.

It felt like her world was opening up now that the cloud of insanity that had enveloped Hannah was gone. The friends she'd made—Irma, Jess, and Ray, even Elmer—brought home how lonely she'd been. But the reality was that she was no more herself now than she'd been before Hannah's murder. She couldn't risk it. Her life was hidden to everyone except Jess, as it always had been. The only difference was that before, she'd hidden her life out of shame. Now, she hid it out of fear. She'd learned to trust Jess, that was progress. Despite that, anxiety stalked her. Life had never been easy, but life with Jess was and that made her anxious. He'd become too important to her, and in the past, that had usually resulted in disaster.

Dani stared at the money. She wanted the truck repaired just in case. *Just in case what?* she wondered. *Are you going to leave once it's fixed? Are you going to leave Jess?*

She shuffled the bills in her hands, then stuck the money in her jeans pocket. *Fix it, just in case,* she thought bundling up and walking over to Ray's garage. Dani pushed through the door to find Ray snoozing in his desk chair. Hearing the door open, he jerked awake and blinked at her several times before saying hello.

"Sorry to startle you, Ray."

"It's okay. I was just taking a little after-lunch snooze. Not very busy today. What can I do for you?"

"I was wondering if you'd order some of the parts for my truck. I have three hundred dollars cash I can give you now. If that won't cover the cost of all the parts, maybe just order what you can. When I save up the rest, you'll have them available to get started fixing it. Jess said you'd estimated the repairs at a thousand. I realize it could be more, but I need transportation."

"Could be less, too," he said.

"Let's hope."

"Planning on getting back on the road to Utah?"

Dani shrugged. "Eventually. Maybe when spring rolls around and the weather improves. I haven't really decided."

"We'd be real sorry to see you go, young lady. You've been a big help to Irma. She's stopped talking about moving to Denver since you began helping her." He winked at her and grinned. "And I know a certain bartender who'd be sorry if you left."

Dani smiled back at him. "Well, I have no transportation at the moment, and spring's a long way off. By then, you'll probably be sick of me. I would like to start getting the truck fixed, if you'd be willing to do it in stages."

"Sure, I can order what it needs. Might just start fixing it when they arrive. This is a pretty dead time of year. It'd give me something to do other than jump-start cars, fix flats, and change oil."

"I may not be able to come up with the rest for a while …"

"Don't worry about it." He laughed. "I have your truck as collateral if you don't pay."

"That's not a very good bargain for you."

That made him laugh again. "I've never been a good negotiator, and I've always been a sucker for a pretty face."

Dani walked in the front door of the bar and was surprised when Polly Letofsky walked out of the office area and into the front of the bar. She was buttoning the top buttons on her café uniform, and her bright-red lipstick was smeared.

She stopped short when she saw Dani and covered the remaining open buttons with her hand. "Oh," she said, looking rattled. "I didn't realize you were here." She pushed past Dani and left a cloud of pungent perfume in her wake.

Dani had witnessed Polly chatting with Jess a lot lately. It was often at the bar, and the conversations hadn't lasted long, but Polly had looked as if she was flirting—touching him, smiling at him. He didn't prolong the conversations—he was busy at the bar—but he didn't put a stop to them either. It rankled her, but Dani had said nothing to Jess. Baffled now by her sudden appearance and behavior, Dani walked toward the office door to see Jess wiping at his lips, which were marked with Polly's lipstick.

"What's going on? What—what was Polly doing here?" she stammered.

A miasma of Polly's perfume filled the office, and it made her stomach turn. Jess looked stunned to see her in the doorway, and Dani's heart lurched painfully. "Dani, it's not what you think. She surprised me … She …" he began holding his hands out to her.

"Looks like I'm the one who got surprised. You missed some of her lipstick," Dani said, glaring at him as she turned toward the kitchen.

Jess moved from behind his desk and followed her. "Dani, listen."

"No! I don't want to hear it. I'll be back before the shift starts."

"Wait," Jess said, reaching out and grasping her shoulder.

Dani whirled and swatted his hand off her shoulder. "Don't touch me!" she shouted at him. "I need the job, but I don't need someone who cheats on me." Jess opened his mouth, and she held up a finger in front of his face. "Don't say anything. It would only be lies. I'm done listening to lies from anyone. I spent my life listening to Hannah's, and I won't listen to yours."

"You're not even going to hear me out?" he asked, his face clouding with anger.

"No. I'll be back at five. You can let me know then if I'm still employed or whether you've called the cops."

Dani pushed out of the back door and stumbled down the road to her apartment, tears building as she walked. In her apartment, she sagged against the door and sobbed. *You can't trust anyone*, she thought. *I was a fool to think you could.* How long had he been seeing Polly behind her back? Why had she thought those conversations were unimportant? He'd probably kept Polly at arm's length in the bar because he knew Dani was there and would see.

Why Polly? I'm an idiot, she thought, *always looking for a happy ending and never finding one.* What she'd had with Jess had been too good to be true. She had to get the truck fixed and leave. There was no way she could stay here now.

She sat on the bed wiping tears from her eyes and rifled through her backpack until she found her wallet. Her one credit card was still there. She'd kept it, although she knew it wasn't safe to use. She looked at the card with Beth Caldwell's name on it and wondered what the credit limit was or whether she could still use it. The motels she'd stayed in had taken it, and there hadn't been a problem, but obviously no one was making payments. It had probably been suspended or whatever they did to cards in arrears. Maybe they just piled on the interest charges for a few months. Dani had no idea; she'd never been late for a payment of any kind. As luck would have it, she'd paid off the small balance on her card before everything had gone to hell. She tapped the fake card on her palm; she'd have to use her real card. As soon as Ray got the parts in, she'd tell him to get the truck fixed, and she'd charge the repairs when he was done.

If she used her card to pay for the repairs when the truck was ready to go, it'd give her time to leave before the charge raised any flags on her account—she hoped. If Ray noticed or commented on the name on the card … well, she'd think of something to tell him. She'd be packed and ready to go, and she'd disappear again. Until then, she'd just survive. She'd done it for years with Hannah, and she could do it for a few weeks more despite Jess's presence. She thought she'd found something special with him, but that had been a fantasy. She didn't know how, only that she'd survive. She was good at surviving; living, not so much.

"Fuck!" he swore and slammed his hand into the back door as it closed on Dani's retreating figure. Polly had been going out of her way to talk to him at every opportunity recently, and he'd made short of her attempts at conversation. *That calculating bitch*, he thought, thinking about Polly's "surprise" visit just minutes before Dani always showed up for work, walking into his office undoing her uniform top, doused in perfume. He'd stood up, about to ask her what the hell she was up to, when she walked up to him, threw her arms around him, and kissed him hard as he clamped his lips shut against her intrusive tongue.

He shoved her away. "What the fuck? What d'you think you're doing? Get out of here!"

She smiled at him like a cat stalking a mouse and backed toward the door. "Just giving you a taste of what you're missing."

"I'm not missing anything. Get the hell out of here," he said, watching her smile and walk out the door.

The next thing he knew, Dani appeared in the doorway as he wiped at his mouth, the back of his hand coming away with a red smear of lipstick.

Christ, she wouldn't even listen to him, although he supposed that shouldn't have surprised him. Polly had set it up so it looked pretty damn incriminating, and from what he knew, Dani had experienced a lot more lying than honesty. *God damn Polly*, he thought as he sat at the desk and held his head in his hands. If it was the last thing he ever did, he was going to see her forced to leave town. He walked to the window and opened it to air out the cheap perfume she'd worn. It made it hard to breathe.

She stood in the office doorway her arms crossed tightly over her chest, and said, "Do I have a job or not?"

"Of course you have a job. Dani, please listen to me."

"I have work to do before the bar opens. Let's keep this impersonal, and as soon as the truck is fixed, I'll be gone and you and Polly can do whatever you like."

He stood up and grasped her by the shoulders and felt her try to pull away. "You at least owe me the chance to explain."

"I don't owe you anything."

"Just listen to me," he pleaded.

"Fine. Explain away."

"It was a setup."

Dani snorted in derision. "I've seen you talking to her. I've seen all those hurried conversations where no one can overhear you two, all her touching and flirting. This isn't new."

"She's been after me since I moved here, and I've *never* been interested. Those weren't conversations—they were her attempts at them. Attempts I brushed off."

"Because you were working and I might overhear the conversation!"

"Dani, there is nothing going on between us. She showed up out of the blue—uninvited. I thought it was you coming in the front. All of a sudden, she was here, her blouse was undone. She shocked the hell out of me by kissing me and making sure she smeared her lipstick all over me." Jess held her arms and searched her face. It was impassive, and his heart took a nosedive. She wasn't listening. She didn't believe him.

"Dani, she did it intentionally. She knew you'd be arriving for work. She wanted you to think exactly what you're thinking, and it isn't true. I would never do that to you."

"You've had your say. Now I have work to do." She pulled away from him and turned toward the kitchen.

"I'm not your fucking sister!" he shouted.

Dani whirled around to face him. "You're just like her. You get caught red-handed—or I guess I should say red-lipped—and then try to lie your way out of it. I'm not stupid, and I'm not blind."

"You're both if you honestly believe that I would do that to you, but have it your way."

"Uh, did you know Beth gave me three hundred bucks to get parts for the truck?" Ray asked Jess at the bar that night. He noticed that Beth was conspicuously absent from the front of the bar. Food was being made, but Jess had to retrieve it. A little ding would be heard from the kitchen, and Jess would go around the corner, return with the food, and distribute it to customers. Beth hadn't been out of the kitchen all night. Something was up; he just wasn't sure what it was.

"No, I didn't. None of my business anyway," Jess snapped.

"She stopped by before she was due here and said to fix the truck when the parts arrived. Said she'd pay for the repairs in full when I was done. Not sure where she'll get the money. Once I get the parts, it won't take more'n a couple days to get the truck fixed."

"Ray, that's between you and her. Repair it or don't repair it. That's not my call, and I'm not paying the bill."

"Uh, what about the storage bill? That's coming due."

Jess pulled his wallet out and slapped a twenty on the bar. "That should take care of next month. My guess is she'll be gone by then. I don't expect a refund."

CHAPTER TWENTY-EIGHT

JESS LEFT RAY MUSING over his beer and worked the bar with an ache in his chest and his stomach in turmoil. He kept trying to figure out a way to convince her that what had happened was not what she thought, what Polly had intentionally hoped she'd think, and he hadn't come up with anything. If she wouldn't take him at his word, he damn well wasn't going to beg. He was short with customers, and his conversation with Ray had been upsetting. She'd asked Ray to repair the truck and planned to pay for it when it was done. *How is she going to do that?* he wondered more than once that night. What puzzled him the most was whether she'd planned on leaving all along, even after they'd connected?

She couldn't leave. The mere thought of it tore him up. No one had ever made him laugh as much as Dani did. He could relax around her and just enjoy her presence; he didn't have to be "on" or guarded. He didn't have to be embarrassed by his scars or his limp. Unlike other women—including his mother and sister—she wasn't repulsed by them. They were just there, and they didn't diminish him in her mind.

He'd been attracted to and at least temporarily involved with a number of women, but had never felt this connected. Even dressed as she was tonight—her hair covered by a baseball cap, her short brown stub of a ponytail pulled through the keyhole closure, wearing a shapeless plaid flannel shirt worn over a T-shirt, and well-worn jeans, her eyes red-rimmed and puffy—he wanted her, badly. Wanted to hold her and make her listen to him, make her tell him she believed him.

She'd been fifteen minutes late coming back to the bar and looked wrung out. There was no smile, no quick private hug or kiss for him. She just began her work and said nothing to him.

"God damn you, Polly," he muttered to himself for the hundredth time that night.

Jess had tried once again to talk to her after the bar had closed that night. "Dani, look at me. Why would I lie about something like this? I wouldn't do this to you."

She gave him a cynical look. "I have watched my sister look me in the eye and lie to me, over and over again. The only time she was ever honest with me was right before she was shot to death. I won't be taken in again, and I'm done being pathetic."

"You honestly believe I would do that to you? Lie to your face?"

"People are capable of anything to get what they want."

Jess reared back, stunned. "You think I befriended you because *that's* what I wanted, just a piece of ass?" He shook his head. "You are unbelievable, lady."

Dani had said nothing as she left out the back door.

Jess hadn't been drunk in a very long time. He'd seen too many drunks at the bar to overindulge, but he'd had a few last night after he'd closed the bar. He'd driven home slowly and carefully. There weren't any cops patrolling the road, but he didn't want to run off it and wreck the truck or himself.

Arriving safely at the cabin, he'd made a serious effort to drink himself unconscious. He hadn't managed to do that, but by nightfall he was pretty shit-faced and the fire in the open grate of the woodstove had mesmerized him. Between the alcohol and the flicker of the flames he realized his leg wasn't bothering him, or maybe it was and he was just too drunk to feel it.

"Only good thing to come of it," he muttered to himself and emptied his glass.

When Dani had walked out the door and left him standing in the kitchen, furious and heartsick at the same time, he felt lost. On the way home, he'd thought about going to Polly's place and ripping her up one side and down the other, but he was so angry he was afraid of what he'd do. When he thought about it, he really didn't want to see her again. Ever. He sure as hell didn't want to give her a chance to call the sheriff on him.

On that thought, he fell asleep. Waking cold and confused in the dark, he pushed a button on the side of his watch to illuminate the face and saw it was four a.m. The cabin was freezing. He hadn't banked the stove for burning overnight like he always did, and it had gone out. The electric heat was set at fifty-five, just high enough to keep the pipes from freezing, but it didn't keep the place warm. Not wanting to deal with the stove or the thermostat, he pushed himself up out of the recliner and staggered to his bedroom, where he crawled into bed fully clothed, pulled the comforter up around himself, and fell asleep.

Someone was tapping his head regularly with a ball-peen

hammer. He opened his eyes to tell the hammer enthusiast to fuck off and leave him alone, and the room whirled around and sent his stomach into revolt. He jolted out of bed and made it to the bathroom in the nick of time. An acid wash of liquor and bile ended up in the toilet. When he quit heaving, Jess blindly felt for the handle, flushed the toilet, lay down on the tiny bathroom floor, and closed his eyes. The cold woke him up half an hour later. He brushed his teeth, trying to remove the vile taste in his mouth, and then staggered into the main room. Christ, the place was freezing. He walked into the kitchen area and turned the tap on. The water ran freely, so the electric heat was working, and the heat tape he'd wrapped the pipes with had kept the pipes from freezing.

I shoulda turned the thermostat on the electric baseboards up last night before I anesthetized myself, he thought. Electric heat wasn't cheap, and he preferred to use the stove. He got the stove going and poured himself a glass of water. Gulping it down, he waited for the coffee to brew. A piece of dry toast and a cup of coffee later, and he felt marginally better, although it was a slim margin. Looking at his watch and seeing it was nearly ten a.m., he walked to his desk and pulled the sat phone out. He raised the antenna and walked out onto the porch in stockinged feet to get better reception.

"Ray? This is Jess. I need you to go over to the bar and put a notice on the front door. The bar's closed today. Say it's closed until further notice. I feel like shit and won't be coming in."

"Okay, do you need anything? You're not bad sick, are you?"

"No, I'm just hungover. I'm pretty sure I locked up last night, but you have the spare keys, so if I didn't, lock it all up for me."

"Everything okay, Jess?"

"No, it's not, but that's not your problem. Thanks for taking care of all that for me."

Elmer took his time sniffing at nearly everything he came to, rolling in the untrampled snow of people's front lawns, and generally enjoying himself as Dani walked morosely behind him. She felt as if a ten-pound weight sat on her chest, and her head ached. Just when she thought she'd cried herself out, something would remind her of Jess, and she'd start again. Sunglasses concealed her puffy, reddened eyes.

When she returned with Elmer, Irma asked her in. "I made a shepherd's pie and figured you could take half home with you. I always make too much," Irma said, waving her into the kitchen.

"Thanks, but I'm just going to go home and rest. I have a splitting headache."

Irma turned and put a hand on her shoulder. "Well, you take it anyway. You'll be hungry later. Gonna tell me what's wrong?"

Dani shook her head, afraid that if she tried, she'd burst into tears.

"I'm here if you need to talk. Take this and take Elmer with you if you want some company." She walked Dani to the door and put the wrapped dish in her hands. Dani nodded numbly. "Honey, I don't know what's happened, but life goes on. Take Elmer with you. He's a comfort," she said with a sad smile.

Dani shook her head no and left. Elmer had followed Dani to the door. When she glanced back from the top of the stairs to her apartment, she saw he remained at the door and looked disappointed that he hadn't been asked to accompany her. Irma watched as well, a worried expression on her face.

Jess was fixing himself some canned chicken noodle soup for a late lunch when a knock on his door surprised him. He was even more surprised to find Irma Hotchkiss standing on his doorstep.

"Irma?" he asked as he held the door for her, puzzled at her appearance. "Uh, come on in. Would you like some coffee?"

"No." She came in, crossed her arms over her chest, and gave him an annoyed frown. "I saw Ray Decker posting a closed sign on the bar. He said you were sick, and Beth won't come out of the apartment. She didn't take Elmer to her apartment last night, which she often does, and I had to walk him this afternoon. I'm not here to complain about the dog. I want to know what the hell happened between you two."

"Why do you think something happened between Da—Beth and me?"

Irma waved a dismissive hand in front of his face. "Oh, for God's sake, Jess Walker, I am not blind. Everybody knows you two have been seein' each other. Now you're "sick," and by the smell of you I'm guessing you're hungover, and Beth won't come out of the apartment. What happened?"

She speared him with a look that rivaled his drill instructor's in boot camp and waited. He motioned her over to the small kitchen table and held a chair out for her. Sitting down opposite her, he told her what had transpired.

"Well you've got yourself into quite the pickle, haven't you?"

"I didn't do anything! I got ambushed," he shouted, then held his hands to either side of his head as it throbbed. "But she doesn't believe me, and I don't know how to convince her."

"It's going to be hard to do that. She's hurting. I don't know what happened to that child, but she's the loneliest person I've ever met." Irma stood up and walked to the door. "Give her a couple days, then talk to her. And you stay away from Polly. I'll take care of that pain in the ass."

"You stay away from Polly, too. She's caused enough trouble as it is."

"Who said I was going to go anywhere near her?"

CHAPTER TWENTY-NINE

SANDERS POKED HIS HEAD into Kaye Jagerski's office. "I just got a call from Michaels. He was supposed to meet a CI, and when he got there the guy was dead, gunshot wound to the head. He asked for you to come out and take over. He's there alone, and he figured it was better if you and I handled it, since he was supposed to be meeting the guy."

"It's protocol. Let's go. The guy was dead when he got there? He didn't shoot him, did he?"

Sanders barked a laugh, then saw Kaye wasn't joking. "He says he found him that way."

"We'll take an unmarked car. You drive and I'll call the ME's office and Forensics while we're on our way."

When they pulled up at the head of the alley and got out of the car, Kaye could see Michaels standing away from the body, hands in his pockets, waiting. Kaye slipped on gloves and pulled an evidence bag from the glove compartment.

Sanders looked surprised. "You don't really think he shot the guy, do you?"

"No, but we have to handle this as if it's a possibility, you know that. So we take his gun and we have Forensics test his hands and clothes for gunshot residue. If they're clean, and the Officer Involved Shooting investigators confirm that the kill shot didn't come from his gun and he wasn't somehow involved, he'll get it back. Call dispatch and have them send some uniforms over to start canvassing the neighborhood and searching the garbage receptacles for a weapon."

She reached Jack and held out the evidence bag. He slipped his gun out of its holster and held it out to her. "So what happened Jack?" she asked as she sealed the evidence bag, and scribbled her name and the date on it. His hands and clothes looked clean; there was no blood that she could see.

"No idea. He called and wanted to meet, said he had some intel on the Alphonse killing—you'll see the call on my phone log and his, unless he wiped it. He wouldn't say what it was he wanted to tell me, said he didn't want to talk on the phone. He seemed pretty freaked out so I agreed to come. He picked the time and place. I showed up on time and found him like that." He lifted his chin toward the corpse. "Seemed like he'd been here a while."

"You handled the corpse?"

"I didn't *handle* it—I felt for a pulse. Pointless, considering the state of his head, but I checked anyway, and there wasn't one. He felt cold, so he's been here a while. For some reason he was here before he'd asked me to meet him."

"Who is he?"

"Dominic Amato. I've used him in the past. His intel is usually reliable, so I came as requested."

"Okay, go sit in my car. I'm going to have Forensics swab your hands for GSR, and you'll need to give a statement to the OIS when we get back."

"Yes, ma'am," he said and gave her a quick salute before he turned and walked toward her car.

Kaye frowned. There it was again, that attitude that never rose to the level of insubordination but held an insolence that grated on her.

An hour and a half later, they left. Michaels's hands had tested negative for GSR, and Kaye would collect his shirt and jacket and take it to Forensics for GSR testing. Forensics had taken his gun, the ME's crew had taken the body away, and the OIS had set up an interview. The crime scene team was still processing the area. He'd let Kaye scan his call log and had fully cooperated. She didn't think for a minute he'd done it, but she had to follow through.

"You're on desk duty till we hear from forensics and the OIS," Kaye said, accepting the evidence bags that held his shirt, pants, and jacket as he walked out of the men's locker room.

"Okay," he said, drawing out the word.

"Do you have a problem with this, Jack?"

He held his hands up and shook his head. "I just think a little trust would be nice. Seriously, you had Sanders watch me take off my clothes?"

Kaye gave him an exasperated look. "This isn't about trust, and you know it. It's protocol. You knew what would happen when you called Sanders about it. If you didn't want to do this, you could have left without calling it in and let some unlucky person stumble onto the scene. No one would have ever known you were there."

"You're right. Sorry," he said, not sounding sorry at all.

Kaye thought about responding and calling him out on his attitude but didn't. It would put her in a defensive position and make her look like a paranoid bitch, so she let it go and let him walk away without comment.

God, she wished she'd had better sense than to sleep with him. This was going to bite her in the ass every time she had to deal with him.

"The slugs retrieved are identical to the ones from Alphonse and the others, so the same gun is being used to take these guys out. My guess is Amato knew who was doing the killing and that's what he wanted to tell you." Kaye sighed and pinched the bridge of her nose. "But we still have no gun and no witnesses, except the elusive Danielle Calderwood. No nothing. Any thoughts or updates?"

"I wish the idiot had talked to me over the phone, but he refused to, and I never figured I'd find him dead." Jack had been cleared. His gun didn't match, his clothes were clean, and Forensics had returned them to him. "As far as Calderwood, who knows?" he said. "Terry in IT was never able to track her phone, and so far no sightings. She probably purchased a burner phone and tossed hers. She's in the wind."

"Whoever is killing these people is pretty serious about not being ID'd. Must have a lot to lose if he is."

"There's a turf war going on. Whoever is doing this will either end up dead or come out on top, and we'll soon know who it is." Jack let out a disgruntled laugh. "By then the fucking gun will be long gone, so these cases are dead in the water unless we find Calderwood or someone else comes out of the woodwork and I can talk to them before they're taken out."

Amato had been dealt with, so one threat had been eliminated. Blackmail had been a very stupid idea, an idea that had gotten Amato killed. Now he just had to figure out who Amato had told and take care of them as well. Guys like Amato always shot their mouth off to someone.

Irma spread the word, about what Polly had done and encouraged people to hit Polly in her wallet. She smiled at how perfect the payback would be as she climbed the stairs to Beth's apartment and knocked on the door.

"Is everything all right?" Dani asked when she opened the door. The last time Irma had made the trip up the stairs had been to show her the apartment.

"Everything's fine—well, mostly fine. Can I come in?"

Dani held the door open. "I'd offer you some coffee or something, but I haven't been to the store."

"Don't worry about that. Come sit down," Irma said walking over to the kitchen chairs. "The bar is closed today. I thought you should know before you walked over there."

"Closed? Why?"

Irma shrugged. "Jess decided to drink his troubles away yesterday. He's feeling pretty miserable … for a lot of reasons, I guess." She waited to see what Dani would say, and when she didn't speak, Irma said, "Somethin' you need to know. Polly's a troublemaker, always has been. She's soured more than one relationship and totally broke up another with her ways. We should have forced her out of town a long time ago. If Jess says he was set up, then I believe him. I know him, and he's a good man."

She saw Dani's face redden. "I've seen the two of them talking—a lot—recently. On Thursday, before the bar opened, they were kissing. She was buttoning up her blouse when she left his office. That doesn't sound like a setup to me."

"Did he act like he enjoyed those conversations? Didja see him kiss her or take advantage of that open blouse?"

"He couldn't very well act like he enjoyed the conversations with her. I work there, and I'd see it if he did. And he had her lipstick all over his lips!" Dani cried. "His office reeked of her perfume. That's no setup—that's getting caught."

"You sure that isn't what Polly wants you to think?"

"People lie, especially when they get caught. I've learned that the hard way."

Irma pushed up from the chair and sighed. "You need to make up your own mind, but if it were me, I'd at least hear Jess out. Or better yet, ask around and see what people tell you about Polly. That might change your mind."

CHAPTER THIRTY

DANI WALKED OVER TO THE GARAGE and found Ray in the repair bay unpacking a large box. Her truck was parked in the bay. She knocked on the doorframe to let him know she was there.

"Hey there, you're just in time. Some of the parts arrived for the truck. I'm waiting on a couple more, but I can at least get started."

"Good." She was relieved that he'd be able to begin repairs and panic stricken that she'd have the ability to leave. "Irma said the bar is closed today … do you know … did Jess say when he planned to reopen it? I don't have a way to reach him."

"I don't know. He told me early this morning it'd be closed until further notice, but I saw him drive by a little while ago. Maybe stop by the bar and find out what his plans are." Dani nodded and turned to go, but stopped when she heard Ray speak. "If I had to choose who to believe, it wouldn't be Polly. Seeing something isn't necessarily seeing the truth of the matter."

Dani nodded her head quickly and left.

She walked toward the bar and drew her coat close. The temperature had dropped in the last hour and more snow was on the way. It felt good to be out of the apartment, but she was dreading seeing Jess. The bar was quiet when she walked in. Lights were on, but Jess was nowhere in sight. Noise was coming from the kitchen, so she headed that way.

There were grocery bags sitting on the counter. Through the open kitchen door, she saw him unloading a couple cases of beer from the back of his truck. He had his back to her. When he turned with the cases in his arms, he stopped. He looked ill, dark circles lay under his eyes, and he was pale. It must have been a whopper of a hangover, Dani thought, surprised that he was even considering opening later. She could see the muscles in his arms flex as he gripped the cases against his chest. He stared at her for a long moment, then came through the door and pushed past her into the bar area.

Dani watched as he took the cases behind the bar, set them on the counter, and began loading the cold chest with the beer. He said nothing to her, and the awkwardness drew out until she couldn't take it anymore.

"Irma said the bar was closed tonight, but ... I saw your truck. I guess you're going to be open?"

"I'm here. It'll be open. You here to quit, or do you plan to show up later?"

"I'll be here." Dani took a deep breath. "Irma and Ray ... well, they don't have a very high opinion of Polly ... and they said—"

Jess stopped loading the cold chest and, turning to her, he cut her off. "You made it pretty clear you didn't want to listen to me, that you think I'm a liar, and that I was screwing around with Polly behind your back. I don't want you to decide I was telling the truth because two people told you Polly might be the liar. If you don't trust me enough to know what I would and wouldn't do to you—without the input of Irma and Ray—then there's nothing to talk about."

"Jess, I—"

His brows were tightly drawn together. "You're not the only one who's been lied to or hurt, but think about this before you come back tonight. *I believed you about what happened in Denver*," he snarled at her. "I believed you with no proof other than a vague "wanted for questioning" in the broadcast to back up your involvement in the murders. I didn't assume you'd killed your sister and her dealer, and I didn't need a pep talk from anyone to convince me you were innocent. I believed you, and you *didn't* believe me. That's pretty hard to swallow."

He turned and walked through the kitchen and out to his truck. His wheels spun as he drove off, spewing snow and gravel in his wake. Dani stood motionless for several minutes, watching as his truck disappeared. She was stunned by the truth of what he'd said, the desolate look on his face, and his abrupt departure. At last, she walked over and locked the front door to keep people out until he returned and was ready to open the bar. On autopilot, she finished putting the beer in the cooler, unsure whether she could face him when he returned or whether she could repair the damage she had caused.

Polly cleared the table with a scowl on her face when she saw the quarter that had been left on the table. A quarter. The tab for Ray and Pat's regular Friday dinner merited at the very least five bucks. That had been happening for the last several days since the incident with Jess. Some customers had left the tip line blank if they used a credit card, and Hal Dearborn's wife Kit and her buddy Rosa Jenkins had left a penny. And nobody would talk to her. Oh, they said "Thank you," when she left their plates on the table—at least some of them did—but no amount of chatter would get them to talk to her.

Storming into the kitchen and depositing the dishes in the sink, she rounded on Harry. "What the hell is going on?" she demanded.

"What d'you mean?"

"This." Polly reached into her apron pocket and pulled out a handful of change that she slammed down on the countertop. One of the pennies rolled off it and Polly made no attempt to pick it up. "These are my tips for today, a handful of change! And nobody will talk to me. What's going on?"

Harry shrugged and returned to the grill he was cleaning for the night. "You done anything to piss people off?"

Polly glared at him. "Jess Walker is at the bottom of this."

"Why would Jess have anything to do with your tips?"

Polly felt heat rise up her neck. "Never mind. This town is nothing but a narrow-minded, hateful bunch of people." Throwing her apron down on the counter, she scooped up her meager tips, collected her coat, and left.

"Ya reap what ya sow, little girl," Harry muttered as he heard the door slam.

Conversation stopped abruptly, and all that could be heard was a song playing on the jukebox. Standing just inside the doorway under the scrutiny of everyone in the bar, Polly wasn't sure coming here to confront Jess about how people were treating her had been a good idea, but it was too late to back down. Jess walked in from the kitchen carrying two plates with burgers and fries on them, stepped around her, and delivered them to a nearby table.

He turned, as did every head in the bar, and glared at her. "You're not welcome here, Polly." His voice carried, and everyone had heard him.

She glared back and set her hands on her hips in defiance. "This isn't your bar, Jess Walker. I can come in here anytime I like."

Jess shrugged. "Make yourself at home, then," he said with a smirk and took his place behind the bar.

Taking a seat at the bar, she watched in embarrassment as the two men who sat on either side of her got up and moved to different seats. "I'd like a glass of white wine," she said, braving it out. Jess took no notice of her and continued about his business. "Did you hear what I said?"

"I heard," he said and did nothing to produce it.

"Are you going to serve me?"

"No."

"No? I'm a paying customer. You can't refuse me service."

Jess cocked his head and pointed to a sign above the bar. "You're mistaken about that."

Polly glanced up. Her brows drew together, and her mouth pulled down in an ugly grimace when she saw the "We reserve the right to refuse service to anyone" sign. She stood up abruptly and shot Jess a withering look. "Fine. You can just go to hell, Jess."

He grinned. "Gladly, as long as you're not there."

Polly barreled out the door to the accompaniment of applause and laughter.

Dani heard the laughing but was puzzled by what she thought was applause and hesitated in the doorway to the bar area. Jess was in his usual spot behind the bar, but she couldn't see any reason for applause. She wasn't entirely sure that's what she'd heard.

"I thought I heard … applause," she said hesitantly to Jess. Conversation between them had been reduced to food orders since Jess had reopened the bar. He refused to talk about anything else, and she'd quit trying. It'd been several days, and she sorely missed closing up for the night and sitting with him at the bar talking, but he'd avoided any conversation with her other than about bar-related issues. "What happened?"

"Nothing serious. I just asked a customer to leave. She wasn't happy, but apparently folks thought it was a good decision."

"Who was it?"

"Ben and Carl want an order of wings," he said, handing her the ticket without answering her. He turned away from her, picked up a rack of glasses, and carried them into the kitchen. She followed and watched his back muscles flex and stretch under his shirt as he loaded the dishwasher. The physical connection they'd had wasn't what she missed most. Dani missed him. Missed his humor and his kindness and his company. Missed having someone she didn't have to hide from, someone who'd wanted her as she was.

He turned the dishwasher on, straightened, and started to step around her.

"Jess." She grabbed his arm, and he halted, giving her a wilting stare. "I'm sorry."

"Good. Thanks."

He's not going to listen, she thought.

He started to walk to the bar, and Dani stepped in front of him. "I deserve you being angry and not wanting anything to do with me, and it may make no difference to you, but I am sorry for not at least giving you the benefit of the doubt."

"That's generous of you."

"Well, for what it's worth, I am sorry. I wish … never mind." She said with a shake of her head. "Ray says he'll have the truck fixed day after tomorrow. I'll be on my way, then. That way neither one of us has to be miserable."

CHAPTER THIRTY-ONE

DOMINIC AMATO WEIGHED ON KAYE'S MIND. What had he known that had gotten him killed? Michaels thought it was related to the Alphonse murder, but what could the guy tell them? He could've given Michaels a name, but without the gun or some other concrete evidence, it wouldn't get them far. They could bring the person in for questioning or put a tail on whoever he implicated, but there'd be no way to arrest and charge anyone with the crimes. It'd be Amato's word against whoever he was implicating. Information from one witness wasn't enough unless he had some hard evidence. Maybe he'd seen something that would give them an avenue to pursue. It was far more likely he'd heard something, and hearsay wasn't much help. If he could have given them a name, though, they could have watched whoever it was and, if they were lucky, gotten a warrant to search for the gun.

In Kaye's experience, the guys running the show didn't bother killing those who stepped out of line. Ordering their murders, yes. But doing the actual killing? Almost never, unless whatever the victim had done was truly personal. They were like Charles Manson; they got their crew to do the dirty work. Keeping the murder weapon was odd as well. Why keep it? Keeping it could be a simple matter of convenience, or, odd as it was, perhaps it was a favorite gun.

That brought her back to Michaels and his being in the alley and finding Amato's body. He said he'd just arrived and found Amato when he called Sanders, and the hood of his car was still warm when they'd arrived—she'd run her hand over it. She'd caught Michaels staring at her when she'd done that, and he'd shaken his head in disbelief.

The ME had determined Amato had died approximately an hour or more before Michaels had called in his discovery, which put Michaels further in the clear, although there was no one to back up any of his story. There was no voice mail from Amato on Jack's phone, but the call logs on both phones verified Michaels's claim about Amato calling him. There was no way to verify what the actual call pertained to, but the OIS had cleared him.

She kept worrying at the puzzle. The memory of him standing with his hands in his pockets across the alley from Amato's body kept floating into her mind. She'd known him for five years, he was a solid cop. Unconventional at times, but then so were most of the Vice cops; they had to be. The memory, however, refused to go away. Perhaps it was because of what had happened between them and the doubts that had stirred up.

Kaye walked over to Homicide and glanced around until her eyes lit on Blake Halloran.

"Kaye," Blake said, standing up and giving her a welcoming smile. "Haven't seen you in a while."

She laughed. "I know. You apparently haven't needed any of my connections to help you pick locks or break into a hotel room."

"Shhh, I don't want people thinking I'm any good at that kind of stuff." He offered her his desk chair but she remained standing and he leaned against the edge of his desk. "What's up?"

"I'm not sure. Can we talk privately?" she asked.

"Sure. Be back shortly, Clark," he said to his partner.

Clark Stevens sketched a two-fingered salute. "Good to see ya, Kaye," he said and went back to the files he had on his desk.

Once they were settled in a conference room, Kaye got down to business. "You heard about the Alphonse killing and the other drug-related murders, right?" Blake nodded. "Do you know an informant named Dominic Amato?"

Blake frowned. "Rumor says he turned up dead, but I don't know him. Why?"

"Well, hear me out, and let me know what your take on this is." Kaye related what she knew of the Alphonse murder and the others and then relayed what had happened to Amato. "We have no idea what he was going to tell Michaels other than it supposedly had to do with the Alphonse murder. I suspect he was murdered because of what he had to tell Jack, but who killed him is unknown. He hadn't been in contact with Michaels in a couple months. It bothers me that out of the blue Amato arranges to meet, and Jack shows up and finds him dead."

Blake looked surprised. "You don't think Michaels had anything to do with it, do you?"

Kaye made a face and shook her head. "No, he was cleared, and I can't think of any reason why Michaels would be involved. I just … it bothers me. Amato could have told Michaels a number of things that would end up getting him killed to prevent him talking. He wouldn't talk to Michaels over the phone, but someone other than Michaels must have known about the meeting."

"Was he a talker?" Blake asked. "He may have dropped hints

or shot his mouth off. These things get around. Maybe it got around to the wrong person."

"That's probably what happened. It makes me wonder, though, if it was a setup so Michaels would get blamed. He deals with a lot of questionable people. Maybe Michaels was getting too close to somebody. Maybe Amato knew who'd killed Alphonse." Kaye ran a hand through her dark curls. "The guy who's cleaning up is pretty thorough. If he got word of the meeting, he'd have killed Amato, and I can see throwing suspicion on Jack because he's working the case. Maybe it was a warning to back off, knowing that it wouldn't support an arrest, but would cause Jack a few days of grief while OIS cleared him. Even crooks are cautious about killing a police officer."

"What can I do to help?" Blake asked.

"Tell me I'm not crazy?"

Blake laughed. "You're not crazy. It's entirely possible. But you didn't come here for reassurance. What do you need?"

"I don't know, put some feelers out? See what you can find out? I wanted to talk to someone outside of my department. I don't want anyone to know I talked to you about this." She rubbed her forehead.

"I'll see what I can find. Captain Obvious here, but whatever the guy had to tell Jack was important enough that someone put a stop to it. You've got no physical evidence to make an arrest, but this guy could have known something that would have enough weight to arrest and maybe convict someone. That'd be worth killing him for."

"Yeah, it would. There were other calls on Amato's phone, but the people who called him—the ones we can locate—have alibis. We just don't know what he knew."

"And can't find out now that he's dead."

"I don't know. This is probably just one more unknowable about these cases. The whole thing—Alphonse, the other drug murders and now this—is just a clusterfuck. We have nothing." Kaye stood up and moved to the door of the conference room. "Thanks, Blake. I needed someone to bounce things off of. Let me know if you hear anything." She turned toward him and asked, "How's Alex?"

She watched as his face lit up and he smiled. "She's great. She's waitressing and going to UCD to get her criminal justice degree, then who knows what she'll do? She's made some noise about the academy. Not sure I'm in favor of that. She'd be good at it, but … we'll see."

"You look happy."

He seemed surprised, as if he'd just realized it. "I am. For the first time in a long time, I am."

Kaye reached out and squeezed his arm. "I'm happy for you. Tell her hi for me."

CHAPTER THIRTY-TWO

THE AMATO ISSUE HAD *been dealt with, permanently. At least he hoped it had. Dom might have told others what he knew, so he'd keep his ears to the ground for any news. He'd started to relax about the Calderwood woman. There'd been no sign of her, no sightings, no nothing. She was either long gone or dead. Remembering what had happened that day, he thought it was unlikely she'd seen anything, but it was anyone's guess and he didn't want to take any chances.*

Dead would be best. What was the saying? Something about the only sure secret is between you and a dead person. Something like that, but it was true—it'd be better if she was dead. For now, at least, no one could find her.

Charlie Sanders pushed some papers around on his desk until he found a sticky note that he held out to Kaye. "You got a call a little while ago from someone named Sally Howard. Said it was urgent she talk to you."

Kaye took the note and frowned. She'd set up a meeting with two other cops who were working a drug bust and didn't want to deal with Sally. "I'll call her after this meeting." She saw the look on Sanders's face. "What?"

"She was pretty upset, said it was urgent. I told her you'd call when you got in."

"Fine, I'll call her, and we'll do the meeting in fifteen minutes. Get the group together."

God only knew what Sally wanted. She'd been an on-again, off-again informant for Kaye for several years. On good days, she often had good information, on bad days, not so much. Sally meant well, but her life as a prostitute who worked the street and liked to get high was pretty dismal from Kaye's perspective. Kaye couldn't blame her. She'd be high most of the time, too, if she had to prostitute herself. As far as Kaye knew, Sally had never gradu-ated to hard drugs, which was a plus.

"Sally? It's Kaye Jagerski. Detective Sanders said you'd called. What's up?"

"I have some info you need to hear, but I need you to keep me out of it. I need to find some place safe to stay until you figure out what to do."

"What's this about?" Kaye asked. Sally didn't sound high, she sounded scared.

"Look, can we meet somewhere, somewhere private?"

"Where?"

"Come to my apartment. Okay?" Sally gave her the address.

"I can probably be there in an hour. Sal, what's this about?"

"Just come. I'll tell you when you get here. Don't tell anyone where you're going."

Kaye hung up and swiveled her chair back and forth thinking about the phone call and what Sally might need to tell her. At last, she picked up the file on her desk and headed to the conference room.

An hour later, on her way to Sally's efficiency apartment in an old building over a liquor store and a Greek restaurant, Kaye wondered what had scared Sally and what she might have to tell her.

Kaye saw the peephole darken as Sally peered through it and then opened the door for Kaye to come in. "Okay, what's going on?"

"I heard something from a john I'm friends with. I was with him a week ago. We came back here … Anyway, he wanted to talk afterward. We smoked a couple of joints and he started talking about a guy taking over Billy Alphonse's territory and how the guy was ruthless, how he'd popped several dealers who were associated with Alphonse, and how he—the guy I was with—had found out who the guy was and was going to blackmail the shit out of him."

"Okay, did he tell you who he was?"

Sally looked at Kaye. "Look, I know you're not going to believe me, but if I tell you this, then you have to protect me. The guy who told me all this was found dead the next morning. I don't see him regularly, so I didn't know he was missing. I heard about it from a friend. I checked it out online and it's true. He was shot and left in an alley not far from here."

"You mean Dominic Amato?"

"Yeah, Dom. He was a repeat customer, and we hit it off. Sometimes if he brought me weed or something else, I'd give it to him free." She gave Kaye a sad smile. "He brought me flowers for my birthday. No one's ever done that before."

"Who'd he say the guy was?"

Sally frowned and wrung her hands. "You gotta protect me, Jagerski.

"I will, Sal. Now who did he say it was?"

"He said it was a cop."

Kaye reared back and frowned. "A cop? Are you sure?" she asked, a look of disbelief on her face.

Sally nodded and then shrugged. "I knew you wouldn't believe me."

"Are you sure you didn't misunderstand? You were high, you said."

"I was high, not unconscious!" Sally shouted. "Yes that's what he said. I even asked him if he meant a cop, and he said yes, but I wasn't supposed to tell anyone because he was going to blackmail the guy. I told him not to, that he should forget about it. But he wouldn't listen and now he's dead." At that she began to cry. "He was a nice guy. I liked him. He was a john, but he liked me. It didn't seem to matter that I was a prostitute. And now he's dead. You gotta protect me."

"He didn't give you a name or a department or a precinct?"

"No. He said it was better if I didn't know, that he'd treat me after he got the first payment."

Kaye looked at Sally incredulously. "What am I supposed to do with this? You don't know who the cop is or where he is—hell, it could be a woman—and I'm supposed to protect you? *From what?* Do you know how many fucking police officers there are in Denver alone?"

Kaye paced around the tiny, cluttered studio apartment, becoming angrier by the minute. "What is this, Sally? A shake-down for a stay at a hotel for a week or two while we try to figure out who the hell this mysterious cop is?"

"I was trying to help you!"

"Well, it's no help. Why are you doing this? Have you got a dealer after your ass for not paying up?"

"Get out! I wanted to help. I want whoever killed Dom to pay for it."

"I want that too, but your info is worthless without a name or a description." Kaye wiped her hand up her forehead and smoothed the hair away from it. "You'll be fine. You haven't ID'd anyone. Just … just do what you usually do, and let me know if you find out anything more helpful."

"Oh fuck you, Jagerski. If it is a cop, and you find out who it is, you aren't going to do anything. All of you protect each other. And Dom? He was nothing to you, just another lowlife. Get out and leave me alone."

Kaye slammed out of the apartment and took the stairs down to her car, going over Amato's murder in her head. A cop. The only cop at the scene was Michaels, but he'd been cleared. The time of death didn't match when Michaels arrived at the meeting place, there was no gunshot residue and no blood anywhere on his clothes or in his car, and his gun wasn't the murder weapon. She had wondered about someone setting Jack up for the murder, and Sally's "information" lent some credence to that.

If the guy Amato was going to rat out was a cop and he found out what Dom was up to, what better way to kill two birds with one stone than to kill Amato and set it up so that Michaels took the heat? He could have arranged to meet Dom earlier and, when they met, forced Amato to call Jack and arrange to meet him, leaving Michaels to find the body and become a suspect. Jack had said Amato had sounded upset when he called.

There was no evidence to support Michaels having killed Amato, but he'd been there and now with Sally's information, the shade was cast. Kaye needed to talk to Jack and warn him he might have been set up.

When she arrived back at the precinct, she saw Michaels

talking to another Vice cop in the hallway and walked up to them. "Jack, when you're finished here, I need to talk to you. I'll be in my office."

He nodded. "Sure. I'll be there in a minute."

It was nearly fifteen minutes before he showed up and Kaye wondered if this was more passive-aggressive behavior, then put that out of her mind. Maybe she was just paranoid.

"So what's up?" he asked, taking a seat in front of her desk.

"I think someone may be trying to set you up for the Amato murder—"

"What?" he interrupted.

"I have some info from a CI that Amato knew who killed Alphonse and the other drug dealers. He told my CI that it was a cop and that he intended to blackmail him."

"A cop," Jack said with a frown on his face. "Did Amato tell the CI who the cop was?"

"No, he said it would be better not to say."

"No department, no info on whether this cop is rank or patrol?" Kaye shook her head no. "Jesus, Kaye, that points a finger at every single one of us, which is of no help whatsoever in finding the guy. How does this somehow point to me?"

"You found Amato. Did it occur to you that maybe that was the idea? You were supposed to meet with Amato, and you find him dead. Who better to implicate for the murder than you?"

"Why me, though?"

"People talk. Amato talked to my CI, and he may have talked to others. If that's the case, then it makes sense to implicate another cop. Amato was a CI who reported to you, you're on the Alphonse case, who better?"

"I suppose. There's no evidence to back up the implication, other than my being there, so that didn't work very well."

"No, thankfully. But, Jack, you need to be careful. If what I've suggested is true, then there may be another more serious attempt to implicate you like planting evidence."

"I'll be as careful as I can, but with no idea who the cop is, how am I supposed to protect myself or work? If I'm the target, it would have to be someone who knows me and knows that I used Amato as a CI, and that could be anybody—Sanders, you, anybody. The clientele we deal with, hell, they probably all'd like to see me go down."

"You're right. It could be anybody, so keep your eyes open and don't go off by yourself. You should take Sanders or someone else from the department."

"I don't work that way."

"For the time being, you do."

Jack shook his head in annoyance and got up. "Thanks for tipping me off about this."

Kaye watched as he left her office, knowing full well he had no intention of taking anyone with him when he met with people or checked in with his CIs. At least she'd warned him. She couldn't do much more than that, and finding out who this cop was would be nearly impossible unless Amato had talked to someone else and named names.

CHAPTER THIRTY-THREE

DANI LAY IN THE DARK and rolled onto her back. The longer she had to think about it, the more she realized that Polly had set both of them up, but she had refused to listen to Jess, and it didn't look like there was any chance of making up. Polly had made herself scarce since that day, and Dani hadn't seen her talking—or trying to talk—to Jess. So she'd been wrong to think he'd betray her like that, wrong not to trust him.

Her lack of trust had been gradually changing since she'd ended up here. Something inside her had been unfurling—slowly, hesitantly, but opening nonetheless. The anxiety she'd lived with all her life was still there, but less intrusive. And then, she'd been triggered by walking in on Polly. She'd hoped that an attempt to apologize would go some way toward reuniting her with Jess, but he wouldn't budge.

She wondered, at times, if her and Hannah's lives would have been different if they'd had someone like Irma for a mother. Irma was no pushover, but she withheld nothing if she liked you, and she trusted you to make good decisions. She didn't need guilt or recriminations to gain your support. Dani marveled at the fact that meeting the people here had been an accident, driven by her desperation, but a blessing nonetheless.

The grief for her sister was still sharp, but it felt as if a thorn had been pulled out of her finger. The wound was there, and it hurt, but the thorn was gone, and the wound was slowly healing instead of festering. The self-inflicted wound she'd caused with Jess wasn't.

She remembered what he'd said one night during their after-work bar conversation when she'd asked what he thought drew people to addictions.

He'd taken a sip of his drink and hadn't replied for a moment. "I think, maybe, they have something broken in them, something that hurts and needs to be deadened, and alcohol and drugs do that. I don't mean physical like my leg, although that can do it, too, but I think something they've known or experienced that's just too painful to address drives them. We all have those places, those injuries, but some are better able to deal with them than others."

He was probably right, Dani thought. It still puzzled her what Hannah had struggled with. The front she presented was that she just wanted to have fun, that she didn't want to live a boring life, but Dani didn't think anyone went to the extremes Hannah had without there being more to it than that.

Dani wondered if their father's disappearance had anything to do with Hannah's self-destructive behavior. She'd been what Dani had always thought of as the "sparkly" one. The one people, especially their father, gravitated to. Dani had been relegated to the background. His disappearance may have affected Hannah more than Dani had ever considered. Now it was too late to ask.

People in town were getting to know her. They were familiar with her, and they knew the truck she had arrived in. That made her uneasy. Jess had used the bar's laptop to check the news each night and no further Crime Stoppers or other announcements related to the murders had been broadcast. He believed the murders had taken place long enough ago that they had probably been put on the back burner as more urgent cases took their place, and the search for her had probably been sidelined as well.

If Crime Stoppers ran another bulletin asking for information, though, Dani was sure that someone in town would recognize her even with the dye job and the stories she'd passed on through Irma—especially if the broadcast mentioned her truck. Dani hoped the police weren't aware of the truck and were still looking for her Fiesta. Depending on how residents felt about her, or if they felt duty bound to call the tip line, someone might report her.

There is nothing I can do about it until the truck is fixed and nothing I can do to fix the mess between Jess and me, she thought as she sat up and swung her legs over the edge of the bed. It'd be time to go walk Elmer soon. He seemed to sense when she was anxious or upset and after their walk would follow her up the stairs and keep her company. Stroking him relaxed her, and talking to him, which initially felt very strange, had begun to feel normal. Feeling almost normal was something she had begun to think she might achieve here. The loss of Jess, and the need to leave, had ended that hope.

Deputy Steve Rollins sat in his cubicle in the Mesa County Sheriff's Office and read the bulletin again. He looked at the photo and the memory of the woman he'd talked to at the rest stop floated to the surface. The woman in the photo was blonde and pretty, while the woman he'd spoken to at the rest stop had been brown haired and looked exhausted. Nothing like the photo.

He frowned and closed his eyes, trying to visualize the truck she'd been driving. He hadn't run her license plate, which had been stupid. Hell, he hadn't even looked at it. He knew better. His only excuse, which the sheriff wouldn't buy, was that it'd been the middle of the night and he'd been so sleep-deprived he could barely function. His newborn kid had been keeping both him and his wife up most of the night since he'd been born. Now, this far out from the encounter, he couldn't even remember what color the truck was, just that it was an old pickup. At the time, all he'd cared about was getting her to leave the rest area.

He shook his head. Not the same woman, and there were so many old pickups in this part of Colorado that the description wasn't worth much without a license number. He got up and walked to the coffee pot. The bulletin slid off his desk and onto the floor as he passed it. If he had time, he'd swing by the town and see if she'd actually stopped there and, if she had, whether anyone knew where she'd been headed.

Jack sat with Charlie in the break room, after meeting with Kaye. "I saw you in Jagerski's office. What was that all about?"

"She got some intel from a CI that made her think I was being set up for Amato's shooting," Jack said.

"Seriously?"

"Yeah. I think it's bogus, but she was worried."

"Probably because of that call that came in before the meeting."

"What call was that?"

"From some woman ... Sally," he said, casting his eyes up in thought. "Sally ... Howard, that's it. Said she had to talk to

Jagerski right away. Kaye left after the meeting to talk to her, and she came back pretty pissed off. Maybe that was why."

"I'd be pissed, too, if the intel I got was as worthless as what this Howard chick had to say."

"A waste of time, huh?"

"Definitely was." Jack stood up and stretched. "Back to the salt mines, my man."

CHAPTER THIRTY-FOUR

THE PHONE RANG AND WOKE KAYE UP. Fumbling for it where it lay on her bedside table, she finally answered.

"Jagerski."

"Kaye, it's Blake Halloran. I thought you should know, Clark and I got called about a homicide a little while ago. It's Sally Howard. I … You know her, right? She's a CI of yours isn't she? I remember you putting me in touch with her during the Jeffries case."

Kaye sat up abruptly, rubbing a hand over her face. It was three a.m. "She's dead?"

"Yeah, strangled. I'm sorry."

"Where are you?" Blake gave her the name of a cheap motel not far from where Sally lived. "I'm coming over. Can you leave things as is until I get there?"

"Of course. See you shortly."

Fuck, Kaye thought. *How had the cop found out? Why would he kill her when she didn't know anything?* And then the guilt hit. Why hadn't she put Sally somewhere safe at least for a week or two until she figured out what to do?

"God, Sally, I'm so sorry," she whispered as she drove through the early morning to the depressing little motel and what awaited her.

It was a tawdry way to end your life, all for a few hundred bucks Kaye thought as she viewed Sally's corpse lying on the bed. "Anybody see who she came with?"

"No, and no security cameras. Place like this, that's the last thing they want. We'll be checking surrounding businesses for security video once they open in the morning. All the guy at the desk said was Sally checked in like she usually does and rented the place for an hour. He never saw who she was with or the car they arrived in. Not surprising. He works out of a small booth in the office that's enclosed in glass. Money and IDs, when he bothers to ask for IDs, are passed through a drawer. He never leaves the office and, as he so succinctly put it, he doesn't care 'who's paying for pussy as long as they pay for the room.' "

"I talked to her just yesterday. She gave me some intel on the Alphonse case. She wanted protection, and I didn't offer her any because she had no names to give me. I didn't think she was in any danger, and now … she's dead." Kaye turned and abruptly left the room to pace outside.

"This is not your fault," Blake said, following her outside and touching her shoulder with his hand. "The life she lived, this was a constant risk. It probably had little to do with whatever she told you."

Kaye shook her head. "I don't think so, Blake. She …" Kaye looked around at the uniformed officer standing at the doorway and the forensic crew milling about. "Let's go sit in my car, I don't want this overheard."

In the car with the heater running, she told him what Sally had said.

"A cop? But no name, no ID? Kaye, what were you supposed to do? If that was all she had, she posed no threat, and she couldn't ID whoever it was. I don't think this has anything to do with what she told you. I think it's just luck of the draw. She went with the wrong person."

"I hope you're right, but I'm not convinced. Any chance there'll be evidence to ID whoever did it?"

Blake shrugged. "We're hoping for DNA from under her nails. Looks like she got in a couple good scrapes. It could be her own skin, people claw at their necks when they're being strangled, but it's the best evidence we have so far. There may be semen to analyze, maybe pubic hair samples, who knows? But honestly, all of those could be from any of her customers. Unless one of them or the killer has been arrested and their DNA is in the database, it's not much help. The forensic team will dust for prints, which no doubt will be everywhere, but a hell of a lot of people pass through a motel room like this. Until the autopsy is done and the forensic evidence comes in, it's all a guessing game. I gotta get back. You okay to drive home?"

Kaye nodded and was surprised when Blake leaned over and gave her a hug. "I'm sorry, Kaye, but again, this wasn't your fault."

Kaye nodded again, wordlessly. It might not have been, but she wasn't convinced.

Another loose end tied up, he thought. He didn't think she'd known anything, but there was no point in taking chances. God bless the police grapevine for giving him the info on her. Dominic had a big mouth, and he knew her, had a bit of a thing for her. He'd have said something to her. Men like him always told someone. It made them feel important, but the reality was that neither one of them was important. They were just problems to be eliminated.

Dani's heart nearly stopped when she began her walk to the bar and saw an SUV with a Mesa County Sheriff's emblem on it. Ducking into Ray's, she saw him working away at her truck. Thank God he had it in the garage and it wasn't sitting in the storage yard for the deputy to see.

"Hey there," he said, poking his head out from under the hood. "Things are perking along, I should have 'er ready in a day or two."

"Any chance it could be sooner?" *Like now?* Dani thought. What if Jess had called them about her? She couldn't believe he would, but why would the sheriff be here?

"No, it's taking some fiddling with. Sure hope you didn't pay much for this. It's a mess."

"No surprise there, I guess. I just hope you can get it working again."

"Well, I like a challenge and this truck is certainly that. I don't feel right about it, though. I worry it'll break down on you again."

"I'm sure you'll get it working again, and it'll be fine." Dani took a quick glance out the window and saw the SUV back out of the bar's parking lot. She held her breath until the driver headed out of town on the main road and didn't head for her apartment. "Any idea why the sheriff showed up at the bar?"

Ray turned and gaped out the window toward the bar, but the SUV was gone. "Didn't know he had. Seems to be gone, so probably nothing serious." He turned back to the truck's engine and leaned over it, apparently not interested in speculation.

"Okay, well keep me posted on the repairs."

Jess had to admit that when the deputy had walked into the bar, he'd had a moment of sheer panic. He wouldn't give her up, but all the guy had to do was ask around town, and anyone he talked to would tell him where Dani lived. When the guy asked about the liquor license, relief washed over Jess and he reached out to steady himself on the bar to keep his knees from buckling.

Jess handed the deputy the liquor, food, and sales licenses. "They're all in order and current. Who turned in the complaint?"

The deputy scanned each of the documents. "I can't give you that information, sir, but everything looks fine, so no harm, no foul, right?"

"Yeah, right."

The deputy turned to go, then paused. "I had to run a woman out of a rest area about a month ago. Looked to me like she was planning on overnighting there. I mentioned this as a place she could gas up and maybe find a place to stay for a bit. She show up?"

Jess frowned. "I haven't seen anyone new here in months, and believe me, it'd be the talk of the town if anyone had. No motels, no place to stay, really. She may have stopped for gas or groceries. My guess is she probably just kept on driving."

"Probably. I felt kinda bad having to roust her out like that, but those areas aren't safe overnight."

"You did her a favor, then."

"Hope so. Sorry to trouble you," he said and left.

Jess walked to the window that faced the main street. He breathed a huge sigh of relief as he saw the SUV turn and head down the road leading out of town.

Walking into the bar felt like walking into Alphonse's house that day—risky and the outcome was just as uncertain.

"Why was the sheriff here?" she blurted at Jess, who was standing behind the bar.

"It was a deputy. Said he'd gotten a call that the bar's liquor license had expired, so he came to check it out." Jess stared at her for a moment. "I didn't call him or turn you in, if that's what you're worried about."

"No … I … it just scared me when I saw his SUV. I didn't think you had." *But you wondered*, she thought with embarrassment. "I think if you were going to do that, you'd have done it a while ago."

"Well, that's progress, I guess."

"Why would anyone tell them the liquor license had expired?"

"I'll give you two guesses, and the first doesn't count. You can be sure it was Polly. It was payback for the other night here at the bar."

Dani nodded and made her way to the kitchen, her heart still pounding away as if it wanted out of her chest.

Polly finished painting her toes and sat back, allowing them to dry while she watched TV. She hated the news, but her favorite show followed this broadcast, so she had it on low, keeping an eye on the clock. It was an old TV, and the picture wasn't the best, but the face on the screen caught her eye … it was so familiar. She turned up the sound and listened as the detective being interviewed discussed why they were looking for the woman. Calderwood … the name struck Polly as sort of familiar.

"The last vehicle we are aware of her driving is a white 1998 Ford F150 pickup truck." He rattled off the temporary license plate number, but Polly had stopped listening. Could Danielle Calderwood be the Beth Caldwell she knew? As unlikely as that might be, the truck was not. It was the truck that Beth had driven into town, which was currently sitting in Ray Decker's garage.

Polly leaped up and ran to the kitchen, where a pen lay on the counter near the wall phone. She snatched it up and ran back. Lacking any available paper, she scribbled the phone number on her palm and then listened to Detective Jack Michaels ask viewers to call the number with any information they had on the woman. The show went to commercial, and Polly shot off the couch and began dancing around her tiny living room.

"Jess Walker, you pissed off the wrong person. Paybacks are hell, baby, but well deserved."

The following night when her shift at the diner was over, Polly walked to Ray Decker's garage. It was nearing six p.m., and it was dark out. She crept around the outside of the garage until she found a side window that allowed her to look inside the garage bay at the truck. Standing on her tiptoes, she couldn't see the front or the tailgate of the truck where a Ford emblem might be, but along the side she saw an F150 emblem and grinned.

"Can I help you?"

Polly spun around and saw Ray Decker standing at the corner of the garage not far from where she stood. "Sorry, I … I was … wondering if … wondering if Beth was going to keep her truck. I … I was thinking about leaving town and I thought maybe she'd sell it."

Ray's eyebrows crawled up his forehead then drew into a

frown. "She's getting it fixed, so I'm guessing the answer's no, but go ask her instead of creeping around here."

"Of course, I'll ask her. I … just wanted a look at it."

Ray gave her a jaded look. "Well, you've had your look, now move along."

Back inside the garage, Ray puzzled over Polly's appearance. Beth's truck had sat in his storage lot for the last three weeks, so why'd she want to look at it now? And after what had happened, Beth would be more likely to run Polly over with the truck than sell it to her. Something was up, and knowing Polly, whatever it was, wasn't good.

Ray locked up and headed home. He'd give it some thought and talk to Jess about it. It was late, and Jess would be busy at the bar. Polly was just a troublemaker. If she was planning on leaving town, hell, he'd give her the truck and pay Beth whatever she'd paid for it. He'd talk to Jess in the morning. Ray was tired and hungry, and as he walked into the house, the smell of his favorite dinner enveloped him. The worry about what Polly was up to faded.

"Smells good enough to eat," he said from the entrance to the kitchen.

Pat rolled her eyes and laughed. "You'd think after all this time you'd have something more original to say."

"But it always makes you laugh," Ray said, giving her a kiss on the cheek and sitting down to dinner.

CHAPTER THIRTY-FIVE

YOU'RE SURE IT'S HER?" Michaels asked the woman who'd been patched through to his extension. The day had not started out well. Jagerski was upset over her CI's murder and had actually quizzed Sanders and him about where they had been the previous night. He'd been seducing a young lady he'd met earlier in the evening and gave her the woman's name to call and verify, and Sanders had been at a friend's house. The fact that she would even ask them for alibis infuriated him.

He'd put in another appearance on a local TV station the night before last in the hope that it would trigger someone to call in with information about Calderwood. After dealing with Jagerski, he'd gotten several calls from the tip line, but none of the people who'd called had provided anything useful. It remained to be seen whether this caller would.

"I'm sure. She looks like that photo on the Crime Stoppers thing. Her hair's a different color and a lot shorter, but … but I'm sure. I know her as Beth Caldwell—at least that's what she told everyone her name is. And she was driving that truck the police detective described on the TV. That was you right? That's who I asked to talk to."

Michaels's interest perked up considerably. Calderwood had used the name Beth Caldwell when she'd purchased the truck. He'd withheld that from the broadcast and had asked each person who'd called to report someone, what the woman had called herself. This woman had provided the correct answer without being asked.

He admitted he was the one who'd appeared on TV. "I'll need your name and location so I can come check things out." The woman who'd identified herself as Polly Letofsky eagerly gave the information to him. She seemed excited about something, maybe she hoped there'd be a reward. They all wanted money.

"I'll head up there as soon as possible. I hope to be there later this afternoon. Please don't tell anyone you called me. We've had a very hard time finding this woman. I don't want to scare her off and lose her again."

Even when Ray got her truck fixed, there was no guarantee Beth Caldwell was going anywhere. Polly had offered to show the cop where Beth—or Danielle or whatever her name was—lived when he got to town and told him where the diner was. She was looking forward to meeting him. Based on his TV appearance, he was a good-looking guy, and he was a cop, which was kinda cool.

She was sure Jess had been about to agree to go out with her before that bitch had arrived and distracted him. She had hoped, with a little patience, she'd be able to get his attention again. Thanks to what she realized now had been a poorly thought-out idea, that hadn't worked. Jess wouldn't even look at her. He had stopped eating at the diner, and that scene at the bar? It still enraged and humiliated her when she thought about it. Calling the cop was a perfectly responsible thing to do to get rid of Beth Caldwell and pay Jess back for the way he had treated her.

She smiled. Beth was probably a criminal. What legit witness ran from the cops?

❧

"Where's Michaels?" Kaye asked Sanders. She had some things to go over with the whole team and he was missing.

"He said he was following up on a tip that had come in via the Crime Stoppers line about Danielle Calderwood."

"Did he say where she was or where he was going?

"No. Said it was somewhere in the mountains. I don't remember him mentioning a town. It must be a drive. He said not to plan on him getting back before late this evening."

"Great. Get Cross and Martin and bring them to the conference room, I've got some new intel on that place we've had staked out."

She was distracted and annoyed by the news that Jack had taken off. Once this meeting was over, she planned to talk to the Crime Stoppers bunch to find out who had called and where they were calling from.

❧

Jack rolled his eyes when he saw "Jagerski" light up his phone's caller ID. God only knew what she wanted He hit speaker phone and answered. "L.T., what's up?"

"Where are you?"

"Heading up into the hills to check out a tip on Danielle Calderwood and bring her back with me if the tip turns out to be valid. Didn't Sanders tell you?"

"He told me. You should have cleared this with me. It would have been better for me to come with you or for you to take a female officer. Christ, Jack, anything could happen before you get back to Denver with her. She could do anything or accuse you of anything, and you'd have no witness or backup. Where are you headed?" Michaels gave her the name of the town. "I want you to update me when you get there and when you leave, then touch base with me periodically so I know where you're at."

That's all he needed, to have to call her every five seconds. Dutifully, he replied, "Okay, I'll keep you posted."

"When do you think you'll get there?"

"Another three hours, I'm guessing. It's about an hour from Grand Junction."

"Okay, touch base when you arrive."

She was treating him like a rookie, like someone who needed to check in every five minutes. That's how it had been since they'd ended up at his place that night. Christ, he should never have fucked her. Dumbest decision he'd ever made.

Kaye hung up, but the unease about what had happened to Sally and Amato and the fact that Jack had gone to bring the witness back to Denver alone would not go away. Going by himself had been stupid. Who knew what the situation was or whether the woman would comply and go with him? Without a partner, Jack was vulnerable. *He knows better*, Kaye thought, thoroughly annoyed with him and his behavior. He should have taken a female officer with him. There was a limit to being a lone wolf.

After another half hour with it nagging at her she decided to follow him and accompany him back to Denver. She'd be seriously behind him if she tried to drive to the town, but there were flights into Grand Junction, which was the nearest airport.

She found a flight leaving in two hours from the Jeffco Airport that wouldn't break the bank and arranged for a seat. Her logical brain kept telling her it was an overreaction, but that nagging little voice kept insisting she go. She stepped out of her office and saw one of her detectives coming into the department.

"Aaron, I've got something I need to take care of, and I'm going to be out of communication for a while. If there are problems go see Lieutenant Walker in Homicide. I let her know."

"Sure. What's up L.T.?"

"I don't know, that's what I need to find out. I'll touch base when I can."

CHAPTER THIRTY-SIX

DANI OPENED THE DOOR to her apartment to head down to Irma's, and her eyes went wide. The stranger standing there with his hand raised to knock on the door reached down, pulled a police badge off the waistband of his slacks, and flashed it at her.

"Ms. Calderwood?" She nodded; her mouth had gone so dry she couldn't have answered if she'd tried. "I'm Detective Michaels from the Denver Police Department. We've been trying to find you to interview you about your sister's murder. May I come in?"

Dani reluctantly stepped back and allowed him in. As she shut the door, she heard Elmer barking frantically. "I can't tell you anything other than Billy Alphonse was killed, as well as my sister."

"So you were there." Dani nodded. "Why'd you take off?"

"I … was afraid to contact the police. I didn't want whoever killed them coming after me if he saw news stories about a witness being present. Then you released a statement saying you were looking for a witness. Then one of you went on TV and let everyone know my name and see my photo during the Crime Stoppers broadcasts. Once the killer saw that, he was sure to come looking for me."

"You said 'he,' so you saw the killer?"

Dani turned on him angrily. "Whether I saw him or not, you said I was a witness, so what else would he assume? You jeopardized my life doing that."

"That wasn't the intention."

"Doesn't matter, does it? You really screwed me over when you did that. What was I supposed to do, wait for the killer to find me?"

"You could have come to us and let us protect you."

Dani made a face as she paced back and forth. "Yeah, you've handled it so well up to now. I should trust you to protect me."

"Do you know who the killer is?"

"No. I never got a good look at him, so I'm not going to be any help to you."

"I need you to come to Denver with me. We need your statement."

"Why do I have to come to Denver? Can't I just give you a statement here?"

"No. The task force officers assigned to this incident all need to hear your testimony. It's better if it's done officially—and we can put you in protective custody."

"I don't want protective custody. I want to give you a statement and when we're done I want you and your colleagues to keep your mouths shut about me so I can come back here and get my truck and disappear. I don't want anyone to know you found me." She heard Elmer barking loudly from inside Irma's house.

Michaels nodded. "If that's what you want, that's fine. But we need to get on the road."

"And I need to let my boss know I won't be in for a day or so." *And,* Dani thought, *I need to let Jess know the police showed up.* How the detective had found her baffled Dani. *It couldn't have been Jess, could it?* She forced the thought away. There had to have been another bulletin, and someone in town must have figured out who she was and turned her in. She started to ask herself who, then realized it must have been Polly.

Dani called the bar, but there was no answer. Thinking she'd leave a message, she wanted to scream when the voice messaging clicked through to tell her the mailbox was full. Jess was awful about checking it, and there was no point in calling Jess's cell; if he was at the cabin, he wouldn't get it.

"He's not answering," she said.

"You can try again later," Michaels said. She grabbed her backpack and followed Michaels out of her apartment and out to his car. Dani could still hear Elmer barking.

She had tried using her phone as they headed out of town, but there was no reception. Holding her currently useless phone in her lap, she began to worry that Jess would be freaked out when she didn't show up at the bar and he discovered she was gone. Once they were on the interstate, she'd try again.

Something about Michaels's voice raised the hair on the back of her neck, but she chalked it up to her own nervousness. She hadn't wanted to leave, but he'd been insistent, and she'd relented. He was a cop; she didn't think refusing to go was an option. He made small talk as he drove down the road away from town, and the more he talked, the more insistently a warning alarm deep inside her sounded. It was nothing he said, really, and she couldn't figure out why she was having a hard time breathing or why her hands had gone cold and her heart had begun to race. She cradled her backpack against her chest and tried to figure out what was wrong.

She turned toward him as he pulled up to the junction that would eventually take them to the interstate. He looked to the left for oncoming traffic, and the alarm went ballistic. *Get out, get out, get out*, she thought frantically. *It's him, I have to get out, get away*. She quietly unlatched her seat belt, let it slip down her arm, and, as he pressed the accelerator to turn onto the highway, she grabbed the door handle, jerked it open, and bailed out of the car.

He lunged for her but missed. His attempt to grab her made him jerk the steering wheel and he lost control of the car as it slid on the icy pavement. He overcorrected, which sent the car into a 360-degree spin across the highway and off the opposite edge of the road.

She landed hard on her left shoulder and hip, her phone skittering out of her hand and across the road as she rolled several feet before coming to a halt. Despite the searing pain in her shoulder, she staggered to her feet, snagged her backpack off the road where it had landed, and took off running into the snow-shrouded trees without a backward glance.

CHAPTER THIRTY-SEVEN

JESS COULD HEAR ELMER barking frantically and leaping at Irma's back door when he arrived at Irma's place. Dani hadn't shown up for the inventory they'd planned to do, and he decided to come check on her, worried there might be something wrong. He still had a couple hours before the bar opened. She was usually so reliable and on time, that for her not to show up puzzled him.

She had a phone and had given him the number, but he'd never seen her use it and had never called it. She might have tried the bar. He'd been out back unloading his truck and thought he'd heard it ringing. He hadn't reached the phone in time, and if she'd called earlier, he hadn't been at the bar to pick up. He called her phone, and it went straight to voice mail. He left a message, not hopeful she'd get it.

"Dani, it's Jess. I'm concerned about where you are. Call me as soon as you get this."

Elmer continued to bark as Jess looked in the garage window. Irma's car was parked inside. She was here. The dog probably was just excited to see him. He took the stairs to Dani's apartment. There was no answer to his knocks, so he tried the door and found it open.

"Dani?" he called. The only place she could be that he couldn't immediately see was the bathroom. He walked over and knocked and, getting no response, he opened the door. Empty. Where the hell was she? It wasn't like her not to show up. Things between them had remained strained, but she'd been as reliable as clockwork even after their blowup. Looking around, he noticed the only thing missing was her backpack. He could still hear Elmer and wondered if Dani might be at Irma's. Maybe Irma was ill.

"Irma? Are you there?" he called, knocking on her back door across from the garage. He could see Elmer, his paws on the door, his face in the door's window, but neither Irma nor Dani had yet to appear. Elmer yipped at him a few more times, and Jess tried the door. It was locked. Something was wrong. He ran his fingers over the ledge of the door trim looking for a key and came up empty. Seeing the large garden gnome sitting next to the porch, he upended it and found the key.

Elmer all but tackled him as he entered the house. "Easy, boy, easy. Where's Irma? Do you need to go out?" He held the door open for the dog to go out into the backyard, but Elmer rushed past him and up the stairs to Dani's place, whining and sniffing around the door.

Jess climbed the stairs and took hold of Elmer's collar. "Easy now, it's okay," he said, trying to speak soothingly to the dog while his own anxiety began to rise. "Let's go find Irma," he said, leading the dog down the stairs. At the bottom of the stairs Elmer pulled out of Jess's grasp and, nose to the ground, ended up at the curb in front of Irma's house, whining and pacing back and forth. Jess's unease ratcheted up. He'd seen K9s in Afghanistan act that way when they were on a scent trail and it disappeared. Jesus, what had happened?

"Irma?" he called out. Elmer appeared at his side and pushed past him, going down the hall to sit by the closed door to what Jess presumed was a bedroom.

"Irma? It's Jess. Everything okay?" Jess called out as he walked down the hall. He knocked quietly and, getting no response, opened the door. Irma was stretched out on the bed sound asleep, hands folded across her midriff. He walked over and bent down, laying his hand on her shoulder. "Irma?"

Her eyes flew open. She let out a startled cry and sat up, nearly banging her head into Jess's.

"God in heaven, Jess, you scared me to death. Hang on a minute." She reached for her hearing aids that lay on the bedside table and inserted them. "There, that's better. Can't hear a damn thing without them. I musta been out cold." She saw the look on his face. "What's wrong?"

"I need to find … Beth. Have you seen her?"

"I saw her a couple hours ago. She was going to take Elmer with her to work tonight, like she does from time to time. She didn't cancel that. What's happened?"

"We were going to do inventory around two, but she didn't show up or call. She's not in her apartment. I can't find her, and I'm worried."

"Well, where on earth would she go? She hasn't got a vehicle." Irma glanced at Elmer. And a frown appeared on her face. "Where would she go?"

"I don't know. I gotta go. If she shows up, call me."

"Ray?" Jess shouted when he didn't see Ray in the office. Ray poked his head around the door to the shop.

"What's up, Jess?"

"Have you seen Beth?"

"She missing?"

"I can't find her, she didn't show up at work, but she's not home and Irma hasn't seen her."

Ray frowned. "I shoulda said something, but it slipped my mind."

"What? What slipped your mind?" Jess's anxiety, which had been running high since his conversation with Irma, spiked higher.

"Polly was snooping around the garage last night, gave me some cock-and-bull story about wanting to buy Beth's truck. I ran her off. I was gonna say something to you this morning, but I forgot."

"She was checking out the truck?"

Ray nodded. "I can't imagine why she'd think Beth would sell it to her. I thought she was up to something …" He saw the look on Jess's face and took a step back. "Jess, what's wrong?"

"That vindictive little bitch," Jess said under his breath. "I gotta go, Ray. Anybody asks, the bars closed till further notice."

Jess ran over and locked up the bar, then headed for the diner. Polly had to have called the cops, Jess thought as he drove to the diner, but how the hell had she found out about what had happened? Then it hit him. He'd stopped checking online for bulletins. It'd been so long since he'd seen anything, he figured they'd given up. Searching the internet felt like a waste of time and, because of what had happened between him and Dani, he felt pathetic combing the internet for news. So he'd stopped. He should have kept looking, there must have been something on the news.

He found Polly behind the counter in the diner and stepped around behind it to block her from leaving.

"Where is she?"

"Who?"

"Beth." The diner was almost empty, but his abrupt questions had attracted the attention of a couple sitting nearby.

"I haven't seen her. She probably went with that cop who showed up looking for her," Polly said offhandedly. "I told him where she lived. He said she was a witness he'd been trying to find to interview."

"How'd he know she was here?"

Polly shrugged, but it wasn't convincing and Jess narrowed his eyes. "You called the tip line, didn't you?" he demanded, grabbing her upper arm and giving her a little shake.

"She's involved in a murder!" Polly hissed at him, pulling her arm out of his grasp. "Little Miss Mysterious could be a killer for all we know, and you're covering for her. I called the tip line. That's what you're *supposed* to do. You're not supposed to harbor a criminal, Jess Walker."

Jess shook his head and scowled at her, lip curling as if he smelled something foul. "You jealous little shit. You may have gotten her killed. You don't even know if the guy was legit."

"He showed me his ID!"

"As if you'd know a legit cop's ID. You just want her gone."

"I do! She's snowed you good and proper, made a fool of you. Good riddance to her."

Jess ignored that. He'd known Polly was jealous and petty, he just hadn't thought she was that vindictive. "What'd he look like? What kind of car was he driving?"

"Gonna run after her?"

Jess grabbed her by both upper arms and leaned in close. "You tell me, Polly, or so help me God, if anything happens to her, I'll make you wish you'd kept your mouth shut."

Polly's eyes flared, and she tried to shrink away from him but couldn't. "D-dark hair ... not as tall as you"

"What was he driving?" Jess shouted.

"A bla-black SUV … I don't know what kind of car other than that."

Jess let go of her, pushed past her, and ran out the door of the diner.

Jess tore off down the road toward the highway, hoping to catch up with the SUV and make sure the guy was legit, make sure Dani wasn't in danger, and insist on going with her wherever the cop was taking her. Twenty minutes later, the sight of fresh tire tracks heading toward the verge of the road and then disappearing over the edge nearly made his heart stop. He pulled to the side of the road and parked, making his way to the drop-off and peering down. The SUV was lodged against a stand of pine trees, the passenger side nearly wrapped around one of the trees, the driver's door hanging open.

If Dani had been in the passenger seat … Jess couldn't finish the thought as he looked for a way to get down to the vehicle. The snow was churned up around the driver's side, and it looked as if someone had made it up to the road. He hadn't seen anyone in his frantic drive out of town and turning in a circle, he still couldn't see any sign of anyone. Where was Dani, and where was the cop?

Slipping as he made his way down through two feet of churned-up snow, he finally reached the SUV only to find it empty. The airbags had deployed, and there was blood on the deflated driver's side airbag that draped over the steering wheel. The passenger door was ajar and bent. Because of the angle of the SUV, he couldn't tell if the door had been opened or if it had popped because of the impact, and he couldn't see whether Dani might be lying in the snow outside the half-opened door.

"Dani? Dani! Answer me. Are you hurt?" No answer. *Don't let her be dead. Please don't let her be dead.*

He couldn't work his way around the back of the car because of the slope and the deep snow and he couldn't get to the passenger side from the front of the SUV, so he jerked the back door open and climbed in. The passenger side of the car was empty, and there was no sign of blood. The door was ajar by about a foot but was wedged against a tree. She wasn't lying in the snow, which was a relief, but how had Dani gotten out? Where was she now?

He climbed back up the embankment to the roadway, shaking snow off his jeans and boots as he scanned the surrounding area. It wasn't too far from his cabin, maybe a mile or two on the road, less if you cut through the trees. Taking that route, though, would be dangerous with the amount of snow that had fallen over the last several weeks covering the ground with its unpredictable surface. If you weren't used to the area or didn't have a compass, you could easily get lost. In this weather you could freeze to death wandering around trying to figure out where you were.

After getting in his truck, he drove back across the highway, parked on the road leading back to town, and got out. He saw something lying by the side of the roadway and walked over. A phone, the screen shattered, lay on the pavement. A phone that looked like Dani's. Jess scanned the area on both sides of the road and saw what looked like a break in the snowbank at the side of the road across from where the phone had landed.

On closer inspection, someone had broken through the snow bank, and he could see a trail that would eventually lead to his cabin, assuming whoever was making the tracks stayed on course. A trail that required breaking through a foot and a half of fallen snow that drifted even higher in some places.

He followed it for ten or fifteen feet and saw drops of blood periodically and remembered the blood on the steering wheel. Broken nose from the airbags deploying? Was the cop tracking Dani, or were they were both trying to get to Jess's cabin? The phone on the roadway bothered him, but the choice of route bothered him more. If they were trying to get back to town, or even his cabin, they should have stuck to the roadway. Someone would have come by eventually and picked them up. Unless Dani was trying to run from the cop, which seemed more likely.

Jess jogged back to his truck, opened the driver's door, and shrugged out of his coat. He pulled his insulated bib overalls from behind the seat, put them on, and zipped the lower legs over his hiking boots. He wasn't dressed for the backcountry—his boots where what he wore daily—but the bibs would help keep snow from getting in them.

After shrugging into his coat, Jess reached across the seat, grabbed a small pair of binoculars from the glove box, and hung them around his neck. He took his rifle from its rack, pulled his wool beanie onto his head, and buttoned up his coat. From the toolbox in the bed of his truck, he grabbed a pair old ski poles that he used when he explored the land around his cabin. Once he'd loaded the rifle, he added extra shells to his coat pocket, and slipped the rifle strap over his shoulder. Donning his gloves— outwardly calm, inwardly dreading what he might have to deal with—he stepped once again into the path he felt sure that Dani, followed by the cop, had taken through the snow and hoped he could find her before the sun went down.

CHAPTER THIRTY-EIGHT

DANI'S BREATHING CAME IN DESPERATE GASPS, and her lungs burned. Something was wrong with her shoulder. She couldn't move her arm without searing pain shooting down her arm and making her feel as if she'd pass out. Cradling her injured arm against her body with her other arm helped some, but each step jarred it. Despite the cold, sweat gathered on her forehead and tracked down her back under her coat. The pain in her shoulder made her sick to her stomach.

Her hip had taken a blow when she'd landed on it. The pain made struggling through snowdrifts and around trees, and occasionally tripping over tree roots or fallen branches concealed by the snow, exhausting. Because of the trees, there were areas with less deep snow, but there were more than enough areas with high drifts that had to be traversed, and the muscles in her legs burned and cramped. Her hip and shoulder had her in agony, but at least she could walk.

She had no idea how long she'd been stumbling through the snow—her phone had been lost in the leap from the SUV, and she had no watch—but it felt like an eternity. And she had no idea where Jess's cabin might be. Dani knew she was on the right side of the road, knew his cabin should be … somewhere in this forest of trees … but she wasn't sure if she was headed in the right direction or how far his cabin might be.

When she'd last stopped to rest, she thought she'd heard noise in the forest behind her. He was following her, and when he found her, he'd kill her. He'd killed Alphonse and her sister. He couldn't let her live. Despite the fact that she hadn't recognized him when he'd first showed up, by leaping from the SUV, she'd made it clear that she had finally figured out who he was.

Having somewhat caught her breath, she bent and scooped snow into her mouth, holding it until it melted before she swallowed it, hoping to relieve the dryness and appease her thirst. It didn't help much, and the cold made her shiver as it slid down her throat. God, what she'd give for a bottle of water. She moved off again, searching as she struggled through the snow for a place to hide. Her jeans were soaked and freezing against her skin. Her boots were never meant for deep snow. They had quickly taken on snow, and her feet were wet and cold. She prayed she'd find Jess's cabin soon so she could get to the satellite phone and get help.

A sob escaped her. The pain in her shoulder and hip made her want to lie down in the snow and rest, but fear kept her moving. She clamped her lips together to prevent making any more noise and pressed on. The cop would have a lovely path to follow, a path that she'd exhausted herself making, but she didn't want to help him by hearing her cry.

Kaye had no idea what to expect of the flight to Grand Junction. She remembered a nail-biting trip to Aspen a few years back, though, and hoped this flight wouldn't be a repeat. She'd had a window seat on that flight and regretted it as soon as the plane neared Aspen. Snow-covered mountains were everywhere. Kaye hadn't seen any flat land that looked like a runway anywhere and wasn't reassured when the flight attendant came on the intercom.

"Folks, please buckle up and stay in your seats until we land. Because of the weather, we may experience some turbulence. That's normal near this airport, but you'll be happy to know that our pilots both have the safety ratings required to fly into Aspen and have done this many times."

"They need special safety ratings?" Panic had made Kaye's voice ratchet up in pitch.

"It's considered a challenging airport at which to land a plane. Short runway and surrounded by mountains, lots of wind, so not just any pilot is allowed to land here," said her boyfriend at the time. He'd suggested a long weekend in Aspen to ski and relax, and the idea had seemed like a good one ... earlier. He returned his tray table to its upright and locked position and put his book in the seat pocket in front of him. He looked calm, which seemed astounding considering the circumstances.

"Are you *serious*?"

"It'll be fine. There hasn't been a fatal accident since 2001."

"Oh, that's reassuring." Kaye had clamped a death grip on the seat's armrest and closed her eyes, preferring not to see her approaching death, and had prayed it would be quick.

The flight to Grand Junction was far less alarming, but she had always been a nervous flyer and was glad to be on terra firma when the plane landed. She exited the plane and picked up her rental car. The guy manning the rental desk insisted on giving her a map and directions to the town where Jack was headed.

"Roads up to the turnoff are good, but after that they're

usually snow packed, so it's good you rented an SUV. I've marked the route on the map."

"I can use my phone's app—"

"Take the map. Reception isn't always dependable, especially in the more remote areas."

"Okay, thanks."

Kaye drove out of the airport and onto the highway seriously questioning her sanity for making this trip, but the uneasy feeling about Jack's decision had never gone away. She was here; may as well follow through. She was pretty sure Jack would be pissed when she showed up.

Jesus, he had not been prepared for her leaping out of the SUV— that took some balls. It had taken him twenty minutes to get out of the SUV and up the slope to the road. He was totally unprepared for tracking her through this godforsaken wilderness. He'd planned to drive to someplace like a remote trailhead or rest area that was unoccupied, force her to walk to an isolated spot, and kill her. Her body wouldn't be found until spring or summer or never if animals found her first. A few more months and there wouldn't have been much left of Billy Alphonse to find.

If anyone from the town talked to that waitress who'd called in the tip and inquired about Calderwood's whereabouts, or if Jagerski questioned his return without the witness, he'd planned to say that he never was able to connect with her. He'd say she wasn't at the apartment where he'd been told she lived and that he thought he'd been misled by the person who'd called in the tip. No one could have proven otherwise. Now he had the car wreck to explain. He'd keep it simple, he thought as he struggled to follow the path Calderwood had made through the snow. He'd tell them he wasn't used to driving in the mountains and had lost control of the car on his way out of town after not finding the woman.

It wasn't far from the truth. After he'd taken care of her, he'd walk back toward town on the highway and find a way to get a vehicle or talk someone into driving him to Grand Junction where he could arrange for a tow truck to get the SUV and rent one to return to Denver.

She'd said she couldn't ID the killer, but when she'd bailed from the SUV, he'd known something had clicked and she'd realized who he was. He couldn't let her live, now, couldn't let her spoil what he'd worked so hard for. He'd taken out all the problem people standing in his way. She was the final problem that needed to be eliminated, and then he'd be able to settle back and enjoy the money coming in from the people he'd set up to run the daily activities involved in selling drugs. In retrospect, it had been a mistake to handle Alphonse by himself. He should have had one of his associates take care of Billy, but he'd wanted to make sure it was done right.

Where they were was probably as good a dump site as any, he thought. Isolated and hard to access. He'd do it here once he caught up to her. Fortunately for him, she was easy to follow. She was breaking a trail that a blind man could track and he didn't have to struggle as much as she had to get through the snow—she'd done it for him..

He stopped and listened, trying to determine how close she might be, and thought he heard something, maybe a gasp or a sob. She was close; all he had to do was pick up his pace. She had to be exhausted. She'd been plowing through knee-deep snow and trees for nearly forty-five minutes now. He didn't know where she was headed. Maybe she knew someone who lived around here, or perhaps she was just blindly trying to escape.

Michaels's nose, which he was sure had been broken when the damned airbag had smashed into his face as the SUV went off the highway, had stopped bleeding finally. It was swollen, breathing through it was difficult, and it forced him to breathe through his mouth. That left it dry, made his lips stick to his teeth, and made him long for a drink. His shoulder was sore as hell from the seat belt locking in place, but he supposed that was preferable to something more serious.

Christ, this whole thing was falling apart, and it pissed him off. He transferred his gun to his left hand and shoved his right into his coat and under his arm to warm it up. He'd been driving without gloves, which were now somewhere on the floor of the SUV, where they'd been sent flying on the ride down the embankment. He hadn't wasted time trying to find them, and now he wished he had. The fucking gun was freezing to the touch, and his hands didn't tolerate holding it out in the open for long, but he wanted it in his hand when he found her. He wanted this over and done with quickly.

He swore under his breath. He'd worked so hard to find two Vice cops who'd been under far too long and were eager to help him set up their own operation. The undercover cops did the face-to-face work. They were presumed to be part of the drug world they hung out with, and Jagerski and the administration had no idea they'd gone rogue, all of which kept him out of the limelight. Alphonse had been the one who'd pissed him off enough to take care of him personally, and it had snowballed from there. But it had been a major mistake. Not a goddamned thing had gone right since he'd popped Alphonse and his girlfriend.

Kaye turned onto the road heading toward the turnoff to the town, and at the intersection she saw a huge area of snow that had been crushed at the side of the road. She parked, walked cautiously toward the edge of the road and glanced down. It was Michaels's SUV, she was sure of it.

She hadn't dressed for exploring the mountains, hadn't imagined she'd be doing anything other than driving to the town, meeting up with Michaels, then driving back to Grand Junction to turn the car in and ride with him to Denver. There was no way she could safely get down to the car, but there didn't seem to be anyone in it as far as she could see. She returned to her car and turned down the road toward the town.

An unoccupied truck was parked at the side of the road. Had it been involved in the accident that had caused Michaels's car to go off the road? She parked and walked up to the truck, then around it, and saw no damage. It was an older model but in good condition. The lockbox in the bed was open. There was nothing much in it except for a box of ammunition that was half empty.

Kaye frowned, deciding the best option was to get to the town and talk to the police or the sheriff, someone who could come and help her look for Jack.

Dani stopped to catch her breath and eat more snow. It wasn't helping; in fact, she felt thirstier than ever and colder. Every time she had to let go of her left arm to use her right hand, her shoulder fired with pain. It was so intense that it had made her throw up just now, and it seemed to be getting worse. She'd broken something in the fall, probably her collarbone or something in her shoulder, but there was nothing to be done about it.

She knew she couldn't keep this up for much longer, and Jess's cabin was nowhere in sight. She didn't even know if she was close. Leaning against a pine tree, she scanned the area. There was nothing but trees and snow as far as she could see. The sun would be going down in an hour or so, if she was judging the time right, and it was getting colder by the minute. She didn't feel the cold when she was struggling through the snow, but now, standing still her sweat turned icy and she began to shiver.

The gun she'd taken the day Hannah had been killed was in her backpack. If she could find a hiding place and wait, when he came into view she could shoot him. If she killed him or badly injured him, she could walk back the way she had come and get to the road. By now she hoped Jess was looking for her. She hadn't shown up for the inventory they'd planned on doing. Maybe he'd somehow figured out what had happened. Surely, despite their falling out, he'd try to find her?

If I have to stay out in this weather much longer, I'll freeze to death. She was exhausted enough and scared enough that the option had some appeal. But now that she knew who the killer was, she'd do whatever was necessary to see that he paid for what he'd done to Hannah. So she kept plowing on through the snow, looking for a place to hide or hoping she'd stumble onto Jess's cabin, while it got colder by the minute.

CHAPTER THIRTY-NINE

THE BLOOD DROPS HAD STOPPED, but there was only one track through the snow, so the presence of blood was irrelevant. Jess was pretty sure Dani was running away from, not accompanying, the cop—if he was a real cop. Something must have scared her badly for her to take off into the woods.

Based on the phone's location, it didn't look to Jess like she'd been in the SUV when it had run off the side of the road. Had she jumped out of the vehicle? Had she opened the door and run when the cop stopped to merge onto the road leading to the highway? It looked to him like she'd bailed while the SUV was in motion. It might explain the car in the ditch on the far side of the highway and Dani's phone being where it was. If she'd seen something or figured out something that scared her, it explained her taking off into the woods rather than sticking with the roadway. And that terrified him.

Just let me find her alive, he thought.

Jess stopped briefly and used the binoculars to scan the area ahead of him but saw no movement. He checked his watch, which had a compass, and knew that, by some miracle, the trail was still heading in the general direction of the cabin, but not on course. If she kept going in that direction, she'd miss the cabin completely.

God only knew how long Dani had been trudging through the snow, but it had to have been at least an hour or more. She'd be tired and cold, probably wet as well. He knew time was running out before she became hypothermic and would be unable to continue. It'd be sunset in another hour. The shadows cast by the trees they were trekking through were growing darker by the minute. His heart rate sped up, and he resumed a brisk pace, using the ski poles to help push him along.

Ten minutes later, he halted. Something had moved up ahead, a flash of dark against the white of the snow. Jess pulled up the binoculars and watched. There it was again. He adjusted the focus and could see a man in the distance moving slowly, but steadily, through the trees, and he saw the gun in the guy's right hand. Jess let the binoculars fall against his chest and began to run, his fucking leg making him limp as he ran. The rifle slapped against his back, held on by the strap that ran across his chest; his breath came fast and harsh.

Dani had found a small outcropping of boulders up against a rise in the surrounding landscape and had moved into its shelter. She scrunched up as small as she could but knew it was not going to keep him from finding her. As soon as he saw that the trail in the snow had ended, he'd know where she was.

She let her backpack slide off her good shoulder and opened it, bracing her left arm against her chest with her knees, searching until she found the gun. The gun was ready to go; Jess had reloaded the clip and returned it to the gun after their last practice session. She'd heard once that cops always kept a round chambered in their guns so they wouldn't have to waste time pulling the slide when seconds counted. Jess had agreed it was a good idea, which was a blessing—she'd never be able to rack the gun with her injured shoulder. Her eyes swam with tears as she thought of Jess and hoped against hope that she'd see him again. She released the safety on the gun and waited.

It had been quiet for what she guessed was ten or fifteen minutes, and she was grateful for the chance to rest. She hoped he had lost the path in the gradually gathering dusk. A few minutes later, she heard footsteps that stopped in the clearing. She could hear his breath coming in short gasps.

"I ... I know you're here ..." Each statement came out between a gasp. "Look ... I don't know why you bailed from the car ... this is ridiculous ... All I want ... all I want, is to take you ... back ... back to Denver ... for a statement."

Dani thought she could hear movement, but she wasn't sure where it was coming from. He was lying, she knew that. As soon as she revealed herself, she'd be dead.

"Boo!" he said, coming around the boulder she was hiding behind. A frightening smile was on his battered face.

Dani screamed, and without thinking, pulled the gun's trigger. He threw himself to the side, rolled, and came to his feet. She'd missed him. He pointed his gun at her.

"Drop the gun and kick it away," he shouted.

"Please," Dani said, doing as he asked and holding her hand out in front of her as if it could deflect a bullet. "Please. No one in town knows about what happened. No one but you knows I'm here. I won't say anything. I won't come back to Denver, ever."

"That's where you're wrong. One of your acquaintances called and turned you in. I don't think she likes you much, so your secret's out." He smiled at her. "It's kind of a shame. You're a pretty lady. I gotta admit I've been impressed by your ability to disappear, but I can't afford to let you live. You said you couldn't identify the killer, but clearly something triggered you into taking off. What was it?"

"Your voice and seeing the side of your face … it just clicked," Dani said. She was so tired and in so much pain, she couldn't think of any way to get out of this alive, but she tried. "Please, I'll say … I'll say you dropped me off at my friend's cabin after we talked …" Fear made it hard to breathe and drawing a deep breath was impossible. She'd begun to shiver as the cold caught up with her now that she wasn't moving. "I'll say that … that I answered your questions, and you went back to Denver … No one will know."

"You'd always be a risk. It'd be stupid leaving you alive. I can't afford you identifying me and ruining everything I've worked so hard for. All that lovely drug money that would end up in some asshole's pocket instead of mine."

"You're not a cop?" Dani asked, puzzled.

"I'm a cop. I just diversified. No point in letting dirtballs live high off the hog while I get paid a pittance to deal with them. I'm sick to death of working like a dog, putting myself at risk of getting killed on a daily basis and living like a poorly paid office worker. So, I put my connections to work. Life's a whole lot better now."

Simultaneously with the sound of a rifle shot, a chip of granite exploded near Michaels's head. A bright-red line streaked across his forehead, which began to bleed profusely. He crouched and moved quickly over to Dani, jerked her up, and held her in front of him. She cried out as the movement made her shoulder explode in pain.

"Who's out there?" he shouted. He had his arm around her neck and pushed Dani toward the edge of the rock outcropping. "I've got her. If you don't drop your weapon, I'll kill her."

Michaels forced her around the rocks and onto the path in

the snow, where Jess stood his rifle raised and braced against his shoulder.

"Jess …" Dani whispered. Dear God, she was going to get them both killed.

Michaels raised the gun and pressed it to Dani's temple. "I said, drop your weapon, or I'll blow her head off."

"You'll be a dead man if you do." Jess's voice had an oddly calm, emotionless tone to it. Standing with his rifle raised and pointed at them, all he was missing was camouflage fatigues and a helmet.

"Drop your weapon, now," Michaels said, breathing rapidly. Dani could feel a slight tremor in his hand as he pressed the gun to her temple.

You have to do something, she thought. She looked at Jess and held his eyes, remembering their conversations and their nights together, remembering how hopeful she'd been that there would be more. *I'm sorry*, she mouthed silently and let her body go limp and her legs collapse. Michaels wasn't prepared for the weight of her as she abruptly sank, which pulled her out of his grasp. She cried out in pain as she collapsed on the ground. It caught Michaels off guard. She heard Jess's rifle fire and felt Michaels drop onto her.

The man from the garage—Ray, she thought his name was—had offered to go with Kaye to find the truck owner, who he called Jess, and the witness he knew as Beth. After a call to someone named Irma, Ray said Irma didn't know where Beth or Jess were. That didn't sound good. Christ there wasn't a police force or a sheriff's office in the town. It was just her.

They reached the abandoned truck and got out of her rental car. "Yep, that's Jess's truck." Ray walked over to the open lockbox and glanced in, then took a look in the cab. "His rifle is gone and so are his bibs and ski poles." He looked around and pointed to the trail of broken snow. "I'm guessing he headed that way." He gave her black leather flats a skeptical look. "Maybe you'd best wait here while I go see where he is."

"I'll be fine. Let's go," Kaye replied, running her hand over her holstered gun, grateful she had it, as they headed through the break in the snow.

CHAPTER FORTY

JESS RAN TO DANI and grabbed Michaels's gun, tossing it away from him and rolling him off Dani. Jess's shot had hit Michaels on the side of his neck, taking out a chunk of it. Blood seemed to be everywhere. Jess went to pull her up to him and she cried out sharply.

"What's wrong—are you hit?"

"My shoulder, I think it's broken. Something's broken." Dani had started shaking. "I'm so cold."

"No bullet holes?"

She grimaced against the pain and shook her head no.

"The cabin's not far, maybe ten minutes, but we have to get going." He tried to figure out how to get her up without causing her more pain or damage her shoulder.

"Is he dead?"

"Yeah. Don't worry about him. First, let's get you upright. You hold your arm tight, and I'll pull you up. Let's do it in one movement if we can. I'm sorry, sweetheart. I know it's gonna hurt." It did hurt, and it killed him to hear her cry out. He steadied her, pulled his jacket off, and draped it around her buttoning it up to keep it in place.

"I can't walk anymore, Jess." Dani began to sob. "I'm sorry. I can barely feel my feet, and my legs are shaking too hard."

Jess shifted the rifle across his back on its strap and turned to Dani, bending at the knees a little to look her in the eyes. "You're not going to walk—I am. I'll carry you. Just hold your arm close to your chest." He picked her up, cradling her good side against him and began to walk. The ski poles were left in the snow.

They'd been walking for about ten minutes, when Kaye stopped and listened. "That was a shot." Then she heard another. "We need to get a move on. Someone's in big trouble. Can you call the local police … sheriff … whoever it is and get them over here?"

"Cell phones don't work in this area. Looks to me like the trail is heading in the direction of Jess Walker's place. He's got a satellite phone. We can call from there."

"Okay, lead the way." He was right about her shoes, and she was grateful that they weren't the first to go through this way. If she stayed on the broken trail, she could avoid deep snow. She kept up with Ray Decker, but the altitude was making her short of breath. God only knew what waited for them; she just hoped Michaels and the woman were safe.

Twenty minutes or more had passed when they came into the clearing where Jess had confronted Michaels.

"Holy shit," Ray said as they stepped into the clearing.

Jack Michaels lay sprawled on his back in the snow, his neck and chest covered in blood. The snow was churned up, a gun lay several feet from his body, and it took Kaye a few seconds to process that there were two ski poles lying nearby. She knelt next to Jack and felt for a pulse, knowing there wouldn't be one considering the size of the neck wound and the coldness of his skin. Shutting down her personal feelings about him, she stood up and turned to Ray.

"Where's this cabin of Walker's?"

Ray pointed behind her. "'Bout ten, fifteen minutes that way. What the hell happened?"

"I don't know, but we need to get to his place now."

"What about him?"

"He's dead. Nothing can be done for him, but I need to find the woman he was with. I need to find out what happened and call the local authorities."

"You're gonna leave him like that? I thought he was a cop you worked with."

"He was. And yes, I'm leaving him like this. I can't do anything for him, and it's a crime scene. I can't mess it up any further than I already have. I need to get to that satellite phone."

Ray looked around and saw a trail that had been cut through the snow. "Jess's cabin is that way. Let's go."

The trip to the cabin could have taken minutes or days. All Dani remembered was the feel of Jess holding her against his chest, the pounding of his heart under her ear, his ragged breathing, the jarring cadence of his walk as he struggled through the snow, his periodic stops to catch his breath, and how much her shoulder hurt.

"We're here, Dani. Just hang on … I'll get you warmed up … and take care of your arm," he gasped between breaths. He maneuvered the hand that was under her knees up to the cabin's doorknob and managed to turn it, pushing the door open with his foot and easing her through it.

He looked exhausted, the hair around his temples wet with sweat, as he placed her gently on the bench by the door and closed it behind him. "Just sit tight and try not to move. I'll be right back."

He disappeared into the bedroom, and she heard him pull something heavy out from under the bed. He was back several minutes later and got a glass of water from the kitchen.

"Here. Take these pills. It'll help with the pain." He placed two of the narcotic pills on her tongue and helped her drink the glass of water, which she gulped down eagerly. He was eternally grateful he'd kept the pills.

"Jess ... I'm so sorry ..."

"Stop. I don't want to hear any more apologies. We're good." He cupped a gentle hand against her cheek and smiled, then seemed to return to the present. "Getting your coat off is going to be a bitch, so I'm going to give the pill a chance to work. Meantime, I need to check your feet."

"Get something to drink, Jess. You need it."

He shook his head. "I'll get something once I've taken care of you." He gently removed her wet boots and socks, and inspected her feet. "I don't think they're frostbitten, but hang on and I'll get them warmed up."

Jess found a large pot in the kitchen and filled it with warm water. While it filled, he drained a glass of water—water that had never tasted so good. He carried the pot over to where she sat and placed both her feet in it. As she sat soaking her feet, he added wood to the stove and set it alight. Returning to her, he unbuttoned his coat that was wrapped around her and eased it off her shoulders.

"Okay," he said, sizing up the situation trying to figure the best way to get her wet coat off her without further injuring her shoulder. His face hadn't lost that intense, determined look she'd seen during the confrontation with the cop, and it made her feel safe. "Here's what we're gonna do. You sit still while I get it undone, then … well … I'll figure something out."

She really couldn't move her injured arm, and moving her good arm meant the injured one was unsupported. He stood up, retrieved a pair of scissors from the kitchen, and walked into his bedroom returning with several rolled elastic bandages.

"What have you got in there, a mini … mini hospital?" Dani asked. She blinked at him slowly, her head nodding a bit, and her words, while not slurred, were hard for her to string together. Good, the pills were working.

"Yeah, I do. Good thing too." He maneuvered himself so he could access the back of her coat. "Hope you're not too attached to this coat."

"Just … a coat."

Jess cut through the collar, down the side near her shoulder, then cut across the shoulder seam and began to cut down the top of the right sleeve until he reached the end of it, leaving it hanging for the time being. He did the same to the left side, carefully cutting as far down the left arm of the coat as he could, and sat back. He began cutting around the sleeve at the elbow, where he'd had to stop. "I'm sorry. This is gonna hurt. I'll be as gentle as I can."

He took hold of the mutilated sleeve and tried to pull it out from under her arm, and she moaned in pain. "Dani, we need to get this wet stuff off you, so take a deep breath and I'm gonna do it quick."

He got the upper part of the coat sleeve off her arm, then let her rest for several minutes. He carefully slid the lower part of the sleeve off her injured arm. Cut by cut, he managed to remove the sweater and shirt she had on. It scared him to see her shoulder. The bruise was shocking, and her shoulder drooped a bit. He draped a blanket around her as he took a closer look. He was pretty sure she'd broken her collarbone. All he could do was secure her arm to her chest to keep the broken bone from moving, but he needed to let her rest before he tackled that.

"Your toes look okay. They don't look frostbitten," he said as he patted them dry with a towel. He heard the sound of someone stepping onto the porch and stood up in one fluid motion, picking up the rifle that leaned against the wall. He moved quietly to the door, jerked it open, and raised the rifle stock to his shoulder. He was shocked to see Ray Decker and a woman with dark, curly hair standing on his porch. The woman had her gun drawn and pointed at him.

"Drop your weapon," she called out.

"Lady, you're on my property and my porch. Put your fucking gun down." He threw an angry look at Ray. Without lowering his rifle he said, "Who the fuck is she and what the hell are you doing here?"

"I'm Lieutenant Kaye Jagerski, Denver Police Department, and I'd appreciate it if you'd lower your rifle," she said before Ray could respond.

"It's okay, Jess. She came to help that other cop take Beth—or Dani, I guess—back to Denver."

Jess kept his rifle aimed at them. "Then she's no friend of mine or Dani's. Your buddy's dead. He tried to kill Dani and me. She's in no condition to travel, thanks to your dead friend, so you may as well forget taking her anywhere."

Kaye holstered her weapon and held out her hands. "I'm well aware he's dead. I understand you have a satellite phone. I need to use it to call the Mesa County Sheriff and get them and their crime scene people on the road before it's dark. No one's going anywhere tonight."

Jess scowled at her and, at last, lowered his rifle. "Get in here so I can close the door before Dani freezes to death. The phone's on the desk over there. You know how to use one?"

Kaye rolled her eyes. "I know how to use one."

"It works best outside. Call 911. They'll hook you through." He leaned the rifle up against the wall and turned to Dani. Her head was tipped back against the wall, her eyes were closed, and her mouth hung open slightly. *Jesus*, he thought, *I hope I didn't overdose her*. "Ray, I need you to step outside for a bit while I get her fixed up here." Ray nodded and went out on the porch to keep Kaye company.

Jess snipped the straps on her bra, undid the front closure, and let it fall away from her.

"What? What're you doing?" she said, coming around.

"I'm going to wrap your arm against your chest. I can't very well wrap you up with a wet bra on."

She giggled. "You jus' wanna see 'em."

He grinned. "Of course I do, darlin', but right now I want to get you fixed up and warm."

When he had her arm secured to her side with the elastic bandages, he helped her stand and slid her jeans and panties off and rewrapped the blanket. God, her hip looked like it had been hit by a truck; the bruise was frighteningly huge.

"What're you doing?" she asked, as he began to walk her to the bedroom.

"Taking you to bed."

She giggled again and then sighed. "Too tired, arm hurts too much ... but m'glad you still want to ..." her voice drifted off.

Then she roused as Jess helped her into his bed and covered her up. "What about the cop and Ray?"

He was surprised she'd even noticed them. "Don't worry about them, Dani. Just sleep." He watched her eyes close and leaned over and kissed the top of her head, grateful she was alive, grateful that he'd have a chance to fix things between them.

CHAPTER FORTY-ONE

DANI ROUSED A LITTLE WHILE LATER when she heard Jess talking to someone. *I didn't think he had phone service out here*, she thought drowsily, then heard other voices and remembered the cop and Ray. They must have been talking to Jess about what had happened.

The bedroom was dark, and she was warm and cozy in the nest of blankets and the down comforter on Jess's bed. She sat up jarring her arm, and moaned. The door opened almost immediately, and he came to the bedside.

"How're you feeling?"

"Not as bad as I did. My leg muscles are sore, and my hip hurts. My arm is the worst of it. Who's out there?"

"The sheriff's here now. The cop from Denver interviewed me, and they wanted to talk to you. I told them to come back in the morning."

"I'm awake. I might as well talk to them." She looked around. "I'm gonna need some clothes."

Jess walked to the cupboard that held his clothes and took out a sweatshirt and a pair of thermal pants and socks. "These will be huge, but they're warm, and your clothes aren't totally dry yet. Never wear jeans when you're breaking a trail in snow trying to escape from someone." The worried look had left him, and he grinned at her.

"I wasn't planning on that, but good to know," she said, yawning. She noticed he'd shed the overalls he'd been wearing and was in jeans and a sweater. He helped her into the clothes, kissing her on her bruises as he worked.

"Kissing them and making them better?" she asked with a smile.

He blushed, which touched her. "It's about all I can do at the moment."

"I've missed you Jess … I …"

He took her head in his hands and cut her off with a kiss full of longing. "I've missed you, too," he said. "Let's talk about this later. I'm just glad you're alive." He pulled the sweatshirt over her head and helped her get her good arm in the sleeve leaving the left arm of the sweatshirt to dangle. "Can I get you anything before you talk to them? Food or something to drink?"

"No," she said. She clutched his arm. "Don't leave me alone with them."

"Wasn't planning on it." He walked her out into the main room. "Dani, this is Lieutenant Kaye Jagerski, and this is Mesa County Sheriff Kent Olson. They have some questions for you."

The woman stepped forward. "I'm glad you're okay. I-I worked with Detective Michaels, and I'd like to hear what happened. Mr. Walker has explained his part. A crime scene team has secured the site of the shooting and is going over it."

The sheriff nodded as Jagerski talked, letting her take the lead. "First, I'd like to hear what happened the day your sister was murdered, then we can get into the rest. Why don't you sit in one of the recliners so you're comfortable. Mr. Walker, can you pull up some chairs so we can all sit down?"

She set her phone on the end table near the recliner and turned the recording app on. "I'm recording this so I get a firsthand account. I'll have you give a formal statement in Denver, but I'd like to get your account of things as soon as possible."

With everyone situated, Jess by her side holding her hand, Dani related what had happened that day. Halfway through, she asked Jess for a glass of water and drank half of it rapidly.

"So you didn't actually see what happened—you heard it, correct?"

"Yes, but I got a glimpse of the killer as he passed the stairwell door, and I heard his voice. It was Michaels. I didn't realize that until we were in his SUV headed for the highway."

"Why'd you run if you didn't know it was Michaels you'd seen? You could have come to us for protection."

"I didn't know who the killer was, but I knew once my identity was revealed as a witness, he'd be looking for me. I couldn't identify him—I had no idea who he was—but he didn't know that. I didn't know what to do, so I ran. Turns out it was the right decision. Michaels would have killed me if I'd stayed. You didn't know he was responsible, so how could you protect me?"

"I don't understand why he killed Alphonse and your sister."

"At the house, I heard Michaels say Alphonse had been warned not to piss him off. Billy did his usual big-man routine and told Michaels that he had to make a living and 'it was his territory.' He taunted Michaels, asking him, 'What're you going to do about it?' Michaels agreed that was the question. That's when I heard the first shot. I guess he had taken over Alphonse's drug territory, and Billy wouldn't back down. And then, he shot my sister." Dani's brows knit together, and she screwed her eyes shut. Jess gave her hand a squeeze.

"Do you need a break?" he asked.

"No, let's get this over with."

Jagerski shook her head and looked pained hearing what Dani had told her. "It's a shame. He was a good cop, for a while at least." She took a deep breath and exhaled, as if bracing for what was to come. "Tell me what happened when he showed up at your door."

"He said I had to come with him to Denver to give a formal statement. I didn't think I had a choice, so I went with him. The more I listened to him talk, the more anxious I got, but I didn't know why. Then he turned his head to look for oncoming traffic. It was similar to the position he was in when I'd seen him at the house, and I recognized him. I opened the door as he hit the gas to enter the highway, and jumped out of the SUV. He grabbed for me but missed, and it jerked the steering wheel, I guess. Anyway, the car spun across the road and off the side, then I ran into the woods.

"He … he followed me into the woods, and although he was about twenty minutes behind me, he made better time. I had a gun. It was in a bag at the house where my sister was killed, and I took it with me. I was so tired, and my shoulder hurt so much, I couldn't go on. I hid behind a rock outcropping hoping he wouldn't find me or, if he did, that I could shoot him. He surprised me, and I fired, more of a reflex to his sudden appearance than aiming, but I missed him. I didn't realize Jess had followed us. When Jess took a shot at him, he grabbed me and pulled me out from behind the rocks and told Jess to drop his rifle. I didn't know what to do, so I just let everything go limp, and my weight pulled me out of his grasp … and Jess shot him. He would have shot Jess if Jess hadn't shot him first. He would have killed both of us."

"Did he admit anything to you prior to that?" Jagerski asked.

"He said he couldn't afford me identifying him and ruining all he'd worked for. He called it 'all that lovely drug money.' I didn't think he was a cop, because of that, but he said he was. He said he'd just diversified so that he could enjoy the money rather than some dirtball getting it. He seemed … bitter about what he was paid to risk policing the offenders."

"Okay, I think that's enough for now. Sheriff, was there anything else you needed?"

"No, ma'am, not tonight. I'll need to talk to you tomorrow about handling the body. Here's my card. Just give me a call."

Jagerski stood up and walked to the door, retrieving her coat from the bench at the door. The sheriff followed. She handed Jess her card.

"The sheriff's deputy said he'd take Ray Decker out to where you left your truck so he could drive it back here. He's going to run Ray and me into town," Kaye said "I'll return to Grand Junction and make arrangements for the three of us to fly to Denver. I'll let you know when I get it arranged."

Jess nodded, noticing her shoes for the first time. "You should get those wet shoes off and dry your feet." He shook his head, seeing her blank look. "Have you got another pair of shoes with you?"

"No, I wasn't planning on staying overnight."

He disappeared into his bedroom and reappeared with a pair of socks. "You can have these. Wear them until your shoes dry out," he said and handed them to her.

"Uh … thanks." She looked puzzled, but took them.

They took their leave, and Jess closed the door after them. "I can't believe you hold her at gunpoint, then give her a pair of your socks," Dani said.

Jess rolled his eyes, a blush creeping up his neck. "Did you notice her damn shoes? They were ruined, soaked through, and she was cold. It's just a pair of socks."

"Still, that was nice of you."

"I'm just glad that's over," he said, changing the subject. "I was worried they'd think you were lying about what happened. If I'm any good at reading people, I don't think she was surprised by what you told her. I think she knew, maybe not until recently, but she knew or suspected that Michaels was crooked."

Dani sighed. "It's over, I guess."

"Thank God. Are you hungry?"

"I'm starved, suddenly. Just no burgers, fries, wings or nachos, please."

Jess laughed. "Will stew do you?"

"Yeah." Dani followed Jess to the kitchen, hitching the waist of Jess's leggings up, and cautiously took a seat at the table. Watching as Jess prepared the food, she said, "Trusting people is incredibly hard for me …"

"Dani, this isn't necessary."

"It is. Please, just listen to me. Dealing with my sister, it was one lie after another. She'd look me in the face and lie and think I didn't know she was lying. It was humiliating. I got to the point where I expect people to lie and disappoint me. It's easier to assume someone is lying than believe them.

"I'd seen you talking to Polly a number of times in public and at the bar. It seemed like she was flirting or that there was more between you than I'd realized. That night when she talked to me in the kitchen, she said to stay away from you, that you were hers. It shocked me to see Polly coming out of the office, buttoning up her shirt, and then find you with her lipstick on your lips, reeking of her perfume. I … I really had no reason not to believe you, but the betrayal—what I thought you'd done—was so familiar. I couldn't—didn't—believe you, and I'm sorry."

"Old patterns, I guess."

"Yeah, old patterns. The funny thing is, I've found people I can trust here and all by chance. If I hadn't been so tired and desperate, I would never have come here, never rented Irma's apartment, never met you. And because of what Polly did, I realize how important you are to me and how important the people I've made friends with are. Bad things aren't necessarily bad, I guess."

Jess raised his eyebrows and gave her a skeptical look. "Sometimes they are," he said rubbing his leg.

"No, not even that's *all* bad. If not for that, you wouldn't be here. I wouldn't have met you. We wouldn't be sitting here now, trying to patch things up. That's good."

"It is. Although I can think of better ways to meet someone I don't want to be without."

Dani looked at him, surprised. "You don't want to be without me?"

Jess looked at her for several moments. "I was so angry when you wouldn't listen to me. I may be a lot of things, but I'm not a liar. I was embarrassed and angry that it had taken two other people to convince you that I might be telling the truth. At that point, my pride took over. I wanted to heal the rift, but I'm stubborn—fair warning. Then you went missing, and I was terrified I might never see you again. I don't want to lose you."

Jess turned back to the stove and brought two bowls of stew to the table, along with glasses of water.

"No beer or wine?" Dani asked

"Not with the pain pills on board. Water will be just fine."

"You don't have to lose me, unless you change your mind."

Jess grinned. "That's highly unlikely."

❧

Kaye was exhausted and depressed. She'd liked Jack a lot, enough to make love to him. He'd been a good cop, but his behavior since the Alphonse murder had become increasingly troublesome. Seeing him stiff and cold in the snow, his once beautiful blue eyes covered in a milky haze, had nearly broken her. She'd been shamed by Ray Decker's comments—*You're gonna leave him like that? I thought he was a cop you worked with*—as if he was affronted by her decision to leave her dead colleague lying in the snow. She hadn't wanted to, but she had a job to do.

Kaye had caught the sheriff's deputies and crime scene people working the area where Jack's body lay sneaking covert glances at her. They'd heard from the sheriff that Jack was a cop on her team, and she guessed they were waiting to see what she'd do. Because she'd been professional, they probably thought she was a cold bitch, but their opinions were irrelevant. She'd never see them again.

She'd watched as the coroner's crew transferred him to a body bag and began to zip it up. Kaye had looked at his face, his forehead streaked with blood, nose swollen and distorted, and taken a shaky breath. What she'd locked onto before the zipper blocked her view was his hair. She remembered the soft feel of it as she'd run her hands through it when he'd first kissed her. Silently, she'd said her goodbyes and returned to her rental car.

Later, as she undressed and got into bed in her Grand Junction hotel room, Kaye thought about her confrontation with Sally Howard and sighed. As much as she didn't want to believe it, the more she'd thought about it, and the more she'd tried to suppress the doubts, in the last few days, she had begun to wonder if the cop Amato had told Sally about was Jack. And now, she had to wonder whether Jack had arranged for someone to kill Sally.

CHAPTER FORTY-TWO

BEFORE FLYING TO DENVER, Jess had insisted Dani be seen by a doctor who ordered X-rays and diagnosed a broken collarbone. Her hip was badly bruised, but the doc said nothing was broken, which was a relief, as he'd also said she was lucky not to have broken her hip or pelvis in the fall.

Jess was unhappy that all the doc did was put her arm in a sling and advise rest, ibuprofen, and ice applied to the areas.

"That's all?" Jess exclaimed.

"The fracture is clean and isn't displaced. A sling is the normal treatment. There's no reason to do anything more. It'll heal. Probably take six to eight weeks, but it'll heal."

"She's in a lot of pain—" And that was as far as he got.

"The prescription NSAID I've given her is strong, and I don't prescribe narcotics for injuries like this. It's not needed."

"Says you. You're not the one who can't use your arm or move it without it causing a hell of a lot of pain."

"Jess, it's okay. The sling helps. Let's go."

Jess scowled at the doctor, and they eventually left after getting care instructions from a nurse, sample packets of pain meds, and a prescription for more.

Sitting in the waiting area before boarding, Jess said he'd be right back. Returning with a paper cup, he handed it to Dani and fished in his coat pocket. He handed her a tablet. "Take this. You can take the med he gave you when we get to Denver, but for the trip I want you comfortable and able to sleep."

"Is this what you gave me last night?"

"Yeah, it's the narcotic he wouldn't prescribe. I know how much bone pain hurts and for right now, after all you've been through, you deserve some decent pain relief."

Dani swallowed the pill. "Why don't you take them?"

"With my chronic pain, it's a slippery slope that can end in addiction. I've seen it happen to guys I met through the VA. A couple doses won't hurt you, and you can sleep during the flight. After that, you can take what the doc prescribed. I imagine there'll be a lot of questions during the interviews, and you need to sleep."

On the trip back to Denver, Kaye realized she should have known something had changed for Jack. Over the last year, he'd regularly disappeared on Sanders without telling him where he was going or why. His presence at the Amato crime scene had raised concerns, as had Sally's death, but not enough to make her think he was dirty. She hadn't thought much about it until lately when his absences began interfering with his job.

She remembered his expensive apartment and his response when she'd commented. It had made sense at the time. After all, she'd inherited her grandmother's place. Being the beneficiary of a life insurance policy was no different. None of that had sent up red flags. It embarrassed her how much she'd failed to see or connect, but the changes had been gradual, and Jack had easily explained it all away. Taken together, they were more damaging.

Confronted with every new revelation about him, she still found it hard to believe that he was crooked, that she had been attracted to and slept with a crooked cop and hadn't known, or had been blind to, what was staring her in the face.

Yesterday morning, she'd finally listened to, rather than ignored, that tiny, persistent doubt and followed him. And now he was dead. He'd murdered eleven people in his bid to take over Alphonse's territory, and had nearly murdered two more. She knew in the back of her mind that he most likely hadn't accomplished this by himself, and she sighed. Internal Affairs would be all over her department trying to figure out what he'd done and who'd helped him.

She wanted to wash her hands of it all, wanted to wash Jack out of her mind, and yet she wanted to grieve for him as well. Such a fucking waste, she thought as she leaned her head against the plane's window and closed her eyes. She fought the sting of the tears she had refused to let fall as she'd knelt near his body in the snow. Now they won and slipped out from under her eyelashes.

No one liked dealing with Internal Affairs, and Kaye was no exception, especially when it meant smearing an officer's memory. She had to keep reminding herself that it had been Jack who'd ruined his reputation and caused his own death. Kaye sat in Lieutenant Dave Beckwith's office and related what had happened. IA would turn Jack's apartment and car inside out and examine his accounts, laptop, and phone in an attempt to find any other evidence of what he'd been doing. All the undercover cops would be under a microscope. She had made arrangements with the Mesa County

Sheriff's Office to have his body returned to Denver for autopsy and had turned his gun and the one Danielle Calderwood had taken from Alphonse's house over to Forensics.

Kaye was sure that Jack had worn old clothes and gloves to the meet with Amato, had shot him, left to dispose of the clothes, and returned to the scene before he called and reported the death. And she was equally sure that they'd never find any of that evidence. The type of gun that had killed Amato and the others matched the gun he'd had with him when he'd tracked Danielle Calderwood through the woods. Ballistics was in the process of confirming that it was the murder weapon. The serial number had been removed, so it was untraceable, but Kaye figured he'd picked it up during one of his deals or gotten it from someone he knew. It was also possible he'd taken it from the evidence files.

Beckwith had warned her to say nothing to anyone about the IA probe of the department. She knew they'd be checking up on her as well, just to make sure she hadn't been involved in his schemes. No one escaped their scrutiny. She also knew it wouldn't be long before everyone in the precinct knew what had happened and IA's involvement.

"Got an ID on the killer who took Sally Howard out," Blake said over the phone.

"Who was it?" she asked, holding her breath, hoping Jack hadn't had anything to do with it.

"Guy named Hector Moore. He's an enforcer, works for whoever needs a job done. We've got an arrest warrant for him. I'll keep you posted if we nab him. He had to know she got a couple good swipes in, so he may have disappeared. He works a lot around here, but we've just never been able to pin anything on him. I figure he'll be back eventually if he took off."

Kaye felt somewhat relieved, but the truth was that Jack could have paid this Hector to kill Sally. If so, he might as well have strangled her himself. "Keep me posted. I'd like to know why he killed her. What's happening to her body?"

Blake took a deep breath. "She's got no family so for the moment, until we get Hector and close the case, she's at the MEs."

"Okay. When she's ready for release, let me know. I'll take care of her."

"I'll let you know," he said and paused. "Kaye, this wasn't your fault."

"It is, but I can't rectify that, so I'll take care of her. It's the least I can do." Kaye hung up and walked to the women's room. Closing herself in a stall, she wept as quietly as possible and hoped that wherever Sally was, she forgave her.

CHAPTER FORTY-THREE

THE INTERVIEW ROOM WAS DRAB, painted a color that Dani thought might be beige or might have been white at one point but had deteriorated with age or lack of cleaning. It clearly wasn't intended to be welcoming. The table was bolted to the floor, and the chairs were hard and made her hip ache. To avoid the discomfort, she stood, leaning against the wall to take the weight off her left hip. The bruise had spread, and the ache it caused had increased over the last twenty-four hours. She cradled her left arm protectively and was glad of the pain pills the doctor in Grand Junction had prescribed. They worked, but not nearly as well as what Jess had given her. All she really wanted to do was go somewhere quiet and lie down.

They'd put her in the room alone and taken Jess to another room. That worried her and made her wonder whether they believed what she and Jess had told Jagerski. As Jagerski and another cop entered the room, Dani's hands went cold and her heart rate spiked.

"Ms. Calderwood, I'm Lieutenant Beckwith. I work in the Internal Affairs department. We handle complaints or concerns about members of the police force in this precinct. I believe you know Lieutenant Jagerski?"

Dani nodded, her mouth dry. There was a bottle of water sitting on the table, but she hadn't touched it, and now she was afraid to pick it up and show that her hands were shaking.

Beckwith indicated the chair with his hand. "Please, have a seat."

She eased onto the chair, shifting her weight onto her right buttocks and listened as he told her the interview was being recorded and read her the Miranda warning.

"Am I being charged with something?"

He ignored her comment and asked if she understood her rights. She nodded, wondering whether she ought to have asked for a lawyer.

"You spoke with Lieutenant Jagerski following the death of Detective Michaels. I'm wondering why neither you nor Mr. Walker called the Mesa County Sheriff when it happened?"

"Please answer my question. Am I being charged with something?"

"No, this is a noncustodial interview—"

"I don't know what that means."

"It means you're not under arrest and have the right to leave at any time, although I hope you'll stay and answer my questions. In situations like this, I like to read the Miranda so that interview subjects understand their rights." Dani nodded, and he continued. "Please tell me why neither you nor Mr. Walker called the Mesa County Sheriff at the time of Detective Michaels's death."

"The cell reception in that area is sporadic and nonexistent in places. I no longer had a phone, and Jess couldn't call anyone from the site either. I had been struggling in the snow to evade Detective Michaels and was wet, cold, and exhausted. I had injured my shoulder and hip in my fall from the SUV, and I was in a lot of pain. It was getting dark, and the temperature was dropping. Jess brought me back to his cabin to warm up. Lieutenant Jagerski and Ray Decker followed us through the snow to Jess's cabin and arrived not long after we got there. There wasn't time to call anyone."

"I've listened to your recorded discussion with Lieutenant Jagerski about what happened. Do you want to listen to it?"

"Why would I need to?"

"I want to know if you have anything to add to it or correct."

"I would like to listen to it."

He played the recording and Dani listened carefully. Beckwith shut the recording off when it was finished. "Is that an accurate description of what happened?"

"Yes."

"Do you have anything to add?"

"No."

"You're sure it was Detective Michaels you heard and that you caught a glimpse of at the house where your sister and Billy Alphonse were killed?"

"Yes. Not immediately. I mean, I didn't realize who he was initially. He seemed legitimate, showed me his badge and talked me into leaving with him, supposedly to come to Denver and give a statement. His voice bothered me—something about it made me uneasy.

"He kept talking as he drove toward the highway, and then he turned and I saw his face at the angle I saw it at the house, and I knew who he was. I jumped out of the SUV and ran. He followed me and admitted he was the killer when he held me at gunpoint. He told me he had to kill me to prevent me from ruining his plans."

"Explain to me why you didn't come to us and identify your-self as a witness."

"I was scared. I couldn't identify the killer at that point, but he knew who I was thanks to you guys and the Crime Stoppers broadcasts. It's a good thing I didn't come to you. If I had, I'd be dead, since one of your officers was the killer." Dani stared at Beckwith until he looked uncomfortable.

"You act like I'm somehow responsible for what happened to my sister and to Michaels, when he's responsible for it all. You have my statement that I gave to Lieutenant Jagerski, and you have my answers to your questions. If you have nothing further, then I'm done with this."

"I think we're done, for now."

"Not for now. We're done, period. If it hadn't been for Jess Walker, I'd be dead, and none of you would be the wiser to the crooked cop in your midst." Dani stood up and held onto the back of the chair for support. "I know how you protect your own, but if you imply to the media that either of us are in any way responsible, I will go to the media and explain exactly what happened and who the killer was. I will then contact a lawyer and see what type of legal action I can bring against this department. Are we clear?"

"I think we're done."

"Good. Now go release Jess, and we'll be on our way."

Beckwith got up and left, but Jagerski remained. She grinned at Dani. "I don't think you or Mr. Walker will be hearing from him again. I'm sorry for what Michaels put you through and for the loss of your sister."

"I appreciate that. I'm sorry that one of your colleagues turned bad. Did you know him well?"

"Apparently not well enough. He was a good cop at one time. I regret losing that cop, but I don't think he'd been that cop for very long time."

"Still, it must be hard for you." Dani picked up her backpack and moved toward the door and stopped. "In all of this, I've been meaning to ask. Where is my sister?"

"At the medical examiner's facility. Once you decide what to do with her body, they'll release her. She's been identified, so you needn't see her unless you want to."

Dani frowned. "I'd like to see her. How do I do that?"

"I'll call over there now and arrange a time. I can take you there."

"Thank you." Dani opened the door, stepped out of the room, and saw Jess coming down the hall toward her. The rush of relief at seeing his face was overwhelming.

"All done?" he asked, giving her a quick kiss on the cheek.

"Not quite." Kaye gave them some privacy, and Dani explained about the morgue. "Kaye will set it up and take me over there. You don't need to come, but I'd like to see her and take care of her one last time."

"I'll come—if you want me to. I don't want to intrude."

She stepped close and let her head fall against his chest as he stroked her back. "You're not intruding. I'd like you to come."

At the morgue, Dani looked through the viewing window at her sister's body. Jess waited for her on the other side of the door. She'd asked him to wait outside the viewing room to give her some time alone. Hannah's body was covered almost her chin with a sheet. Dani could see a dark discoloring to the left side of her face and neck where she'd rested on the floor after she'd been shot.

"Thank you for saving my life," Dani whispered, placing her palm against the glass window separating them. "And thank you for forcing me to get a life."

She stayed for a few more minutes, then left.

After signing a multitude of papers to arrange for her sister's cremation and receipt of the ashes, Dani stood outside the morgue with Jess and Kaye Jagerski. The day was clear and, despite the sunshine, cold.

"On a brighter note," Jagerski said, "your car was in the impound lot. I had it brought to the station."

"My car? The car dealer didn't dismantle her and sell her for parts?" Dani felt the prick of tears at the thought that Berry hadn't been lost.

"No, he says he intended to call and let us know because he thought the car was stolen, but he forgot until he saw the Crime Stoppers announcement, which convinced him to call us. It should be in the parking garage. I arranged for it to be brought over." She handed Dani the keys. "Let's go get your car."

CHAPTER FORTY-FOUR

WE DON'T NEED TO SPEND two days here. I'm perfectly capable of surviving the drive back home," Dani said as Jess pulled into the hotel parking lot.

"Think of it as a vacation. The hotel room has a Jacuzzi tub, which will be good for both of us. And then Sunday, we can head back."

Dani opened her backpack and pulled out a piece of paper, handing it to Jess.

"What's this?"

"The phone number for a pain clinic in Grand Junction. I talked to the ER doc and asked if there was a way for you to get help for the pain in your leg. He said there was a pain clinic at the hospital and to call and set up an appointment for an assessment."

"And you want me to go?"

"It can't hurt to talk to them, and you wouldn't have to stay in Denver."

Jess eyed Dani for a moment and then added the number to his phone. "Okay, if that's what you want."

"I don't want you to be in pain."

Jess nodded and seemed disconcerted. "Jagerski told me your belongings from the apartment are in your storage locker there and that we can pick them up on the way out of town."

Noting the abrupt change of subject, Dani chose to say nothing further about the pain clinic.

"There's not a lot to collect."

Jess shrugged. "It's yours. We might as well pick it up. You may want it later."

"Maybe," she replied, as Jess opened the door to the hotel room.

Getting comfortable in bed was not easy. Jess had joked that making love, or doing anything else with her, was like handling a porcupine—you had to do it carefully. She couldn't tolerate removing the sling and couldn't get it wet, but she was able to sit in the Jacuzzi tub far enough to let the hot water soothe her hip, while Jess lounged much more comfortably in it.

"Some vacation. More like a weekend at an assisted living facility."

"Now don't get crabby," Jess said, piling pillows up against the bed's headboard. "Better?"

"Yes." She closed her eyes and sighed, then looked at Jess. "I'm sorry."

"For what?"

"For everything. For almost getting you killed, for having to shut the bar down and come here, for this," she said, waving her right hand at her arm in its sling. "You should never have stopped to check out my truck that night. I'd have frozen to death and you wouldn't be tangled up in all this."

Jess took airplane-sized bottles of scotch and red wine out of the small fridge in the room. He turned to look at her and grinned. "We're feeling very sorry for ourselves tonight, aren't we? This should help." He poured the scotch and wine into plastic glasses and sat down on the bed next to her.

"I guess it's all caught up with me—how close we both came to dying, seeing my sister …" She didn't finish the sentence as they sipped at their drinks. At last, Dani said, "How did you get through what happened to you? My injury is nothing compared to that, and here I sit, whining."

"I didn't do a lot of whining—you know, big tough Marine, whining isn't acceptable—but I sure as hell was hard to live with. Still am, so don't be surprised if I get grumpy." He leaned in and kissed her. "It'll get better." He grinned at her. "Maybe you can come get assessed at the pain clinic, too."

News of Jack's death had hit the department hard. Details about the why of it had been kept close, but not close enough. By now, everyone in the department—probably the entire precinct—knew what had happened. Unfortunately, that had made identifying any of Jack's partners difficult, but IA was putting everyone through the wringer, especially the undercover cops.

Kaye sat in the observation room and listened to Blake and Stevens interview Hector Moore. They had finally found and arrested him. He was intimidating; despite being only five foot eight, his arms and shoulders strained the jacket he wore. His face was expressionless as he listened to Blake.

"So tell us how you know Sally Howard," Blake said.

"I don't know anyone named Sally Howard."

"The prostitute you were with a week ago at the Sleepy Time Motel. Ring any bells?"

"They're prostitutes. I don't ask for names."

"But you were with her, correct?"

"I may have been. I like prostitutes. Keeps life simple."

Blake pushed a photo of Sally in better times across the table. "Look familiar?"

Hector shrugged. "Ya know, they all kinda look alike to me. As long as they aren't total dogs, I don't pay much attention to them. It's not their faces I'm paying for."

"Well, Sally here was strangled, and interestingly enough she had tissue under her nails and the DNA ID'd you. Remember her now?"

"Sometimes they get a little carried away in their excitement. What can I say?"

"Yeah, being strangled is probably pretty exciting. What I'm curious about is whether you just got carried away or whether someone paid you to get rid of her."

"She was fine when I left her. Nobody paid me to do anything to her."

"That's not what I've been told." With all that had come to light regarding Jack Michaels and Kaye's telling him about Dominic Amato, Blake decided to try bluffing Moore.

"Who says I had anything to do with it?"

"According to Detective Jack Michaels from Vice you offed Dominic Amato and Sally Howard."

Moore's eyes went hard and his lips thinned. That had struck a nerve. "Well that's interesting. I have some information about the murder for you guys."

"Which is?"

"I need to hear the words *deal* from you before I tell you."

Kaye got up and left. She knew how this would end, and she knew Jack had set up Sally's murder. He hadn't done it himself, but he was responsible. What the hell had happened to him? What had pushed him over the line? He had been a good person, at one time, and had been good at what he did. But there was often a fine line that separated cops from the bad guys; they were two sides of the same coin. It didn't take much to flip some of them. Kaye would never know, but she would always wonder what had flipped Jack.

⌒

Polly opened the door and found Irma standing on the doorstep. "What d'you want?" Seeing Irma had given her a start. Irma had never liked her or been friendly. Her appearance on Polly's doorstep was worrisome.

"I think you know why I'm here."

"Gonna give me a lecture?"

"I doubt that'd do any good."

"Have you convinced everyone in town to stop tipping me? I know you were the one who talked them into stiffing me on tips."

"Seems like appropriate payback for what you did. But that's not why I'm here. Jess and Dani will be back day after tomorrow, and you're going to be gone."

Polly didn't allow Irma to continue. "Jess put you up to this, didn't he? He's just a vindictive—"

"Jess didn't have anything to do with this. What you did—out of pure spite—nearly got Jess and Dani killed. That's not going to be tolerated."

"You can't make me leave. Besides, I have no transportation!" Polly said, her voice rising in panic.

"I'm going to give you until tomorrow morning to pack up your belongings. I'll be back for you at ten and take you to Grand Junction. From there you can do as you like, but you're not staying here." Irma reached into her coat pocket and pulled out an envelope, holding it out to Polly. "Harry gave me your pay for what you've worked this week and very generously added two weeks' severance pay and his estimate of what your tips might have been."

"You meddling old bitch. I don't have to leave just because you say so."

Irma crossed her arms over her chest and gave Polly a steely glare. "This is nonnegotiable, young lady. No one in town wants you here. Harry doesn't want you working for him, and no one else will hire you. So pack up and be ready to go, or I'll have a deputy from the sheriff's office come get you."

"Fine. I never liked this place anyway."

CHAPTER FORTY-FIVE

ON THEIR RETURN FROM DENVER, Jess wanted Dani to move in with him and was a bit frustrated when she turned him down.

"Irma needs help, Jess, and she needs someone nearby. I can't abandon her and Elmer, not when she helped me so much. When spring rolls around and the weather is better, then we'll see how she is."

"Never thought I'd be less important than an old woman and a dog," Jess groused.

"Oh, stop. You're not less important, and you know it. Don't be a baby about this. We'll still be together, some nights here, some nights at your place."

"Promise?" Dani nodded, and Jess finally acquiesced. "You can come hang out at the bar, but no working until your shoulder has settled down."

Jess ran a hand through his beard and looked a bit sheepish. "Bob called me last night. He and his wife are enjoying the warmer climate a lot. He asked if I would take over running the bar as a partner. I think I'll take him up on it."

"I think you'd be pretty good at it. D'you need an accountant?"

Jess laughed. "I'm sure I will come tax time."

Dani asked Irma to drive her into Grand Junction where she had a stylist cut off as much as possible of her dyed hair and return what was left to her original blonde. The look on Jess's face when she walked into the bar had made her laugh.

"What the hell have you done with your hair, woman?"

"I wanted my blonde back, and the stylist suggested getting rid of the dyed hair rather than trying to take it all back to blonde."

"You look like a boy."

"It'll grow out," she said, running a hand through the top self-consciously. "I didn't want to see the brown and be reminded of why I dyed it."

Jess tilted his head from one side to the other, scrutinizing her new look. "It is kinda sexy. Makes you look like Tinker Bell, without that little bun on her head."

"You know what Tinker Bell looks like?"

He blushed. "I liked Peter Pan when I was a kid. At one point I wanted to be him. I liked Wendy, but I thought Tinker Bell was pretty cute."

"See, I knew you'd come around."

He laughed. "Sweetheart, you could be bald, and I'd still find you sexy. But," he quickly added, "don't get any ideas."

A few weeks after their return, Hannah's ashes arrived. Dani held the box and wondered how an entire person could be reduced to a box she could hold in her hands.

"I don't know what to do with the ashes. She'd hate them being spread in Nebraska, and Denver doesn't feel right. I have no idea where I'd even spread them there," Dani said as she and Jess sat at the bar talking.

"I don't think she cares now. She's past all that. I think it should be someplace that gives you comfort, maybe some peace about what happened."

Dani sighed and took a sip of her wine. "I may have to wait until spring so we can take some hikes and find a place. This town is the only place I've found peace and friends and you. You're the best part of it all."

Jess grinned at her. "Good, 'cause I have plans."

"You do, do you?"

"Oh yeah, short-term and long-term plans," he said taking her in his arms.

"I love a man with plans."

ACKNOWLEDGMENTS

I HAVE A LONG LIST of people to thank. Thanks to the fans who read my books—I couldn't do this without you.

A huge thanks to my beta readers, Lois Miller, D'n, Karen Michaud, and Donna Lefferdo—you keep me focused and give great feedback (i.e., all the tips on geography and mountain living). Thanks to my editor, Julie Cameron, at Landon Literary, for her guidance, astute comments, and her humor. Thanks to KB Jensen, for her help with all the details needed to get a book published. Thanks to Victoria Wolf, at Wolf Design and Marketing, for the formatting and another great cover.

This book is a work of fiction, people, places, and names (except for Polly Letofsky who won the 'name a character after you' contest), are my imagination alone and any mistakes are mine. PS: Polly's really a great gal, unlike the Polly in the book.

ABOUT THE AUTHOR

COLORADO NATIVE AND FORMER OR nurse, Helen Starbuck is an award-winning author of The *Annie Collins Mystery Series,* contemporary romantic suspense, and the *Denver Major Crimes Series.* Of no relation to the coffee bunch, she (sadly) doesn't get free coffee. When she's not writing, you can find her ballroom dancing, gardening, reading books about strong women and interesting men who find themselves in suspense-filled situations, and being her cat Bean's servant.

Follow her on Facebook (facebook.com/helensstarbuck —yes two s's), Instagram (instagram.com/helenstarbuck_author/), and her website (helenstarbuck.com), where you can sign up for her newsletter to be the first to hear about new books, events, cover reveals, and freebies.

Turn the page to read the first chapter of *Finding Alex*
available on Amazon in ebook, paperback, and audiobook
https://www.amazon.com/dp/B08MCGK837.

FINDING ALEX

Who is it that can tell me who I am?
—William Shakespeare

PROLOGUE

"Wake up! Please wake up!"

The voice sounded frightened and far away. "Can't," *she mumbled, her mind clouded, drifting, wanting nothing more than to drop back into nothingness and get away from the pain.*

"No!" the voice sounded ... worried ... familiar. "Wake up! You have to wake up and get away ... please ... he'll come back! He'll hurt you." The voice faded into the nothingness.

Cold. So cold and dark, she thought. The pain in her head felt as if her skull would explode with each beat of her heart. *Have to get away, have to get help. Someone had told her that ... someone ... someone.* She rolled onto her side and managed to get to her hands and knees before becoming violently ill. The pain in her head surged with each retch.

She waited for the nausea to pass, swaying on her hands and knees, her head hanging down. Slowly she lifted it and saw she was at the bottom of a deep culvert. Overhead, the moon was partly hidden by clouds. She crawled away from the vomit and made her way slowly up the incline, feeling the dry grass and dirt under her hands and knees, feeling the rocks that punctured and scratched them. It would take an eternity to reach the top. Was it worth the effort?

"Move, keep moving," the voice said. So, she moved.

CHAPTER ONE

H E'D BEEN LOST IN thought when he damn near hit the woman. If he hadn't had his headlights on high he would have. It was midnight and almost nothing was visible outside the twin beams of his car's headlights.

The fields on either side of Highway 93 and the foothills to the west were invisible in the darkness. In the distance to the east were glimpses of the multicolored lights of Denver. Clouds periodically obscured the moon. His was the only car on the road.

Detective Blake Halloran had been thinking about the case he'd been working on for the last week as he drove on autopilot toward Boulder and the woman he'd been seeing for a couple of months.

Movement from the side of the road at the edges of his headlights brought him out of his thoughts. A woman staggered out onto the highway, into the path of his car. He stood hard on the brake pedal, his tires screamed, and the car fishtailed. His heart was slamming against his chest as the car came juddering to a stop only feet from her.

As he got out of the car on shaky legs, the scent of burnt rubber from his tires surrounded him. The woman's head, face, and neck were bloody, and she swayed as she stood in front of the car. She raised a scraped and bloody arm to shield her eyes from the headlights. Before he could round the front of the car, her legs gave way and she collapsed.

He fished his phone out of his jacket pocket and dialed 911.

"This is Detective Blake Halloran with the Denver Police Department," he said, giving the operator his badge number. "I have an injured pedestrian and need an ambulance south of the entrance to the Leyden dump on Highway 93 going north toward Boulder."

"Is this a pedestrian motor vehicle accident?"

There was no other car in sight. "I don't know," he said his breath uneven, a tremor in his hand made holding the phone difficult. "It could be a hit-and-run, but she's on the highway so it's urgent that emergency services and the police or the sheriff's office are notified." Blake couldn't remember who had jurisdiction on this stretch of highway.

"Is the victim breathing?"

"Yes, but unconscious. Tell them to hurry," he said, disconnecting and dropping his phone into his jacket pocket.

He knelt beside her in the glare of the headlights and felt under her jaw for a pulse to reassure himself that she was, in fact, just unconscious. She was deathly pale. Blood matted her dark red hair and had run down her neck and onto her chest. Purplish-blue bruises wrapped around her neck. Not a hit-and-run then, some sort of assault. He took a deep breath and exhaled, trying to slow his breathing and his heartbeat. He hoped she was strong enough to hold on until help got there.

She wore a very short, tight skirt and a tight stretchy top that didn't leave much to the imagination. Working girl was his first assumption, but he'd seen some high school and college-age girls who wore similar outfits. There was a gash on the side of her head. The palms of her hands and her elbows and knees were scraped and covered in blood and ground-in dirt. Several of her fingernails were broken, and there was a deep cut near the last joint of her left index finger.

Her elbows and knees were still bleeding. He stood up and retrieved his phone activating its flashlight and shining it off the side of the road. The ground dropped off into a deep culvert. Maybe the injuries to her hands, arms, and knees were from crawling up the side of the culvert. The bleeding from the head wound had stopped, so whatever had caused it had happened a while ago.

He ran back to the car, hit his hazard lights, and opened the trunk to extract his triangular hazard warning signs and a blanket. He set up the warning triangles, hoping to prevent any approaching cars from hitting them.

Covering her with the blanket would screw up any trace evidence on her, but she was ice-cold. Figuring it was damned if you did and damned if you didn't, he went with the blanket. Once she was covered, he knelt beside her again to wait for emergency responders.

She moaned and, unable to restrain himself, he stroked the uninjured side of her face. "Help is on the way, hang in there," he said.

He had no idea whether she'd heard him. She seemed to have lost consciousness again, and he wasn't sure whether he'd said it to reassure the woman or himself. He took his phone and briefly peeled back the blanket to photograph her injuries and check that there were no other wounds. Replacing it, he tucked the blanket in around her and waited feeling a familiar numbness creep over him.

Five minutes later he saw flashing lights in the distance and heard sirens. A fire truck arrived with lights flashing and fire fighters emerged and began blocking the highway to divert traffic. Mercifully, there wasn't any at the moment. EMTs unloaded a stretcher from the ambulance that had arrived with the fire truck and a black SUV with a local police emblem on it pulled up. EMTs rolled the stretcher over to where the woman lay and Halloran was still kneeling.

"What happened?" the EMT asked as he pulled the blanket off and replaced it with a reflective blanket that would help keep her body heat in. He began examining the woman as the other one took the transport board off the stretcher and placed it beside her. They transferred her onto it and the first EMT began taking her vital signs as the other hooked her up to oxygen.

Blake stood up and stared down at the EMT blankly for a moment. It was as if his brain had momentarily short circuited.

The EMT shot him a concerned look. "Are you okay? Any injuries that need looking at?"

Blake shook his head to clear it. "I'm fine, no injuries."

"Can you tell me what happened?"

"She … she stumbled out into the road as I was driving. I damn near hit her." He picked up the blanket and held it against his belly as if for comfort.

A cop appeared at Blake's side and asked, "Where'd she come from?"

"I don't know where she came from. There's a fairly steep culvert leading down from the highway, she could have been down there. She's got bruises around her neck. It looks like an assault to me. Maybe whoever did it left her there, thinking she was dead."

"Dispatch said you're a cop."

"Yeah, DPD. Homicide." Blake pulled his jacket back to show his badge.

"What were you doing up here?"

"I was on my way to Boulder to a friend's house."

"That's quite a drive, and it's late," the cop said, giving him an impassive stare.

"You know the job. It isn't bankers' hours." Blake eyed the guy for a minute. "You asking me for an alibi?"

"You got one?"

"Talk to my partner. I was with him until half an hour ago, when I left to head up to Boulder." He provided his partner Clark Stevens' name and phone number. "If I was the one who did this, why the hell would I call 911 or stick around?"

The cop shrugged. "Stranger things have happened."

He walked back to his SUV, slid into the driver's side, and pulled out a phone. *Jesus, no trust in a fellow officer at all,* Blake thought. Still, he grudgingly admitted he'd have probably done the same thing. He watched as the EMTs wheeled the stretcher toward the ambulance and loaded her in. Christ, he'd nearly killed her. He followed them to the door of the ambulance.

"Where are you taking her?"

"Saint A's. They're Level 1 trauma."

"Is she going to be okay?"

"We'll do everything we can, sir," the EMT said, climbing into the back of the ambulance and shutting the doors in Blake's face.

The lack of expression on the EMT's face and their rush to leave worried Blake. Would she be okay? The ambulance made a U-turn and took off, lights flashing and siren wailing. Blake watched as the ambulance's lights faded. He knew the lights and the siren meant 'critical patient, no time to lose.'

The sense of responsibility for her and the urge to follow the ambulance washed over him. Maybe he'd call the ER when he got to Fleur's place and see how she was doing. He rubbed his forehead. He must be tired or more shook up than he realized. No one at the ER was going to give him any information over the phone. The question was, did he let this go or stop at the hospital and see what her prognosis was?

"Gonna need you to give me a statement, tell me what happened. I'll let you know when it's ready for you to sign. Gonna need contact info as well," the cop said interrupting Blake's thoughts. He eyed Blake carefully. "You okay?"

"Yeah, just a little rattled," Blake said. He related what had happened and gave the officer his info.

A fireman walked up and stopped. "Need you to get your car off the highway," he said to Blake. "And the sooner you can finish this up, we can get the scene secured and take off, unless you need us to stick around?" he asked the cop.

"No, thanks for the backup. We're almost done here."

The guy nodded and returned to confer with the firemen stationed around the accident scene while they waited. Blake got back into his car and pulled forward into the breakdown lane. He opened the driver's door and waited for the cop to walk over. When finished questioning Blake, the cop handed him a card and said he'd be in touch.

"What happened to your hand?" Blake asked noticing the scratch marks on the back of it.

The cop gave him an appraising stare. "I had a little confrontation with someone earlier who objected to being arrested."

"You might want to have them looked at. They look serious."

The cop raised his eyebrows at Blake. "Thanks, I will," he said. He got back into his car, made a U-turn, and drove away, shortly followed by the fire truck.

Blake realized he was still clutching the blanket. He supposed he should have given it to the cop but was too tired to turn the car around and follow. He'd give it to the guy when he went in to sign the statement. A few minutes passed before he realized he'd forgotten about his emergency triangles. Resignedly he got out of the car, retrieved them, and threw them into the trunk.

On top of the tiredness, the adrenaline was still humming. He sat in his car and looked at his hands on the steering wheel and watched them shake. It'd be a while yet before he could sleep. *You'd think I'd be used to this kinda shit by now*, he thought. Being called to a crime scene never bothered him like this, primarily because he knew what he was getting into. But this had been so unexpected and jarring. Maybe you were never used to emergencies that actually involved you.

As a cop he'd handled other people's emergencies, but only one of his own, and that had been one too many. Lindsey had been the last time he'd allowed anyone to mean anything to him. It was the last time he'd been close to anyone or felt responsible for anyone. He had fucked that up royally, so he'd made sure no one got close enough for it to happen again. He closed his eyes tightly, frowning, his breathing speeding up as he fought the images of holding Lindsey in his arms, unable to do anything, as she bled to death.

He forced his eyes open and focused on the interior of the car, remembering what the therapist had said—focus on your surroundings, where you're at, why you're not with Lindsey. *I'm in the car. I'm on the road to Boulder. I'm … here, not there*, he said to himself to counteract the panic that he felt building. He sat and breathed slowly, repeating the phrases, and waiting for his heart rate to drop.

Almost forty minutes later, surprised by the insistent ringing of his cell phone, he didn't know where he was for a moment until he remembered what had happened. Had he fallen asleep? He pulled his phone out of his jacket pocket. Glancing at the screen he saw it was Fleur. He'd planned to pick her up and have dinner, but those plans had been derailed early in the evening. She'd been pissed but told him to come up when he could. She was going to be even more pissed now.

"Where are you?" she demanded, "It's almost two a.m. This is the second time I've called. Are you all right?"

The second time she'd called? He hadn't heard the phone if she'd called before. He wiped a hand over his face. It had been more than a year since he'd had a flashback or lost time after one. Christ, he hoped that wasn't going to start up again.

"I'm sorry, babe, I can't make it," he said rubbing the heel of his hand on his forehead. "Something … came up on the way to your place." There was dead silence.

Finally, she said, "This is getting old, Blake, but whatever. Let me know when you can make some time for me," and disconnected.

He sighed, closing his eyes. Maybe it was time to call it quits and end this. She wasn't happy, and he wasn't entertained enough to continue enduring the sulks and tantrums when he couldn't make whatever they had arranged. Even the sex wasn't enough anymore. Initially it'd been fun, but it wasn't worth all the other nonsense, he thought irritably as he put the car in gear, made a U-turn, and drove toward home.

He'd been seeing her for not quite two months. She was a twenty-four-year-old grad student at the University of Colorado, and he was ten years older. He'd been uncomfortable with the age difference from the beginning. He hadn't thought it would be a huge problem, but it was becoming one rather quickly. Her outlook on life in general was that of someone who hadn't had reality bash her in the head yet. Unfortunately, he had.

He'd met her at a friend's house in Denver. They'd chatted, seemed to hit it off, and exchanged numbers. He'd always been a sucker for blond hair, long legs, and blue eyes, so they had reconnected a week later. The 'relationship'—and he always saw air quotes around it when he thought about it—had sort of evolved from dinner and movies to sleeping together over the course of a couple weekends.

He didn't have a goal in mind in regard to Fleur, and he'd been honest about that, but it seemed she had one. He worried that he'd become the fish she was determined to catch and not release. She'd been more and more frustrated and angry as she realized what his job entailed and that he wasn't going to commit or take their relationship any further than it was. He always kept women at a distance, something many of them complained bitterly about before they left or he did. For some reason, women never seemed to believe that he had no interest in a long-term relationship. No matter what he told them.

At first glance, Blake Halloran wasn't a classically handsome man. He was tall and well-built but he could blend in enough to go unnoticed. Unnoticed until he displayed his quirky smile that, when truly amused, lit up his deep blue eyes and made a dimple appear on his left cheek.

Women seemed to like his startlingly blue eyes and dark blond hair that looked as if he combed it with his fingers, which, about half the time, was true. He liked women, too but between his aversion to getting too close and his job, relationships never lasted long and there were often hard feelings on the woman's part when things ended.